Ransom was struck ⸻ vu as he approached the scene.

The body had already been moved so that more detailed photographs could be taken. It was lying at the foot of the Dumpster. It was a young man who looked not quite as angelic as the first victim, but they did have things in common: There were holes driven through the hands and feet, and the head had been severely battered. The boy's face looked as if it reflected some of the agony it had suffered in passing, as if it had not achieved complete repose in death. There was one major difference between this body and the first: Ransom felt fairly sure he knew who this was.

★

FRED W. HUNTER

RANSOM FOR OUR *Sins*

WORLDWIDE.

TORONTO • NEW YORK • LONDON
AMSTERDAM • PARIS • SYDNEY • HAMBURG
STOCKHOLM • ATHENS • TOKYO • MILAN
MADRID • WARSAW • BUDAPEST • AUCKLAND

RANSOM FOR OUR SINS

A Worldwide Mystery/September 1997

This edition is published by arrangement with Walker and Company.

ISBN 0-373-26249-3

Printed in U.S.A.

In memory of Ivy Travis

ONE

WHACK!

He bit down on the cloth between his teeth; it smelled faintly of feces and was shoved far enough into his mouth to prevent his crying out, but not far enough to prevent his breathing.

Whack!

He had passed the point of pain—or at least, the point at which his mind could still grasp the pain. He had passed the point at which he could grasp anything else, for that matter. The pain itself had transformed from agony to a bright burning in the center of his palms, flaring at regular intervals with each strike of the hammer.

Whack!

As for grasping anything else, he could feel intermittent spasms in his hands, but didn't know if he could exercise any control over them. With great difficulty, he turned his head as far to the right as possible. Just above the rope that bound his wrist, he could see the involuntary twitching of his fingers. His fevered mind likened the sight to a crab, impaled on its back and left to die. He was not sure if he could still voluntarily move his hands, and the excruciating burning in his palms seemed to drain all his strength, leaving him too weak to try.

Whack!

He could feel the bones in his left hand separate as the long, thick nail was driven deeper. He wondered if this really was the punishment for his sins, as he had often heard it described. Although he had understood that at times like this one's life would pass before one's eyes, he found this not to be true: Only his sins were displayed before them. As he mentally recounted every act of his life

that could possibly be considered a "trespass," he began
to sincerely doubt that he could have been so bad that he
deserved an end like this and was horrified to find that he
was thinking of himself in the past tense.

Whack!

And yet, he was sure it was the end. He heard the wood
begin to splinter. He watched through bleary, streaming
eyes the dark, furtive figure working over him like a sweat-
ing, demonic rail-splitter.

He bit harder into the cloth and thought again of his sins.
He was sure they were numerous, but he found that he
could no longer call a single incident clearly into his rapidly
accelerating thoughts. A sob welled up in his throat and
threatened to finish the job the cloth had started.

Whack!

He was sure now; even though his sins had been driven
through his mind like a spike through a board, he was sure
that he couldn't be the recipient of such harsh punishment
without having committed the appropriate crime, in his in-
creasing delirium comparing his situation to a cross between *The Mikado* and the New Testament. He was sure
that he was the hopeless sinner he'd always been led to
believe. There was some sort of incongruous comfort in
this realization, as if merely being able to grasp that there
was, somewhere, sense and logic to this outcome of his
life, even if he didn't remember the details.

Whack!

All at once his vision began to clear. The last tears ran
out of his eyes and were not replaced. His pupils enlarged
and he stared, saucer-eyed, at the ceiling. As he watched,
the chipped paint and plaster melted away, and a huge, oval
hole spread open through the ceiling and the floor above—
like a movie-inspired dream sequence being superimposed
upon reality. But this was no dream. The hole continued to
dissolve upward through the ceiling of the next level and
the roof, until he could see the stars. And still the hole
traveled upward, like an oval window opening the heavens
to him. Onward and upward it went until he was not seeing

the heavens, but Heaven itself. And he could see the Son
seated at the right hand of the Father. And it was the last
thing he *did* see.
Whack!

VOICES RANG OUT in discordant tones. Not music. Not
chords. No melodies at all. Not even words, really. It
sounded more like bits of words: disconnected syllables
sung out in a cacophony of keys. Every now and then an
"Alleluia" could be discerned in the midst of the din.

This was the hardest part of the service for Nicholas
Bremmen, the part in which hands were raised in praise
and voices were raised in the Spirit, creating a sound that
seemed more like madness than music to him. This "release of the Spirit" as they called it, experienced at least
once in every "meeting" (the word they insisted on using
for the service) was an alarming departure from the structure that Nicholas had sought in joining the church.

In fact, the floating mass of disconnected noise reminded
him more of his life before the church than after. Perhaps
that's what he found so alarming. Before joining, he had
been floating: not causing anyone harm, but not doing anyone any good, either. Least of all himself. He considered
himself happy, but knew at the same time that an aimless
life was just that: aimless. And he'd become tired and bored
with going on from year to year in no particular direction,
mattering to nobody and with no attachments of his own.
It was one thing to not want to be tied down, it was quite
another to find at the age of thirty that you had no ties at
all.

Nicholas had drifted into the church the way he had
drifted into most everything else in his life: completely by
chance and with no prior design in mind. He had simply
been invited by a coworker to attend a service, and not
having anything else to do, had agreed to come.

What had impressed him the most about this church was
the way the people had left him alone. At first. There didn't
seem to be any pressure for him to do or be anything, or

to participate in any way. Mostly, he was allowed to sit
and watch with little if any encouragement to join in. And
watch he did. What he saw was a group of people who
seemed to have something indefinable resting between
them: he supposed that in laymen's terms he would have
called it friendship, but that was a description that even at
the time seemed inadequate and now, a year after he'd
joined them, seemed totally inappropriate. He supposed the
precise term would have been commitment. These people
did not necessarily give the outward, worldly signs of
friendship (in fact, now that he knew them, he realized that
many times it was exactly the opposite), but what they did
seem to exude was a sense of commitment to each other.
Then again, now that he'd been with them a year, he wasn't
even sure that "commitment" was the appropriate word,
either. He had long since discovered that their particular
brand of commitment did not encompass friendship. Now
that he thought of it, he wasn't sure he wanted to know the
appropriate word.

The confusion of voices reached its apex. The occasional
"Alleluia" was something that Nicholas could hold onto
as a remembrance of his Catholic upbringing. He tried to
hide the smile that stole across his face when he realized
that he was not remembering his own childhood experi-
ences, but, rather, superimposing *The Sound of Music* over
them. As so often happens when an adult comes to a new
understanding of a long-forgotten incident, Nicholas found
himself precariously close to infusing disproportionate importance into a childhood event. He realized he had been
profoundly affected by seeing *The Sound of Music,* not because the story was so moving (which it was, if he remembered correctly), but because the comical singing nuns of
the movie served as such a sharp contrast to the reality of
the Nazi nuns of his schooling. No shimmering "Alleluias"
soared from these women; instead his lessons had been
croaked at him by an army of identically clad elderly
women, who looked as if they'd been carved out of dried
apples. After seeing the movie, he'd been sure the fault lay

within himself: that if only he could have broken into song like the Von Trapp family children, the nuns would have showered him with their understanding affection, and perhaps have provided harmonies. He hadn't and they hadn't. He considered that his lack of musical ability and subsequent dearth of nunly understanding were jointly responsible for his falling away from the church at the earliest possible age.

If Nicholas could, however whimsically, come to some understanding of why he'd forsaken the church to begin with, he could not fully understand what had brought him back. He would have liked to believe it was the "deep longing" that the Rev. Sam—the Reverend Samuel Draper to the uninitiated—often spoke of, but he knew in his case this wasn't true. Nicholas had been drifting, not longing. He prided himself on having been perfectly up-front with Rev. Sam about this when they'd first met. But the reverend had somehow dazzled him with the explanation that everyone had the same longing, whether they recognized it or not, and were seeking, also whether they knew it or not. The reverend had further explained that people often used the term "drifting" to deny the fact that they were actually seeking (for drifting is, after all, movement in some direction), and that it didn't matter what word you used for the journey as long as one ended up at the proper destination. He then added with a profundity that Nicholas had found perfectly startling the "deep calleth unto deep." Though Nicholas couldn't admit that he understood little of what was said, the reverend's words touched something inside him, giving him the impression that something inexplicable and of the utmost importance had happened by his stumbling upon the church: that he was destined or fated to find his home there. This left Nicholas with the feeling that he'd been on a pilgrimage without ever having known it. It also left him with the uncomfortable feeling that he'd arrived without his luggage.

If Nicholas was unsure of exactly how he'd ended up in the church, he definitely knew why he stayed. Pamela Frazier stood by his side. Her face was upturned, her eyes closed, her lips slightly parted in a smile. The overhead lights reflected highlights in her golden hair. She looked as if she were quite happy, and Nicholas wondered if it went any deeper than that. Not a sound escaped her lips. Nicholas thought, not without a twinge of guilt, that he would be happy when the service—meeting—was over and they could go out to dinner.

The group as a whole could hardly be called a congregation, although its number hovered around a hundred members. Their dress and their manner were simply too casual for such a formal term, and most members would have blanched at the idea of having such an ecclesiastical word applied to them. They prided themselves, forgetting the inherent sin, on being different (read "holier") than the average mainstream churches among America's various brands of Christianity. This difference was most readily reflected in their language; they had meetings instead of services, they "got into the Word" instead of simply reading the Bible, but, most important, they were a Community instead of a church. It was with an almost superstitious pertinacity that they steered away from using terms common to mainstream religion, substituting words which they believed had more substance. If pressed they would insist that this was not just a matter of semantics. Most members of the Community truly believed that their beliefs and their Community had greater depth than their more mundane brethren. Most members would also explain that their stubborn insistence on holding their meetings on Saturday nights instead of Sunday mornings was not merely to differ from mainstream Protestant churches, but to free up Sundays as a day of rest. The irony of this choice was not lost on Nicholas, the former Catholic.

Their one concession to the mainstream world had been the recent purchase of an actual church building. After years of prayer, the church leadership had decided that the Lord wanted them to have a home, a building that would serve their needs (and demonstrate to the outside world that they were, indeed, a church). And after many special collections (above and beyond their usual tithes) and bake sale-type fund-raising, they had finally managed to put a down payment on a long since abandoned Methodist church. However, acquisition of the building would be where the concessions to the mainstream ended. They had immediately removed the pews, which they replaced with ordinary padded moveable chairs. They had gutted the sanctuary, leaving only a small podium in the center from which the Rev. Sam could deliver his weekly "lessons" (their term for sermons). The "opening up" of this room had made it seem much more like an auditorium than a church. An auditorium with stained-glass windows.

During the noisy release of the Spirit that Nicholas found so disturbing, the Community members stood before their chairs, which were arranged in an abbreviated semicircle around the podium. As the singing began to die down, Nicholas's hand stole its way into Pamela's, whose smile broadened perceptibly. At the opposite end of the semicircle, though her face was upturned and her eyes appeared to be closed, this action was noted by Sarah Bennett. Her cheeks puckered and her lips grew thinner.

The voices swelled once again in a final crescendo, then slowly moved from their various points along the chromatic scale until all were joined in various octaves on the same note. The collective note petered out, leaving behind a peace that Nicholas found particularly blessed. After a lengthy pause, an inexplicable sense of expectation permeated the room, and then passed, leaving in its wake a mixture of relief, release, and just a little touch of disappointment. There had been no manifestation.

The Reverend Samuel Draper, who had stepped back from the podium during the release of the Spirit, now returned to his position. Rev. Sam was a medium-built man with a curiously sharp nose in the middle of his rounded face. He had muddy-brown receding hair, with a fair amount of waves that he tried unsuccessfully to straighten out each morning, parting it on the right and brushing it

vigorously to the side. He had about him the air of a rather
self-assured insurance salesman who was convinced that his
existence did not depend on whether or not you bought
what he was selling. The one thing that belied his serenity
was his eyes: they were dark brown and alive with an intensity that could easily discomfit even the most willful
sheep. It was well known among the Community that if
Rev. Sam was moved to anger, an astute observer could
detect a sudden pulsing twinge around the rim of his eyes,
something like an electrical surge. But the good reverend
was seldom moved to anger.

As he stepped up to the podium, he raised both his arms
in benediction.

"May the Lord be with you," his voice pealed authori-
tatively.

"And also with you," thought Nicholas despite himself.

"Turn and offer each other the hand of fellowship."

At this point the Community, on cue as was their weekly
custom, broke into something resembling a rather over-
heated family reunion. Each member turned to his or her
closest counterpart, in proximity and relationship, and
greeted the other with either a handshake or an embrace.
Husbands turned first to wives, boyfriends to girlfriends,
and roommates to roommates. Greetings were then exchanged with those on the other side. Needless to say, Pamela turned first to Nicholas. As they hugged warmly,
Nicholas whispered, "Let's eat." Pamela smiled and turned
to the man on her right, who gently shook her hand. There
was nobody on Nicholas's left.

Gradually the Community broke into small groups that
stood chatting together. Children chased each other about
their parents' legs, and readily availed themselves of the
cakes, cookies, and punch supplied in liberal quantities by
the women of the Community and left for "self-service"
on a long folding table at the back of the room.

"No, really, let's go," said Nicholas, contriving to add
a pleading note to his voice.

Pamela found him particularly hard to resist when he got

that hangdog, slightly petulant look. It added a boyish charm to his otherwise striking looks. He had a ruddy complexion, with the unusual, alluring combination of straight dark hair and light blue eyes. When he purposely curled his lips into a pout, as he did now, he looked like a luridly continental child.

"Honestly, sometimes I think the only reason you come to church is so you can go out to eat."

Nicholas flushed guiltily. "No, I come to church so I can go out *with you.*"

"You're shameless," she replied, pleased nonetheless.

"Uh-huh."

"And you know it."

"Uh-huh."

Pamela pushed the long blond hair back off her shoulder. She looked at Nicholas's expectant face and smiled despite herself.

"All right, we can go."

She slipped her arm through his and together they started for the door. There seemed to be an unspoken agreement between them that their exit should be as unobtrusive as possible. In this they were unsuccessful. Michael Franklin appeared in the doorway just as they reached it, much to their dismay, not out of any dislike for the young man, but because they were anxious to leave and even more anxious that their leaving not be noticed.

Michael Franklin was a reedy young man in his early twenties, pale and nervous, whose dishwater hair dangled just short of the tiny beads of sweat that formed on his brow.

"Michael!" Pamela exclaimed, surprised by his sudden appearance. "Where did you spring from?"

It was a fair question, since from the way he wavered in the doorway it was impossible to tell if he was entering or leaving.

"Weren't you at the meeting?"

"Yes...yes." His anxious eyes scanned the room.

"I wondered. We saw Barbara just before the meeting, but we didn't see you."

"I was a little late. I sat at the back." Michael turned and looked directly at Pamela for the first time. "Why, are you watching me?"

"No, of course not," Pamela stammered. "I just meant…"

"Is something wrong?" said Nicholas.

"No. Sorry. I didn't mean to…isn't Danny here?"

"We haven't seen him."

Michael looked around the room as if he thought the couple might have carelessly overlooked the man in question. "He isn't *here?*"

"What's the problem, Mike? Danny's missed meetings before."

"Didn't he tell you he wouldn't be here?" asked Pamela.

"No. No, he didn't."

Michael's eyes stopped suddenly. Nicholas and Pamela followed his gaze across the room to a small group of women who stood talking quietly in a corner. Four of the five women had small white lace caps pinned in their hair, the head coverings that they believed were a sign of their devotion. The one without a cap had her back turned to Nicholas and Pamela, and was speaking spiritedly but quietly to the other four. Over her shoulder could be seen the object of Michael's scrutiny.

Barbara Searly looked toward him with a combination of sadness and dismay. Michael had once said of her that with one look she could make even total strangers feel they'd let her down. Michael could bear the looks more than the tears, but in his case he didn't think he could blame her for either.

"That's your fiancée," said Nicholas with a grin.

"What?"

"You looked as if you didn't recognize her."

Michael lowered his eyes to the floor and sighed quietly, like a mournful puppy. There was an uncomfortable silence.

"Well," said Nicholas finally, "we have to get going."

Michael started to walk reluctantly away from them. "I suppose I should join Barbara." He said this so quietly they barely heard him.

Nicholas and Pamela watched him for a moment. Then Nicholas took her hand, and without another word they disappeared through the doorway.

ALTHOUGH THEIR EXIT was performed as unobtrusively as possible, the couple's leaving did not go unnoticed, with varying degrees of interest.

William and Janet Clayton, a recently married young couple, noticed Nicholas and Pamela in passing, and smiled at each other as William's hand tightened around Janet's.

On the other side of the room, directly to the left of the dais where a font had once stood, Sarah Bennett peered at the couple as they passed through the door. With a slight inclination of the head she drew the attention of the Beckmans to the event.

"That's becoming a habit," said Sarah in a voice that was half whisper and half hiss, but all condemnation. "They leave earlier and earlier every week! I'm surprised they stay for the end of the meeting!"

With a glance at her husband, Stephanie Beckman said, "Now, Sarah, they always come to the meetings even if they don't stay for the afters."

"I'm sure they're devoted to the Community," added Howard Beckman, tucking his thumbs under his belt and giving it a little tug.

"They never stay for the fellowship afterwards," said Sarah hotly. "I don't think that shows any devotion."

Stephanie pursed her lips, the right corner of her mouth curled upward doubtfully. "I think it shows another kind of devotion. You know how it is..." She stopped, realizing to her embarrassment that this was an unfortunate beginning when talking to Sarah. But she realized it was too late to stop. She began again, dismissing the preamble. "When you're in the earlier stages of love..."

"Or even later," interrupted her husband with a twinkle in his eye.

"...in the early stages, sometimes it seems like you're the only two people in the world."

"But they're not," said Sarah, "they're not alone, they're part of a Community."

She narrowed her eyes as if she could crush the couple between her lids. "But you'd never know it!"

THERE WAS ONE other person who noted with interest the departure of Nicholas and Pamela. Samuel Draper, the Rev. Sam, stood tall and erect, his right hand resting on the podium. Saul Berne, a small-group leader, stood talking to him quietly but fervently. Though Rev. Sam heard every word Saul said, he didn't appear to be listening. Instead, all of his interest seemed to be directed to the brief scene by the doorway. It was said among the Community that Rev. Sam saw everything. And they were right.

TWO

SUMMER HAD GIVEN way to fall. The signs of the changing seasons were not as obvious on Ransom's "beat," where trees were few and far between, and the ones that did exist were cultivated in such unnatural circumstances—such as the marbleized entryways of vertical malls—that they were, in turn, loathe to follow the natural progression of their suburban cousins, preferring to remain green when yellow or brown would have been more appropriate. In downtown Chicago, the change from summer to fall is felt rather than seen: The air seems alive with expectation.

Jeremy Ransom remembered with a sigh the pallid young Sunday school teacher of his early childhood who had delighted in telling the class that the change was in anticipation of death, hence Halloween, the celebration of death, stood as a doorway to winter, while Easter, a celebration of renewal, performed the same function for spring. The young Ransom had found the idea disturbing, but not as interesting as the tattoo of a naked woman that undulated on the teacher's arm as he physically punctuated the lessons. His sleeve would inch up in jerks as he gestured, presenting the female form in a sort of inverted striptease, where the clothing went up instead of down. Ransom later realized that the light blue tattoo had taught him the real meaning of anticipation (though for what he wasn't sure).

It had been many years since Ransom had thought of the Sunday school teacher with the exotic arm. To most people, memories of this kind would seem highly appropriate to a drive through the autumnal colors of Lincoln Park. To Ransom they were just another reminder of the inevitability of change, whether for bad or for worse. At least the seasonal change was expected.

Instead of enjoying the slow drive through the red- and gold-hued trees that adorned the mid-city oasis, Ransom castigated himself for choosing this route on a day when he should have known it would be choked with traffic. Thousands of parents with straggling children seemed to be swarming the grounds of the park and the entrance to the zoo, reluctantly heading home from trying to savor what could easily turn out to be the last decent Sunday of the year. Chicago's weather being known to change with the alacrity of a manic-depressive's moods, it was quite possible that the pleasant sixty-degree temperature of this Sunday would give way to sub-zero weather on the next.

The turning colors and the slow drive served to accentuate the long ordeal through which Ransom had passed during the past three days. The anticipation of the event had been bad enough, bringing with it an uncertainty that was totally foreign to the detective, but Friday had been, by far, the longest day of his life. Saturday had been slightly shorter and Sunday shorter still (though not short enough). His days, he thought reflectively, had become a microcosm for the changing season, as if he'd lived a year in one week, and his own days were shortening with the coming winter. Now that it was early Sunday evening, and the danger had passed, time seemed to be returning to its normal sphere, and his anxiety waned like the memory of a particularly virulent headache.

Ransom finally reached Diversey Parkway and turned right. The small bouquet of flowers wrapped in paper slid forward on the passenger seat, but did not go over the edge. He gently slid it back. He hung a left onto inner Lake Shore Drive, and then left again into the parking lot of St. Joseph's Hospital. This had become the only place that Ransom did not exercise his badge-given right to park wherever he pleased, but chose instead to play by the rules and "pay the man the two dollars." It somehow seemed more respectful under the circumstances. He pulled into a slot and climbed out of his aging Nova, retrieving the flowers from the seat and a shallow box wrapped in white-and-gold paper from the floor. One package in each hand, he walked swiftly to the main entrance and followed the quiet hallway that had become regretfully familiar to him over the past few days, finally coming to the elevators. After a brief wait, he found himself at the nurses' station on the fifth floor.

"Hello, Mr. Ransom," said a melodic voice. The voice belonged to Nurse Carter, a young black woman who was perhaps a little too fond of ruby-red lipstick, but whose smile could be forgiven anything: it cut a wide swath across her oval face. Her eyes danced above it like two happily startled shoe buttons. As she came out from behind the desk, she pulled more closely around her the navy blue cardigan that always hung about her shoulders. She had once explained to Ransom that even in the dead of summer, she could still feel chilly.

Ransom returned her smile. "How is she?" he asked as they walked down the hallway.

"I looked in on her about a quarter to five—she hadn't eaten much of anything yet."

"Does that mean anything?"

The nurse smiled. "It's hard to tell. I don't know how much she normally eats. She may just not be hungry. She may just be tired. She's been through a lot, but she's one tough old woman. She's coming along pretty well—but even the toughest of us get tired."

They came to a stop outside the second-to-last room at the end of the hall. "Like you," added Nurse Carter, her smile waning slightly.

"Me?"

"You look pretty tired. You been getting any sleep at all?"

"Not a lot," he said with a rueful smile. "Maybe I should see a doctor."

"You've come to the right place," she laughed. She had a healthy, throaty laugh that rang like happiness itself. "But really, you should get some rest."

"My work is tiring."

"I know, I know, I sound like your old mama hen." She waved her hands as if chasing away flies. "I'll let it go."

Ransom nodded and proffered the white-and-gold box to her.

"These are for you and the rest of the staff."

"Chocolates!" said Carter, her eye widening. "Whatever kind they are, they're my favorite!"

"I just wanted...I appreciate how well you've taken care of her."

Nurse Carter smiled broadly and hugged the box like a happy child.

"We frown on these in the cardiac unit, but there isn't a nurse on the floor who can resist. I'm afraid this falls under the heading of 'do as I say, not as I do.'"

Ransom returned the smile, but his eyes wandered from the nurse to the room whose occupant awaited him. Carter studied his face for a moment with a scrutiny that would have surprised the detective, and noted the wear and worry that would have escaped a less trained eye.

"And you don't have to worry," she said as if there'd been no pause in the conversation, "she is a doll to take care of. She's quite a remarkable woman."

"That she is," he said.

Nurse Carter gave him a tap on the shoulder with the candy box. "Now you get in there. She's waiting for you." She started down the hall, then called back to him. "And get some rest. You don't want to collapse in a hospital!"

Ransom hesitated in the doorway. He never knew what he would find when he visited Emily anymore: at least, that's the way he felt. When he'd stopped by to see her Wednesday evening, she was having what she calmly referred to as heart palpitations, but she looked so weak and frightened he rushed her to the hospital. Thursday she'd spent placidly reading Shakespeare's *Much Ado About Nothing* in between tests, the results of which found four of the arteries in her heart too blocked to be dealt with in any of the less intrusive ways. Friday she'd spent in the operating room.

Ransom had been unprepared for her physical appearance when he'd finally been allowed to visit her in the ICU that evening. It seemed that Emily Charters, the feisty elderly woman who'd been willing to face a murderer head-on when she and Ransom had first become acquainted, had been robbed of every vestige of strength and vitality. Her hair seemed white instead of gray, and her dusty blue eyes, when they'd finally opened, were more dust than blue.

It was during that time in the ICU that thoughts of his Sunday school days had first returned to Ransom, tinged with regret that those simple times, with the accompanying obliviousness to the dangers of the world, would never come again. And for the first time since his parents had died, he said a prayer. In substance it resembled more of a command regarding Emily's outcome, but it was a prayer nonetheless.

Now as he entered Emily's hospital room, with only a little over one full day since her surgery, Ransom was amazed to find her sitting up in bed, moving the food around on her plate as if she were trying to discern its origins.

"Jeremy! How nice to see you!"

However off the color of her eyes might be, they visibly brightened at the sight of the tired detective.

"Emily, even though I come to visit you every evening, you always sound surprised to see me."

"I always *am* surprised. Pleasantly."

"I've brought you some fresh flowers."

"So I see."

Ransom removed the previous days' flowers—which hadn't had near enough time to even begin to wilt—from the glass vase that rested on Emily's bedside table. He dropped them carelessly into the tiny garbage can that jutted from beneath the table, and replaced them with the fresh arrangement.

"You really don't need to bring new flowers every day."

"I know that," said Ransom austerely as he crumpled the paper wrapper and dropped it in the can. He brushed his hands on his navy blue slacks and sat on the orange vinyl chair that comprised the only remaining nonmedical furniture in Emily's half of the room. The other half, thankfully, was unoccupied.

"I understand that you haven't been eating."

Emily smiled at him knowingly. "Is that a bit of observation on your part, or have you been running an investigation?"

Ransom returned her smile. "I ran into Nurse Carter on my way in."

"Ah, Nurse Carter. She's a lovely girl, and very efficient."

"Yes..."

"It's nice to have young nurses. They are not as inclined to address me with the royal 'we,' which under the circumstances I would find very irritating."

"I thought nurses only did that in post-Victorian novels."

"My dear Jeremy, that is because you're still young. You'll find when you become an antiquated old thing like myself, it is not only nurses who will refer to you that way."

Ransom crossed his legs and folded his hands in his lap. "You're very crafty."

Emily raised her eyebrows, feigning surprise. "I beg your pardon?"

"You think you're distracting me, but you're not."

"I'm sure I don't know what you're talking about."

"I suppose I should take it as a sign that you're on the road to recovery, but I'm not going to be sidetracked. You didn't answer my question."

"What was your question?" asked Emily with a slight smile.

Ransom sighed. "Is it true that you're not eating?"

"You make it sound as if I've committed a crime."

Ransom made an exasperated noise, and Emily raised a hand to quell his wrath.

"Don't worry, Jeremy, I have not gone on a hunger

strike. In fact, I was just thinking how nice it would be to be sitting in my own kitchen having a fresh omelette and a nice cup of tea.''

"Well, I call that a good sign. But you should eat anyway. Isn't the food here any good?''

Emily rested back against her pillows and sighed, "The food is fine, it just isn't...home.''

"You'll be going home soon.''

"Soon," Emily echoed him faintly, her gaze traveling to the window where the striking lake view was quickly fading from sight as the sun set. "Everything is done so quickly nowadays, it's difficult not to feel that one is being left behind.''

"Hmm?''

"It was barely five days ago that I thought I was fine, and in a matter of hours I was having a bypass operation. In my day, that sort of thing was unheard of. When you were having heart trouble, you were put in the hospital 'under observation.' By the time the doctors decided what should be done about you, you'd had some time to get used to the seriousness of the situation. But now everything happens so quickly you hardly have time to realize there's a problem before you're having open-heart surgery. Progress is a wonderful thing, I suppose, but too often it runs faster than the human mind can accept. We don't have time to take in the danger before it's upon us." She paused and appeared to be deep in thought. "'The thing I have greatly feared has come upon me,''' she said absently. "I've always found that one of the most haunting passages of scripture. I suppose it becomes truer as time goes on.''

Ransom studied his adopted grandmother with a practiced eye. Her face was still turned toward the window, vacantly watching the rapidly dimming scene. Everything that Ransom had come to rely upon was still embodied in the little woman: the courage, the intelligence; there was even evidence that her vitality and strength were returning. But there was something else as well: some added facet that Ransom found vaguely disturbing, if for no other reason than that it was foreign to Emily.

After a moment's consideration, Ransom was able to identify this new attribute: it was resignation. Since her operation, Emily seemed as if she'd become resigned to something that was inevitable. Ransom wasn't sure what the object of this resignation was, but he was sure that he didn't like it. He firmly believed that unlike "acceptance," which allows an individual to deal with unalterable circumstances, "resignation" was a sign of giving up: and giving up was not in Emily's character.

Emily turned away from the window and looked fondly at the careworn detective. A benignant smile spread across her face. As if reading his mind, she said, "I know this is a ridiculous thing for a woman in her seventies to say, but I think I've finally realized that I won't live forever."

Ransom hoped the concern he felt didn't show on his face.

"None of us will," he said softly.

As if the cosmos would offer further proof of Ransom and Emily's newfound awareness, the next morning the human tendency toward mortality was demonstrated to yet another unsuspecting Chicagoan.

A large blue truck pulled off Washington Street into the dank alley between Wabash and Michigan Avenues. The alleys of downtown Chicago are throwbacks to the early days of the city: Fire escapes cling precariously to aging bricks that seem to be forgotten during the periodic sandblastings received by the facades fronting the wealthy thoroughfares. Face-lifts do not apply to alleys. The ground looks wet and fetid, as if grime had slithered down the buildings and run into greasy pools.

Each building was supplied with a loading dock commensurate with the size of the building: and each dock was in the same state of disrepair, the wood splintered and permeated with a damp so pervasive that no amount of heat would ever dry it.

The truck moved directly to the third building from the corner, and stopped just beyond it. The driver then backed the truck into the dock, slamming loudly into a mid-sized Dumpster that bore a gold shield matching the one emblazoned across the side of the truck. Both shields displayed the words "Donaldson Brothers Waste Removal Company" in vivid red letters.

Jim Bowman lowered himself heavily from the driver's seat of the truck's cab. He paused only long enough to wipe the greasy sweat from his brow with a smudged handkerchief, which he then stuffed in his back pocket. He glanced up at the strip of sky visible between the buildings, muttered something unintelligible, and spat on the ground. The orange-tinged sunlight was far too bright already: he was running late.

Grumbling to himself, he maneuvered the Dumpster into position, flipped the lid back, and hooked chains on either side of its back. He then stepped back to the side of the truck and threw a lever. With a loud thrumming noise, the chains tightened and drew up the Dumpster, spilling its contents into the back of the truck. The usual assortment of plastic bags and wet garbage rolled reluctantly out of the receptacle.

There was a slight hesitation in the proceedings, as if the truck were taking a deep breath before heaving the heaviest part of its load, then continued to pull on its chains with renewed vigor.

Bowman thrust his large gloved hands into the mess to give the more reluctant waste a helping push. He reached around a particularly stubborn large black garbage bag that seemed to be caught on something, and touched what he took to be the leg of a chair or small table. He cursed to himself and gave the object a tug, but it didn't budge. It figured, he thought: The occupants of these Michigan Avenue office buildings could afford premium rents, but only seemed to be able to afford the cheapest garbage bags, which were forever becoming impaled on things like this.

He gave the object under the bag another tug, and tumbled back as the object suddenly dislodged, and the bag fell forward into the truck. The object twisted awkwardly in Bowman's right hand, and he grabbed at it with his left to keep whatever it was from tumbling out on top of him.

It was then that he realized to his horror that the object in his hands was not a chair or table leg, but a human arm.

Bowman let out a booming yell and leapt back as the naked corpse fell at his feet.

THREE

RANSOM WASN'T SURE whether or not he missed them most while he was reading. Of late he had taken to blaming them for the fact that the time he spent with his beloved Dickens had dwindled to almost nothing. But, with his usual acute sense of self-awareness, he realized that this idea was—he cringed when he thought it—all smoke and mirrors. He was simply—God, could he not get away from these allusions— blowing smoke at the real reasons. In his more cogent moments he would admit that his reading had diminished along with his time. After spending all day investigating murders and all evening (sometimes all night) at the hospital with Emily, there was no time left for leisurely evenings in the bathtub with Dickens and cigars. He sighed. Or without cigars. He sighed even more heavily. Nothing was more relaxing than lying in a hot tub with a good book and filling the room with smoke. Those were the days.

It was not simply because Emily was in the hospital that Ransom was trying once again to give up cigars, but because of Emily herself: She had been after him almost since they'd first met to stop what she considered an unseemly, unsightly, and potentially dangerous habit.

Ransom was loath to admit that giving up smoking had been one of the few areas of failure in his life. His one previous attempt at smoking cessation had led him instead to bigger and blacker cigars, and to Emily's continued disapproving frowns. He thought the problem would be solved by simply not smoking around Emily—or within an hour of seeing her. But he needn't have bothered: The old lady had all the better attributes of a bloodhound, and could unfailingly sniff him out every time. And within the antiseptic confines of the hospital, he seemed to emit fumes from every pore a full four hours after his last cigar. With Emily in the hospital and his newfound sense of mortality, Ransom knew there was nothing for it: He had to give up smoking.

No, he thought with a disgruntled "hrmph," this was when he missed them most: on the way to the scene of a crime.

Gerald's smile rose like a lopsided crescent moon over the steering wheel. It wasn't that he was unsympathetic to his partner's condition, it was just that he couldn't help himself. It was always nice to see signs of humanity in the "master detective." And it was nice to be in a car polluted only with smog and exhaust fumes. But as glad as Gerald might be with the absence of smoke, he would not have had anything happen to Emily for any price. He had a healthy respect for the elderly woman who'd proven instrumental in solving the Pennington Players case.

Then there was Ransom's disposition: On a good day Ransom could be difficult, as Gerald would put it with typical diplomacy. Under the current strain, without benefit of smoke, Ransom was downright irksome.

"Can't this thing go any faster?" said Ransom, drumming his fingers on the armrest.

Gerald's smile disappeared in a sea of gritted teeth.

"It *can* go faster," he replied evenly, "but the victim will still be dead if we get there a few minutes later."

Ransom registered his displeasure at this reply with a brief pause in his drumming, after which he resumed.

"I really hate getting a new murder dumped on me first thing on Monday morning."

"That's the trouble with—"

"Other people get to ease into the morning. Other people get to sit at their desks in peace for a while and have a quiet cup of coffee. I'd like to do that now and then—have a cup of coffee, put my feet up, and read the paper."

"You wouldn't like it. All the news is bad."

Ransom exhaled testily. "Gerald, as time goes by you

get more and more like me which in your case has not been an improvement.''

Gerald smiled, which only served to further irritate his partner. Ransom had often thought Gerald White's face to be a veritable map of childhood: His face was as pale as Elmer's paste, and his lips were the shade of the erasers that topped Ticonderoga pencils. When his lips formed that knowing smile, it was like being mocked by a schoolboy.

Gerald's smile waned as he steered the car onto Washington Street.

"How is Miss Emily doing?" he asked.

There was a brief pause during which Ransom seemed to harden slightly.

"She seems to be recovering since her...incident."

Gerald glanced at Ransom out of the corner of his eye.

"She wants to go home."

Gerald shrugged slightly and said, "Hmm, that's a good sign."

"I suppose."

There followed the type of strained silence that occasionally falls between two normally communicative people who can think of nothing more to say on a volatile subject. The silence remained unbroken for the few remaining moments it took to reach their destination.

"Here we are," said Gerald as he pulled the car to a stop by the squad car that was already blocking the alley.

As they emerged from their car, the detectives were met by officers Layton and Carmody.

"What do you have?" said Gerald, taking care of the mundane while Ransom abstracted himself to the side.

"Young kid," Layton answered, jerking his thumb in the direction of the Dumpster, which now lay on its side where it had fallen from the back of the truck when in his shock Jim Bowman had neglected to stop it as the chains drew it up. Soiled paper and assorted garbage trailed away from it like spilled entrails. A police photographer appeared to be engrossed in capturing the debris on film.

"It's just a kid," Carmody continued for his partner,

whose voice was showing signs of emotion, "and you've never seen anything like it."

Ransom shot a glance at the uniformed officer.

"At least I haven't," Layton added impotently.

"Guy from the garbage company found the body when he was emptying the trash. He's over there," said Carmody.

Ransom eyed the large man who sat in the open door of the squad car's backseat. The man had a large and rather nasty-looking damp stain across the stomach of his coveralls.

"He's pretty shaken up," Carmody added in a voice that made it unclear as to which man he was referring.

There was a brief pause during which the officers were at a loss for what else to say, and the detectives (especially Ransom) seemed anxious to get on with the work at hand.

"The wagon's on the way to pick up the body," said Layton. "I suppose they'll take him to the hospital to be pronounced, but they don't...there's not..." His voice trailed off.

Ransom said "Yes, thank you" rather tersely and headed for the scene, followed by Gerald, who paused only long enough to give a more sympathetic "thank you" to the officers, both of whom appeared a bit green in more ways than one.

The ground felt slippery under the detective's feet, like snot on a doorknob thought Ransom, remembering the phrase from his high school days. He passed a particularly vile Dumpster with a large hole in the top, into which grease was normally poured. It looked as if it had vomited scum. He barely missed slipping into a rat that had been run over so many times it looked like road kill twice removed.

"Are you having a good time, Ferman?" asked Ransom as he reached the photographer.

"It's less frustrating than doing weddings," Ferman replied. "My subjects don't move around."

"Hi, Ferman," said Gerald, joining them.

"My subjects are also more interesting," said Ferman

with a smile as rumpled as his mustard yellow suit, which looked as if it had been designed for a slightly smaller and younger man. "Like this one. I don't know what this kid was into, but it must have been some pretty weird shit."

"Hmm," said Ransom.

"It's a shame, too. He doesn't look like he was much over twenty. A bit young to end up like this." The photographer clucked his tongue and set about putting his camera back in its case. "Then again, when you're older, I suppose you know better than to get involved in things that would make you end up like this. I'm done here."

The photographer ambled away from them.

The body lay at their feet, swaddled in a bed of crumpled papers. What could have been a picture of a young man in repose was ruined by the severe bashing the head had received. However, his face was relatively unharmed, and bore the inscrutability that only a few days of death can bring. It was no longer the face and body of a young man; it was a travesty of a young man, crowned in crusted blood.

"Barely twenty-five," said Ransom, ruminating.

Gerald snorted and said, "I wouldn't think he was even twenty." They were silent for a moment longer, then Gerald added, "But the uniforms were right about one thing: There's no doubt about the cause."

Ransom, who had been stooping over the body for closer examination, raised an eyebrow and stood to face his partner.

"Really?"

Gerald faltered, realizing from Ransom's tone that he'd missed something. He decided to continue with all the force of someone who realizes he's playing a losing game.

"Of course, look at his head."

"Look at his hands," said Ransom with irritating coyness, "and his feet."

Gerald looked more closely at these appendages. From a distance they'd merely looked stained, the fingers curled as if they had been clutching something that had been released only in death, but had not fallen away. On closer inspection,

Gerald found that the palms and feet were not stained, but pierced.

"My God," he said, "what is this?"

"The stigmata," Ransom replied matter-of-factly.

Gerald's eyebrows drew together, giving him the appearance of a flaccid, quizzical owl.

"He may have been killed by blows to the head, but this boy has been crucified."

Gerald let out a low whistle. "Jesus."

"WE QUESTIONED JIM BOWMAN, the man who found the body."

"And?"

"And I think we can be fairly sure that all he did was find the body."

"We can?"

Ransom began to slowly drum his fingers on the arm of the chair as he sat facing Newman across the sergeant's desk.

"The only thing he contributed to the scene was his breakfast, most of which he managed to get on himself. Murderers don't generally vomit when they've done the deed."

"Thanks for the description," said Sergeant Newman, pushing his oily, graying hair back off his forehead. "What've you got?"

Ransom mentally rolled his eyes, though his face remained impassive.

"We canvased the buildings along the alley...at least, the receiving areas for the buildings. Nobody heard or saw anything unusual. But, of course, it must have happened over the weekend sometime—"

"Wait a minute, wait a minute!" said Newman, straightening himself in his chair as if excited to find a point on which to challenge his star detective. "How do you know that? You can't have the doctor's report yet."

Ransom sighed and the speed of his drumming fingers increased.

"Even..." Ransom began, but then checked himself before putting this in the personal. "Even Gerald could see that though the body was stiff, it was on its way to flaccidity."

Newman eyed Ransom as if he was not quite decided on whether or not to let this go. But Newman was never one to cut off his nose to spite his face—especially with Ransom. He didn't push it.

Ransom smiled inwardly.

"So," said Newman, "how do you plan to proceed? Canvas the rest of the occupants of the buildings?"

"I don't think that would give us anything. I think there are a few other things we can assume."

"You're just chock-full of surprises today, aren't you? I didn't think you ever assumed anything."

If Newman had known Ransom's state of mind, he would have known how dangerous the momentary pause in his drumming was. When Ransom resumed tapping his rhythm, there was something slow and spiderlike about the motion.

"We can assume that the murder did not take place in the alley."

Newman started to protest, but Ransom interrupted him.

"We can assume that he was not stripped naked and crucified in that alley."

"We can't assume that he was crucified."

"Something was driven through his hands and feet. If it wasn't literal, it was certainly symbolic. And there were rope burns around the wrists and ankles; my guess would be to hold them in place while the deed was done."

"His head was bashed in, wasn't it?"

"But not in that alley. There were no signs that it was done there. The process must have been very noisy...or at least messy. And you know the Loop as well as I do. Even in the dead of night there are people down there. Too big a risk. The murder was done somewhere private, and then the body was dumped there."

"And so?"

"So, though I'll, of course, canvas the rest of the building's tenants, I'm sure the effort will be worthless. Only a lunatic would have dumped a dead body there while the businesses were open."

"Only a lunatic would crucify a young kid."

Ransom's fingers ceased their slow drumming, and a smile crept across his face. "Isn't it amazing how intelligent a lunatic can be?"

Newman's expression seemed caught somewhere between puzzlement and anger. He settled for movement. He rose from his chair, sending it scraping loudly back into the wall of his musty office.

"And so far we don't have any identification on this kid?"

Ransom's smile broadened. "He didn't have any tattoos."

Newman turned and looked down on the seated detective. Ransom had a talent for appearing authoritative, even from a sitting position. Newman overcompensated by adopting an attitude of exaggerated superiority.

"So it looks like after the doctor's through with him, it's off to the icebox for this boy. When you're through canvasing the neighborhood, you'll have to get together with Missing Persons to see if anyone's been looking for the kid."

"Yes, sir," said Ransom.

Newman rested his hands on the desk and leaned in toward Ransom, a smirk playing about his lips. Although Newman liked nothing less than an unsolved case, he knew the detective's one weak spot, and couldn't help going for it, he wanted so badly to wipe the smile from the detective's face.

"It looks as if this might be one of the ones that stays on ice. Maybe we should take a loss on this one and get on to the next."

Ransom sighed. His smile was unaffected.

"I don't know. Someone's bound to come looking for

him...eventually.'' Ransom raised an eyebrow in mock wonder. ''That is what we want, isn't it?''

''DID YOU GET on to the goddam doctor?'' Ransom snapped at his reclining partner.

Gerald White swung his feet to the floor and sat up, brushing at a crease on his right pant's leg. The couch made rude Naugahyde noises beneath him.

''They just got the body this morning. You know as well as I do that it's too early for results. You also know as well as I do what the verdict will be: death by blunt trauma to the head.''

''Ah, you haven't just been lying there in my absence.''

Gerald replied with more irritation than was his norm, ''It's late and I'm tired.''

Ransom emitted an acerbic ''Hmm'' as he dropped into the chair behind his desk.

''You know,'' said Gerald, ''I wish to God you would smoke.''

''What?''

''It's bad for you, but it's good for me.''

''You're going to have to explain that.''

''Since you've stopped, you haven't been your usual...self.''

Ransom laid his right hand flat on the desk, his fingers looking as if they fairly itched to start a tune.

''I will admit...'' Ransom said slowly through gritted teeth, ''...to being a bit peckish, nothing more, this week. But it hasn't been without reason.''

''I know that...''

''What with Emily's incident and everything.''

''Incident?''

''But that is not what's on my mind now. I just had one of my more circular discussions with your friend Sergeant Newman.''

''*My* friend?''

''Insufferable idiot! I mean Newman, not you.''

Ransom's right hand swung mechanically to his breast

pocket before he realized what he was doing. He frowned and dropped his hand back to the desktop, which he began to lightly tap with his index finger.

Gerald broke the silence.

"I take it this wasn't just another sparring match?"

Ransom heaved a sigh. "It was the usual. He wanted a report, I gave it to him. He offered us some marvelous suggestions for proceeding with the investigation, including canvasing the rest of the neighborhood."

Gerald groaned.

"Which I assured him would be a waste of time, given the facts that we have so far, but then again, if we're going to be good little detectives..."

Gerald groaned more forcibly.

Ransom continued, "One of the sad facts of our fascinating profession, my dear Gerald, is that it is not as fascinating as the books would have us believe."

Gerald pursed his lips at his partner. "Did Newman offer any other suggestions?"

"Yes. In lieu of tattoos, we should contact Missing Persons."

"Huh?"

Ransom smiled. "Never mind, Gerald."

"Anything else?"

Ransom swung his chair around to face the window. As he did so, he dragged his fingernail across the desk with enough force to leave a long, thin scratch. As he spoke, he continued to dig his nail further into the wood, his finger reddening with the effort.

"Only one thing...he issued me a challenge."

"A challenge?"

"He suggested that this case would prove unsolvable, and that we should probably pack it in and move on to the next one."

Gerald smiled. "Oh. He did."

"It was a blatant appeal to my vanity, so patently obvious, in fact, that you would think the good sergeant would blush to use it."

Gerald scrutinized his partner for a moment, his smile broadening.

"Did it work?"

At this point the tip of Ransom's fingernail snapped off. No further reply was necessary.

FOUR

EARLY MONDAY EVENING Michael Franklin hesitated on the doorstep. He knew what he was about to do—or what he intended to do—but whenever he came here, things had a way of not turning out the way he intended. He swallowed hard, took a deep breath, and knocked tentatively on the door.

After a brief wait, during which Michael half hoped that nobody was home, the door swung open. A large figure stood framed in the doorway, imposingly backlit by the bright houselights that spilled out into the darkness.

"Why Michael, what a pleasant surprise," said a measured voice that displayed neither pleasure nor surprise.

"Reverend...I...I need to talk to you."

"Come in, come in."

A shadowed arm gestured smoothly back into the light. Michael hesitated for only a moment before passing the reverend into the house.

"We're in the living room," said Reverend Sam as he closed the door behind them.

Michael stopped in his tracks and looked back at the reverend over his shoulder. Reverend Sam returned the look with a smile that was infused with confidence and superiority. To Michael, that smile had always held a touch of malice. As if on cue, he felt guilt at the thought.

"Your small-group leader is here," Rev. Sam continued as he shepherded Michael into the living room.

At the first sight of Michael, the squat man who sat uncomfortably on the maroon upholstered couch leapt to his feet. The movement seemed to accentuate the thickness of his legs.

"Michael. This is a surprise," said Saul Berne in a tone

that registered genuine surprise. His scraggly red goatee quivered as he spoke.

"I didn't know you were here," stammered Michael.

"Um-hmm," said Saul, his eyes narrowing behind his thick glasses. In contrast to the cool authority that emanated from the reverend, Saul Berne exuded a more manic intensity.

"What brings you here this evening?" said Rev. Sam, gesturing for Michael to sit in a low-seated chair with burnt orange cushions. Saul resumed his seat on the couch.

"I...there's something I need to talk to you about."

Rev. Sam glanced at Saul.

"Then you should have come to me first," said Saul, reddening. "And if I thought it was important, I would bring it to the attention of Rev. Sam. You know the procedures."

"Well, I didn't...want to wait. I thought I might save time."

"You're familiar with the structure of our Community," Saul countered, then added as if to himself, "though we all know you don't always follow it. We've had this discussion before."

"I just...I'm sorry." Michael lowered his head.

The reverend stood waiting stoically until the dialogue between the two ended. Satisfied with the conclusion, he turned his gaze on Michael.

"Yes?"

"It's about Danny. I think he's...I haven't seen him for days."

"What are you saying?" said the reverend, resting an arm on the bric-a-brac laden mantle. "You have a tendency to not express yourself clearly, you know. If this is important, then you need to be clear."

Michael swallowed again and took another deep breath that sounded more like a sigh. He collected his thoughts—or tried to—then continued carefully.

"I haven't seen Danny since Friday night. He came

home for dinner, and left not long after, and I haven't seen him since."

Reverend Sam stared fixedly at Michael as if the boy should have more to say.

"And this worries you?"

Michael looked up at the reverend incredulously and spoke more sharply to him than he had ever before dared.

"Of course it worries me! Doesn't it worry you?"

"Not particularly," the reverend replied with rather pointed tolerance.

"It doesn't?" said Michael, somewhat deflated.

"Not at all."

"But why?"

The reverend adopted the attitude of an ever-patient elder statesman trying to explain quantum physics to an autistic child.

"We only moved you in with Danny about...seven months ago, but Danny has been with the Community for two years. We do know him, I think, better than you. Danny has difficulty at times dealing with authority, and has a tendency to disappear on occasion. He goes off on his own and...gets his head clear. He usually comes back after a while. I don't find it to be of particular concern."

Saul cut in, "This is something you could easily have discussed with me, Michael."

"He's never disappeared before," said Michael in a burst of courage.

"As I said," the reverend replied evenly, "we know him better than you do."

"It's just that..." Michael began, but his voice trailed off.

"What?" said the reverend.

"He told me he was coming to see you Friday night, and I thought maybe he said something to you about where he was going."

"No, he didn't say anything to me about leaving."

"What *did* he say?"

Reverend Sam's face transformed into a mask of patronizing incongruity.

"Michael, I am Danny's spiritual leader and he came here to consult with me. Obviously I am not going to discuss with you the nature of our conversation."

Michael shifted uneasily in his chair and focused his attention on the tip of his right shoe.

"I understand," he stammered. "It's just he's been gone for three days and I'm worried." He then added barely audibly, "I'm just surprised you're not."

The reverend smoothly removed his arm from the mantle and rested his hands on his hips. His eyes bored into Michael's head.

"Actually," he said evenly, "what concerns me...is you."

Michael looked up cautiously.

"Me?"

"Why does Danny's leaving cause you so much anxiety?"

Michael looked at him blankly.

"Has anything...happened between the two of you?"

There was a brief pause, then Michael stammered, "What do you mean?"

The left corner of the reverend's mouth twisted upward in a smile.

"I only meant, did you have a falling-out of some sort?"

The meaning of this question appeared to cause the young sheep considerable confusion and fear. It was as if he were afraid of the meaning of the reverend's words. The reverend, for his part, seemed to be enjoying the young man's discomfort.

"I've been meaning to ask you," said the reverend with rather purposeful nonchalance, "how are you and Barbara getting along?"

"What do you mean?"

The reverend laughed gently, "You keep asking me what I mean, and what I said was perfectly clear. How are you and Barbara getting along?"

"We...I guess we're fine."

"Fine?" the reverend repeated, rolling the word around in his mouth like a morsel whose taste he could not quite discern. "The two of you have been together for quite some time now. I'm sure that you understand the importance of the relationship between a man and a woman."

"Rev. Sam, that's not why I came here. I don't understand..."

The reverend cut him off without a thought. "I'm also sure you understand that unlike relationships in the secular world, we do not believe in...casual dating."

Michael resumed the in-depth study of his shoe. "Yes," he said weakly.

The reverend sighed, "We've been wondering about when the two of you will be setting a date."

"Setting...a date."

"Yes. I've been thinking more and more that it's important for you and Barbara to take the next...natural step in your relationship."

Michael's face had completely drained of color. As he had feared, the point of his visit had been completely deflected.

"And," the reverend continued, "in light of your visit this evening, I think it more important than ever that you and Barbara proceed."

"I don't understand."

The reverend folded his arms across his chest.

"The Bible is quite clear in these matters. The Apostle Paul says that though it is better to remain single, if you cannot control your sexual appetites, then you should marry. I've always thought that this is especially important in someone of your nature. Your excessive anxiety about Danny leads me to believe that you haven't mastered yourself. I'll say it again: I think it's time that you and Barbara proceed."

"I'm in complete agreement with you," said Saul Berne, nodding his head vigorously, "it's just as I've been telling you."

Michael slowly rose from his chair. A tear hung in the corner of his left eye. He walked slowly to the doorway, swaying slightly as if he'd just been roused from a drugged sleep. He braced himself against the doorjamb with his left hand and looked dejectedly back at the two religious leaders.

"Whatever...whatever you may think, I'm...I'm really worried about Danny...whatever you might think."

The reverend smiled at him.

"Sometimes it's very difficult to truly know your heart."

Michael left without another word. It can only be assumed that he found his way out by following the indentations in the carpet: He didn't raise his eyes again until he was well away from the reverend's house.

Reverend Sam sighed as the door closed after Michael.

"Somehow I just don't think Michael is as committed to our Community as he should be."

"I don't think he's turned his whole heart over to the Lord," said Saul, his beard quivering as he shook his head. "He's never really subjected himself to authority."

"No," said the reverend as if receiving Divine inspiration, "it's not that. Michael is still holding on to his former life. The Bible says we have to die to this life in order to be born again. It's clear that he hasn't entirely died to his old life."

Saul nodded thoughtfully.

As MICHAEL SLOUCHED off into the night, Ransom arrived at the hospital.

"She isn't progressing as steadily as we would hope," Nurse Carter said with uncharacteristic gravity during their brief exchange in the hallway.

None of us are, Ransom thought wryly, his mind still on his unproductive day's work. After his meeting with Sergeant Newman, he had spent the rest of the afternoon conferring with Missing Persons, and arranging for pictures of the body to be distributed to all the city's police stations. Despite the usual bravado he displayed before Newman,

Ransom was not all that sure that even with his obvious talents, the nameless crucified body they'd found in a Dumpster might not remain just that: nameless. Ransom couldn't reconcile himself to leaving it that way, especially under the circumstances in which the body had been disposed of. He felt that the inability to put a name to that young life would be to doom the boy to being nothing more than so much trash.

But Nurse Carter's words quickly sank in, and alarm registered on the detective's face.

"Now, now…" said Carter softly, "it's nothing to be too worried about yet. Old people don't always mend as quickly as others."

This statement had brought Ransom up short. He had not made the mistake of thinking of Emily as old since they'd first met. Not that it was a mistake: Emily *was* old. But her ingenuity and vitality had gone a long way in altering Ransom's understanding of the elderly.

"If you want to know what I think," the nurse continued after a pregnant pause, "I don't think it always has to do with their health. I think sometimes it's their minds."

"Their minds?" said Ransom sharply. "There's nothing wrong with Emily's mind."

"No, no, no, I don't mean something wrong with their minds—I mean something wrong with the way they think."

Ransom raised an eyebrow. Nurse Carter hugged herself beneath her ample chest and leaned in toward the detective.

"I mean, sometimes they think it's time to go. Sometimes they think they don't have anything more to live for."

Ransom couldn't believe that the people Nurse Carter described could bear any resemblance to Emily Charters, until he entered her room. Now, as he sat in the lone guest chair, he wondered. Emily looked worse today than she had the day before. Surely, she should look better, not worse. Lying there on the bed she looked almost lifeless rather than asleep. Her complexion was colorless and her hair—if it were possible—was whiter than before. The wrinkles that ran across her forehead, as well as the crow's-feet that lent her character, and the tiny lines at the corners of her mouth, had sunk deeper; and her cheeks seemed to have lowered at least an inch. She looks old, thought Ransom, she looks old.

As this thought floated through the detective's mind, one of the floor nurses entered the room, looked at Emily for a few moments, and then jotted something down on her chart. Then she turned and saw Ransom.

"Oh! I didn't realize you were here. You really shouldn't let her sleep away your visit."

"It's all right," said Ransom, with barely a glance at the nurse.

"No, really, I'll wake her up."

She craned her neck in Emily's direction and called out, "Miss Charters! Miss Charters!"

"No!" said Ransom warmly. "It's all right. Let her sleep."

The nurse straightened herself up and looked properly affronted. She looked at Ransom for a moment, then turned on her soft white heels and marched out of the room.

Ransom watched the retreating figure out of the corner of his eye, then turned his full attention back to the figure lying on the bed. The fingers of Emily's right hand twitched involuntarily, and after a moment the hand moved from her side and rested on her stomach. Ransom registered the movement with a sense of relief. It wasn't much, but at least it was a sign of life. He settled back in his chair and sighed. It would be a long night.

FIVE

TUESDAY PROVED TO be the exercise in futility that Ransom
had expected. The day consisted of an exhaustive canvas
of the occupants of the buildings on Michigan and Wabash
Avenues, which surrounded the alley between Monroe and
Madison Streets. The ground floor of each building was
embedded with small shops and fast food restaurants, all
of which closed too early in the evening to be of any help.
Both of the detectives felt it was most probable that disposal of the body had taken place at some time over Friday
or Saturday night.

They stopped in the University Club on Monroe Street,
which backed about the first 150 feet of the alley. Ransom
was struck by the austere, Old World feeling of the lobby,
with its lush dark wood and wide, red-carpeted stairway
leading to the upper regions. It was reminiscent of a more
elegant time, when gentlemen's clubs were frequented by
rather desiccated elderly men who quietly read newspapers
while pipes dangled from their lips, and a time when luxury
hotels were the norm instead of the exception. The club
was the only building on the block in which patrons could
reside overnight.

The front-desk clerk was a pleasant and professional
young man, with just a hint of reservation at the appearance
of the detectives and at answering their questions. He quietly informed them that while the club did entertain a variety of guests over the weekend, none of the guest rooms
overlooked the alley.

"You know," said Gerald as they spun back to the street
through the revolving door, "there's nothing to say that the
boy wasn't murdered in there. It's possible."

"Did you hear how quiet it was in there, Gerald?"

"So?"

"I think they would have noticed a crucifixion being performed, don't you?"

"Well, maybe it was done quietly."

With tired exasperation, Ransom eyed his partner and said, "In two thousand years of carpentry, no one has yet devised a way to quietly drive a nail through somebody's hand. And besides, what if they could? Quietly crucify the boy and then quietly carry the naked body through the lobby, past the security guard and front desk and out to the back of the building where he was quietly dropped in a Dumpster?"

"All right!" said Gerald. "I know it sounds stupid when you put it that way, but stranger things have happened."

They had walked to the alley side of the building, and looked up. Ransom clucked his tongue.

"It wouldn't matter if someone did look out the window," Gerald observed, "the alley's so narrow and the windows start so high up, you couldn't see the ground unless you opened the window and leaned way out."

"Hmm," was Ransom's noncommittal response. "Let's get on with it."

The remainder of their task was made somewhat easier by the fact that all of the large office buildings in the area had twenty-four-hour security. On weekday evenings and all weekend long they kept scrupulous logs of the comings and goings in the buildings. The logs greatly narrowed the field of possible witnesses. Ransom thought ruefully that "witness" in this case was an oxymoron, since he was sure that nobody had witnessed the disposal of the body.

None of the logs revealed anything but the usual limited weekend traffic one would expect: until they reached Willoughby Tower at 8 South Michigan.

When Ransom flipped through the weekend log, he found one notation that stood out: The signature read "Richard Larkin," with the time in at 11:58 p.m., and the time out at 12:47 a.m. On the destination line, Mr. Stevens had written "Model Americans."

"'Model Americans?'" said Ransom, raising an eyebrow.

The security guard smirked ingratiatingly and explained, "It's a modeling agency on the tenth floor. A little place. Suite 1008."

The detectives rode the old, whisper-quiet elevator to the tenth floor. Though the ride was short, Ransom had time to reflect that even the office buildings of old Chicago displayed an elegance that you couldn't find in their more modern counterparts. The so-called efficiency of state of the art technology was simply no substitute for plain elegance. Ransom doubted if the occupants of this building could ever learn to dread coming to work in the morning the way modern office workers do.

The doors quietly opened, and the detectives quickly located suite 1008. The door bore the words, "Model Americans, Inc." in letters so clean and demure that one expected it to open upon hoards of freshly scrubbed Aryan youths.

As Gerald swung the door open, Ransom was slightly disappointed to find only one, although he did fit the Aryan bill to a degree that Ransom found slightly nauseating. The young man, presumably receptionist for the agency, was fair and slender, pale-skinned and blue-eyed, with very light blond hair. One would not have been surprised if he had spontaneously broken into a chorus of "Tomorrow Belongs to Me." He sat behind a nondescript office desk that was completely clear except for a phone, a blotter, a pen, and a legal pad. A Selectric rested, covered, on a stand behind the desk.

"Can I help you?" he said with a receptionist's smile. Ransom couldn't help thinking that the smile made the young man look vacuous to the point of stupidity.

Ransom flipped his badge at him and said, "We're looking for Richard Larkin."

The young man seemed to turn whiter, which, given his complexion, hardly seemed possible.

"That's me," he said breathlessly.

"Could we speak to you somewhere privately?"

"What've I done?" said Larkin, his eyes widening so that they looked like blue saucers left out in the snow.

"We just want to ask you a few questions."

As if in a trance, Larkin kept his eyes on the detectives as he lifted the phone from its cradle and pressed a white button. After a moment, he said, "Maggie, can you spot me for a minute?"

He paused for a moment, listening, and then nodded as if the person on the other end of the line would be able to hear the movement of his head. He replaced the receiver without saying another word, and then pressed a couple of buttons on the phone and rose from behind the desk.

"There. She'll be able to pick up the phone from back there," he said vacantly, as if the detectives would know where "back there" was. He then led them down a short, quiet hallway with doors interspersed on either side, and went into the last room on the right. Gerald closed the door behind them and they found themselves in a small, comfortable, sparsely furnished room that appeared to serve as a lunchroom/lounge for the firm's employees. A rather grimy window looked out on the alley.

"What's going on?" said Larkin nervously.

Ransom assessed the youth for a moment. Though he didn't think he would give Larkin high marks for intelligence, at first glance he at least seemed to possess the credulous honesty of an altar boy who had not yet reached puberty. Ransom summed him up as reliable, if a bit too pretty.

"Exactly what sort of firm is this?" asked Ransom.

"This? Well, it's a modeling agency," said Larkin blankly, then reddening slightly, he added, "Well, sort of a modeling agency."

"Sort of?" said Ransom.

Larkin said quickly, "No, I mean, it's a modeling agency, but not, you know, one of the big ones. I mean, we supply, you know, models who hand out food samples at grocery stores and who demonstrate rotisseries and things like that at the big, you know, houseware shows and things over at McCormick Place.''

"I see," said Ransom. "And does that involve a lot of weekend work?"

"Weekend work?" said Larkin, his face once again a blank.

Gerald couldn't help but smile as Ransom, with an effort, remained patient.

"Yes. Do you ever have to work on weekends? It's a simple question.''

"Well, I never really have to work on weekends. I mean, I would if I had to, but I never really have to." He stopped for a moment, then as if a thought had suddenly struck him, he rushed to add, "But, I mean, I don't mean that I never come in on weekends. I do. I mean, I do sometimes when I have work I want to do." He stopped and took a breath. "What's going on?"

"What kind of work would have brought you down here at midnight on Saturday?"

The remainder of the color drained from Larkin's cheeks.

"Oh, my God, you mean they know? They know and they called the police? Jeez! They wouldn't call the police over a thing like that, would they?"

"Mr. Larkin," said Ransom calmly, "I'm afraid I don't know what you're talking about."

"The photocopies!" said Larkin, a faint tremor in his voice. His baby-blue eyes had misted over and Ransom had the uncomfortable feeling that the boy would burst into tears.

"Photocopies?"

"I'm a writer," said Larking haltingly, "at least, I mean, I want to be a writer. And I've just finished my first book. And I, you know, have to send copies out to the publishers. And I can't afford one of those copy services, so I have to make them here. Only they don't allow that.''

Ransom and Gerald exchanged glances and it was only with an effort that they both were able to refrain from laughing out loud.

"No, Mr. Larkin, that isn't what brought us here. It doesn't have anything directly to do with you."

Richard Larkin blinked and his lanky frame seemed about to go limp with relief. He was only held back by a lingering sense of caution.

"Then what is it?" he said. "I mean, why did you want to talk to me?"

Ransom took a deep breath and said, "Undoubtedly you've heard that a body was found in the alley behind these buildings yesterday morning."

"Oh, yeah," he replied, sounding more relieved than Ransom thought anyone should sound when discussing a murder.

"We've been trying to find anyone who *might* have been around when the body was…dropped off."

Larkin's face registered a sudden onset of shock. "Oh no! No! I didn't…I wasn't down here then, I know it!"

Ransom considered Larkin for a moment, his patience beginning to wane. He said in a measured tone, "I assume you mean to say that you didn't hear or see anything out of the ordinary while you were in the building."

"Yeah, that's what I mean. I mean, there wasn't anything! And I was too worried about somebody walking in and catching me copying."

"In the middle of the night?"

"Well, you never know, you know?"

Ransom glanced at Gerald and then back to Larkin. "Yes. Would you show us this copier you were using?"

"The copier? You want to see the copier?" From his tone, you would have thought he had a dead body hidden in the machine.

"Yes."

Larkin nodded none too happily, and led the detectives from the lounge to the room directly next door. The room had the same decor as the rest of the suite, but was empty except for a high wooden stool, painted black, and a large multipurpose photocopier. Like the lounge, there was a window looking out toward the alley. Ransom wandered over to the window while Gerald showed an inordinate interest in the copier.

"How does this thing work?" he said, crouching beside the machine.

Larkin grabbed a handful of papers and demonstrated how to work the copier with the practiced efficiency of a shill at a trade show.

"You put the pages you want to copy here, and press this button."

The machine sprang loudly into action, sucking the pages one by one from the feeder. After a moment, sheets of paper began to clank into the sorter bins like slightly muffled pistol shots.

"Very nice," said Gerald, like a disinterested buyer.

Ransom turned away from the window and looked at his partner, his expression tired and amused.

"If you're quite finished, Gerald, we can go."

"Oh, sure."

Larkin saw them to the door, all the while telling them with an almost frantic eagerness that he hoped he'd been able to help.

"And if you need anything else, I mean, if you need to talk to me again, I'll be glad to. I mean, I'll help if I can," he said, his tone so overwrought that Ransom thought the boy might have a heart attack if they took him up on the offer. It was tempting, but Ransom let it go.

On their way down to the lobby, Ransom said, "I certainly hope that young man writes better than he speaks."

"He wouldn't have heard anything with that damn machine going, anyway," said Gerald.

"He couldn't have seen anything, either," Ransom added wearily. "While you were engrossed in the glories of modern photocopying, I checked the window. It's just as we thought. You can't see the ground, and the window wouldn't budge."

The elevator doors slid open and Ransom and Gerald stepped out into the lobby. Willoughby Tower has an L-shaped lobby with an entrance on Michigan Avenue, the one through which the detectives had entered, with another on Madison Street. They left through the Madison door, which brought them to the opposite end of the alley.

"What I don't understand," said Gerald, "is why drop the body here?"

"Hmm?"

"Well, why drop it in this alley, in the middle of the Loop? It's awfully open here."

"I doubt if he did it during the middle of the day while goods were being delivered," Ransom observed wryly, "and it's a good sight darker in there in the middle of the night."

"Yeah, but why not just dump the body in the underground streets?"

Ransom eyed his partner with amusement. "You mean by the police auto pound under Michigan Avenue?"

Gerald sighed heavily and replied, "There's always Lower Wacker Drive."

"Perhaps our murderer reads."

"What do you mean?"

"For one thing, at last count about fifty people were making their homes in boxes on Lower Wacker. Second, there is almost always traffic down there, day or night." Ransom paused and looked down the dank alley, which even in the light of day was one of the darker regions of the city. "No, I think he may have been smart. I think if I were going to dispose of a body, I might give serious consideration to doing it this way."

Gerald himself gazed down the alley, and he could hardly disagree with Ransom's assessment.

"So, where does that leave us?"

"With one very happy sergeant."

"Huh?"

"Newman will be absolutely thrilled that we've wasted a day on his little canvasing project. Let's get out of here."

Ransom rode back to area headquarters with Gerald, staying just long enough to pick up his car. He left Gerald with the pleasant task of reporting their lack of findings to Sergeant Newman.

Ransom climbed into his car, his mood darker than it had been for days. He didn't like being at a standstill on a case, or worse yet the possibility of having to let the case go, even momentarily. But even worse, he didn't like the standstill Emily seemed to have reached. For the first time he found himself not exactly looking forward to visiting his aged friend, for no other reason than that he wanted so badly for her to return to her former self, and was increasingly worried as time went on that she never would.

With a heavy sigh he threw his old reliable Nova into gear and headed for the hospital.

As RANSOM SETTLED in for his quiet evening vigil with Emily, there was considerably more activity in Pamela Frazier's apartment as she busied herself with dinner preparations: a broccoli-and-cauliflower combination was steaming in a pot atop the stove, and a pair of butterfly pork chops were on the road to perfection under the broiler.

Pamela retrieved two potatoes from the vegetable keeper and laid them out to be baked the new-fashioned way, in the microwave. She frowned despite herself. The enjoyment she found in cooking, especially for Nicholas, was tainted by the fact that the other women of the Community would undoubtedly find her dinner preparation "quaint" and indicative of where she was headed with Nicholas—and she could tolerate anything but being found quaint. But in addition to all that, she was irritated with herself for letting the opinions of others affect her enjoyment.

At this she stamped her foot and shook her head, her hair shimmering in the remaining sunlight that shifted low through the kitchen window. No, she would not let them spoil her enjoyment. She glanced at the potatoes and a smile crept across her face. The women would be appalled that she would "bake" them in a microwave. That was enough for her.

"Do you need any help?" called a voice from the doorway.

Pamela started, her hand going up to her heart.

"Sarah, one of these days you're going to give me a heart attack."

It wasn't all that surprising that Sarah Bennett moved so soundlessly: Everything about her was muted. Her hair was the color of wet sand, and pulled back and clipped at the back of her head with a mock-gold barrette. It hung straight and lifeless down her back to her waist. She wore a dark tan cardigan and a dark brown, knee-length skirt above khaki kneesocks. She smiled crookedly. It looked as if the action hurt her face.

"I guess my feet just don't touch the ground."

Pamela grimaced inwardly and gave her full attention to the vegetables.

Sarah came into the kitchen and looked over Pamela's shoulder.

"They look like they're almost done."

Pamela tried not to sigh.

"I know."

"Is Nicholas here already? I didn't see him."

"No, he's not here yet."

Sarah's eyes widened. "You probably should have waited until he got here before you started, since you're not making anything especially difficult."

Pamela allowed herself to sigh openly this time.

"I want to have things ready for him when he gets here."

"But he might be late and then your dinner would be ruined."

"I'm sure he'll be on time."

"I'm sure he will," Sarah replied, her smile crooking upward.

Pamela stopped stirring and put the lid back on the pot. As quietly as she could she took a deep breath, then forced herself to smile.

"So, where are you going this evening?" It was all she could do not to add, "And aren't you going to be late?"

"I'm going to fellowship with the sisters at a movie."

"You're going to 'fellowship' at a movie?"

"You don't need to speak to fellowship with each other. We'll be sharing an experience together."

"What are you going to see?"

"We haven't decided that yet. We'll decide that when we get together."

Let me see, thought Pamela, it's almost six o'clock now—they should be able to agree on something by midnight.

There was an uncomfortable silence during which Sarah's eyes followed Pamela around the room like searchlights as Pamela pulled condiments from the upper right-hand kitchen cabinet and placed them on the table.

"Are you sure you don't need my help?" said Sarah slowly.

"No. Thank you."

Pamela retrieved a handful of silverware from the Rubbermaid tray in the drawer and began laying out place settings.

"It wouldn't be any trouble. I wouldn't mind staying to help you out."

A spoon clanked onto the table. Pamela picked it up and gently put it in its proper place.

"I really don't need any help, thank you."

Sarah moved back to the doorway and hesitated, her manner so intense it reminded Pamela rather uncomfortably of H. P. Lovecraft's Lurker in "Lurker at the Threshold."

"Are you sure I shouldn't stay?" said Sarah, her tone pointedly concerned.

Pamela feigned perplexity. "As you said, I'm not preparing anything particularly difficult. Why on earth would I need you to stay?"

"Well…I don't know whether or not you should be alone in the apartment with a man."

"Surely you don't mean you think Nick is anything but a gentleman?"

"No, of course not," said Sarah, her cheeks turning an unlovely pink.

"Is it me that you don't trust?"

Sarah smoothed the front of her dress. "It has nothing to do with trust. It just might not look right."

"Look right?"

"A young man and woman alone in an apartment. Aren't you afraid people might talk?"

Pamela's smile broadened.

"Like the Bible says, I care not how I look in the eyes of the world."

"But people might talk."

"I don't think my Christian brothers and sisters would gossip about me like that, do you?"

"Well, I..."

"And besides, *you're* the only one who knows about it, and I know I can trust that you won't gossip, can't I?"

"Well...of course," Sarah stammered, "I wouldn't think of talking about my brothers and sisters...or anyone else. I was just concerned about you."

"I appreciate that," said Pamela, confident that she'd scored.

"I guess I'd better get going."

Sarah started through the doorway but paused once again, resting a hand on the jamb.

"Of course, if I thought there was something amiss with you and Nicholas, I would discuss it with the sisters so that we could pray about it...but that wouldn't be gossiping."

Pamela eyed her roommate shrewdly.

"Of course not."

The two women seemed held in place for a moment, as if captured in an overly tense, modern-dress French Impressionist painting representing two women at cross-purposes. The tableau dispersed with the sound of the doorbell.

"That'll be Nick," said Pamela with barely forced nonchalance. "Could you let him in on your way out?"

The implication hardly escapable without creating a scene, Sarah's smile snaked upward. "Certainly."

With this, she left, still managing to make her departure as reluctant as possible.

As Pamela took down the plates from the cupboard and laid them out, she could hear the front door open and the exchange of reserved pleasantries. Then the door closed.

Nicholas entered the kitchen in his usual breezy manner, his smile broad and his hair tousled. He was dressed in a denim shirt and trousers and a dark blue striped tie, all of which served to accentuate his eyes. He swiped his dark hair back off his forehead and took Pamela in his arms, kissing her lightly on the nose.

Pamela pushed him back slightly and glanced over his shoulder.

"Is she gone?"

"She went out as I came in."

She sighed and drew him into an embrace. "Good."

Nicholas laughed lightly. "Has she been giving you trouble?"

"No more than usual," said Pamela with a halfhearted laugh. She moved to break away from him but he held onto her hand.

"What was it this time?"

"I have to turn the pork."

He released her hand and she opened the oven, then turned the chops over with a long-handled, two-tined fork.

"What was it," Nick pursued, "did she catch you applying a particularly sinful shade of lipstick?"

"Oh, Nick!"

"Was your rouge a touch too red? Or did she catch you reading a questionable novelette—one peppered with four-letter words?"

"Stop!"

"Well, what was it?"

"It's not important."

"Come on, Pam."

Pamela laid the fork on the counter, her back to him, and sighed heavily.

"Apparently we're in need of a chaperon."

"You're kidding!"

"Apparently we're in danger of reverting to savages, ripping off all our clothes and having our way with each other if she's not here to watch."

"Perhaps she'd like that."

"Nick!"

"It would really give the evil-minded little crow something to talk about!"

"Nick, please!"

He looked at her for a moment and then sighed: a short, heavy breath that fell just short of being a snort.

"Sorry, sweetheart, I'm just tired."

"Hard day at the office?" Pamela replied playfully as she placed the potatoes in the microwave and set the timer.

"I don't mean that and you know it."

"What do you mean, then?"

"I'm tired of this whole damn 'Community' and everyone in it!"

"Nick!" Pamela exclaimed, more surprised than shocked.

"Well, honestly! Can't we have any sort of honest, human feelings for each other without it being tainted by some...dried-up, underaged spinster?"

"Oh, Nick, you know Sarah...she's different."

"If only she were."

Nicholas dropped into a seat at the table and appeared to engage himself in a sullen scrutiny of its faux-wooden top.

"Pam," he said slowly, "have you ever thought about leaving the church?"

Pamela wheeled around to face him, her usually smooth, creamy brow furrowed with concern and her light blue eyes tinged with sadness.

"No, of course not." She went to him and gently laid her slim white hand on his shoulder. "Ever since I was a little girl—ever since I can remember—I've believed in God. Don't laugh—I was one of those children who feels they have a guardian angel watching out over them. And I always—even when my mother died—I never stopped believing in Him. I don't know, maybe I needed Him even more then. And I still believe in Him with all my heart— maybe not as intrusively as the rest of the Community, but I still believe."

Nicholas laid his hand on hers and looked up into her eyes: In them he saw twin images of himself overlaid with love.

"But I'm not talking about leaving God," he said quietly, "or the church. I'm talking about leaving this Community."

The touch of her hand slackened, and Nick caught her hand and held it tighter in response. Her expression was somber and confused, and maybe even a little fearful.

"I've been a member of the Community for five years now. I don't know..."

"Pam..."

"...somehow I think I would feel like I was leaving God. Even though I know that's not..."

"Pam, I've always believed in God, too—more or less. Maybe without always being aware of it. But I've always thought of Him as a kind, benevolent being," his voice hardened, "but that's not what I feel here. In the year I've been with this group I've come to feel more and more like I'm being watched—and not by a loving, caring God who's concerned about my welfare—I mean *watched*—like a criminal on parole who has to be kept strictly under thumb!"

"Oh, Nick," said Pamela, pulling away from him.

"You can't tell me you haven't felt it, too."

There was a long silence during which Pamela seemed to be of two minds, in part hoping to frame a rebuttal. But she couldn't, and to Nicholas her silence was enough. It was at that moment that the doorbell rang.

"Who could that be?"

"I'll get it," said Nicholas. He went into the hallway, an elongated, wooden-floored passageway of the type common to the roomy old four-flats of the northwest side of Chicago, and when he returned to the kitchen he was accompanied by Michael Franklin.

"Michael!" said Pamela, mentally kicking herself for always managing to sound surprised when she saw him.

But this time she could be excused, for Michael's appearance was indeed surprising. Though normally reedy, he was beginning to look painfully thin. His eyes seemed to have sunk into his skull, and there were dark crescents beneath them. He wore a dull white-and-black checkered flannel shirt, with half of the front shirttail hanging out limply. His black denim pants were unfashionably wrinkled. Nick hovered behind him trying not to look too solicitous.

"Is anything wrong?" said Pamela, with another mental kick.

"I've got to talk to you two," said Michael breathily. Then he glanced at Nicholas. "Actually, it's you I need to talk to."

"What's the matter?"

Michael took a shallow breath. "Have either of you seen Danny?"

"Danny?" said Pamela, knitting her eyebrows. "You always seem to be looking for him lately."

Michael turned his moist brown eyes upon her. "Still. He still hasn't come home."

"Since when?"

"Since Friday night! He hasn't been home since Friday night!"

"That doesn't sound good," said Nick.

"Now wait, now wait," said Pamela, holding up a hand like a young crossing guard, "maybe he's just visiting friends."

"Who?" said Michael desperately. "He's just like the rest of us. He's been here long enough to get cut off."

"You make it sound like we're in prison."

Michael glanced at her out of the corner of his eye, not

quite sure whether or not she was serious. Pamela caught his glance and realized her error. When she continued, she moderated her tone.

"I mean, we're perfectly free to see people outside the Community. You know that."

"That may be true," Nick cut in, "but our time tends not to be our own, as *you* know, and you can lose track of your outside friends. In fact, it seems that happens too regularly."

Pamela acquiesced, thinking the better of continuing.

"Have you called the police?" asked Nick.

"No."

"Haven't you done anything?"

Michael's eyes traveled down to the yellow tiled floor.

"I went and talked to Rev. Sam last night."

"Well, what did he say?"

"He said a lot. He seemed to think I was worrying about nothing. He said I...he implied...he said it was like Danny to disappear."

"Hrmph," said Nick.

"Well," said Pamela slowly, finding this a little more difficult to defend, "you haven't lived with him all that long. Maybe it *is* like him."

Michael looked at her sharply. "You've known him longer. Does it sound like him to you?"

"No, it doesn't," Nick said. "I've always known Danny to be pretty reliable. I can't imagine him running away."

"Running away?" Pamela said, exasperated.

"Running away...disappearing...whatever you want to call it."

"That's why I came to see you," said Michael, "I thought..."

"What?"

"I thought maybe you could do something about it."

Nick laughed ruefully. "I wouldn't be able to get any farther with Rev. Sam than you did."

Michael ran his hand through his hair, pushing it back off his forehead. There were traces of grease where it had been hanging. Though his face was still turned to the floor, his eyes rolled up to Nick's.

"Well, you worked with Danny, didn't you?" Though his tone was sheepish, he somehow made this sound like an accusation.

"Until a few months ago, yeah."

"Didn't you introduce him to the Community?"

"No," said Nicholas slowly, "you've got that backward. Danny brought me here."

Michael's voice took on a pleading tone. "Don't you know anything about where...don't you have any idea how I can find him?"

"Well," Nick said after a moment, "I don't know that much about him...his life...but..." He furrowed his brow for a moment, then an idea came to him. "But, as a matter of fact, I think I remember where his parents lived—at least, his mother. I think they were from Cicero."

Michael brightened slightly, as if hope were something he would only accept on sufferance. "You think so? You think she might know something?"

Nicholas nodded his head slowly. "I'm not sure that's where she lives, I'll have to look her up. But I can give it a try. I'll see if I can track her down and give her a call. Maybe she knows where he is."

"But wait a minute," Pamela broke in, "what if she doesn't know? You don't want to panic the woman, do you?"

"Danny's been missing since Friday," said Nicholas sharply, "it might be time to panic."

"But he may be gone for some good reason. Maybe he just didn't have time to tell anyone."

"Danny wouldn't do that!" said Michael. "He wouldn't just go away. I know him!"

"Don't you think you should check this out with Rev. Sam first?" said Pamela. The two men stopped and looked at her, both of their expressions a mixture of disbelief and irritation.

"He's already been approached," said Nick curtly.

Pamela looked properly rebuffed, but Nick was too pre-occupied to notice.

"You go home now," he said to Michael, "you look like you haven't slept in a week."

"A little less," said Michael with a sad smile.

"At least you'll be able to get some rest tomorrow."

Michael looked up at him quizzically. "What do you mean?"

"Didn't you hear—the 'work party' tomorrow night—to work on the church basement—it's been called off. Rev. Sam has decided to have a leaders' meeting, so we peons are off tomorrow night."

"Not me," said Michael sardonically.

"What do you mean?"

"I'm never 'off,' Nick. Working with my hands—doing manly work is the best thing for someone like me. At least that's what I'm told. There's no rest for the wicked."

With this, Michael slouched out of the kitchen, down the hallway, and out the front door.

"What did he mean by that?" asked Pamela.

SIX

"I SUPPOSE HE never really did belong to us," said the woman as she blew her nose halfheartedly into an already damp pink tissue. Her most outstanding feature was that she had no outstanding features. She was plump but not fat, pale but not wan, and well dressed but not tailored. She looked as if she'd come fully assembled off the center of the rack. "I suppose every mother feels that way at a time like this."

"How do you mean?"

"Well," she sniffed and looked vacantly at the corner of the desk through watery brown eyes, "I feel as if I never knew my son. I feel as if he was a total stranger. I feel as if I had a son at one time but something happened to him and he was replaced by a stranger...by the body of a stranger."

"What happened?"

"I'm not a weepy woman as a rule. I don't usually cry."

"What happened?"

"I thought I could come down here, and look at him, and it would be just like seeing a stranger for the first time—at least, I hoped it would be a stranger—and I could look at him and it would have no effect on me at all." Tears began to well up in her eyes again. "The last thing I would have expected was that I would fall apart like this."

"It's perfectly understandable."

"But I saw him, and it all just came back to me...it all came back to me...everything...and it was like he...like nothing had ever happened."

Ransom rested his arms on the desk and leaned in toward the woman.

"What *did* happen?"

The woman dabbed her eyes and then dropped the tissue in her lap, her hands falling limply to the arms of her chair. She said nothing.

Ransom checked himself in the act of drumming his fingers on the top of his desk. He had no desire to appear irritated with a bereaved mother, but he really wished she would get on with it.

Wednesday morning had proven long and frustrating. The report on the crime scene, or disposal scene, as Ransom had come to think of it, had come back from the crime lab. The Dumpster and the surrounding area had yielded a virtual smorgasbord of fingerprints, all of which were smeared, smudged, grimy, and unidentifiable. Dusting for prints must have been a challenge, thought Ransom, since he couldn't believe that any powder or dust would be able to adhere to anything in that alley. Still, it was work that had to be done: the crime lab's version of canvasing the neighborhood. Prints on prints on prints, as one would expect to find in an area frequented by trash disposers, trash collectors, and trash connoisseurs (the term by which Ransom sardonically referred to the homeless).

With each new impasse he encountered, the memory of Newman's none-too-subtle and all-too-smug challenge reverberated through his mind. And the hot breath of other cases was breathing down the necks of Detectives Ransom and White.

To add to Ransom's frustration, Emily continued to show an uncharacteristic lack of progress. On his Tuesday night visit she'd seemed sullen and lethargic, neither of which states were natural to her, with barely a trace of her usual spark. The nursing staff had assured him that this was not uncommon after major surgery, and was even more common in the elderly, who tended to take longer to recover anyway. But though the staff was fond of Emily, they didn't know her as he did: and he knew that her condition was worrisome, if not dangerous.

He would have thought that a woman of Emily's indomitable character would have snapped back after the crisis.

Instead, she seemed to have reached a plateau from which she wouldn't or couldn't budge. Yes, he thought, "worrisome" was the word. What to do about it was another matter.

All of these things were going through Ransom's mind early Wednesday afternoon when he received the call from Youth Division, the department that encompassed Missing Persons. "Youth" believed they had identified the murdered boy when a middle-aged woman appeared at a southwest-side police station to report her son missing.

Though Ransom attributed his professional success to his wits and wisdom, he was not averse to accepting good luck when it came his way. And the nondescript woman seated before him could prove to be his lucky break. It was his responsibility to call her in to make a positive ID. And she did.

Since the direct approach did not appear to be working, Ransom decided to try a more indirect route, somewhat like a dentist who has to carve his way around a bothersome extraction.

"We were wondering if you could tell us a little about your son," said Ransom with what he hoped was a reassuring smile.

"My son?" replied Mrs. Lyman with a sniff, "I don't think I really knew him."

Ransom spread his hands. "After all, he *was* your son."

"Was..." she said softly, trying to put together the remnants of the tissue to dab her eyes. "He was my son. He was a good boy. He stayed with me...he was one of those boys who knew right from wrong. That might not sound like much, but nowadays I say it's quite an achievement, so many children seem to..."

Her voice trailed off and tears overflowed, streaming down her cheeks and leaving unattractive tracks in her makeup.

Ransom waited for a moment to see if she'd continue unprompted, then said slowly, "He was a good boy?"

She nodded and said, "Top marks in school, top of his class. He wasn't...he was a good boy."

"So, he never got himself into trouble?"

Of necessity Mrs. Lyman had given up trying to use the tissue, little pieces of which still clung to her fingers. She ran the back of her hands across her cheeks.

"Oh, I didn't say that. He's been in...well, I guess you could call it trouble."

"Of what kind?"

Mrs. Lyman looked a little nervously from Ransom to Gerald, who sat on the couch along the side wall of the office unobtrusively taking notes. For a moment, the bereaved mother looked as if she'd forgotten that her son was beyond the long arm of the law. She turned back to Ransom, straightened up in her chair, and replied with a modest measure of pride in her voice:

"He was arrested once at a pro-choice rally in Washington, and he was arrested a second time (that I know of) at a demonstration at the site of a proposed nuclear power plant...out west somewhere. I don't remember exactly where."

Ransom could barely hide his disappointment, and hoped he had successfully managed to remain expressionless. But Mrs. Lyman's eyelids drooped and her hands clenched.

"Before his father died," she said truculently, "we tried to instill in him the...we tried to give him a sense of values, and we tried to teach him to stand up for...to fight for what he believed in."

"Apparently, you were successful."

Mrs. Lyman's expression softened.

"Thank you."

"It sounds as if your son's 'exploits' were more altruism than trouble."

Gerald looked up from his palm-sized spiral notebook. He could feel the slackening of tension in the room.

"His father and I...we thought at one time that he'd go to law school—that he'd go into law, because he had such a sense of...such a profound sense of justice. But he didn't have the stomach for it. At least that's what he told us…that's what he told us."

"Didn't you believe him?"

Mrs. Lyman straightened up, looking slightly affronted. "Of course we did."

"It's just you sounded…"

"Danny never lied. Never. I've never known him to lie." Ransom looked the woman pointedly in the eye and held her gaze. "I'm sorry, I really didn't mean anything."

She softened and looked away from him. "It's all right. I suppose you…I guess you have to ask questions like that."

After giving her a moment, Ransom continued, "What did your son go into?"

"What do you mean?"

"Instead of law."

"Oh. Oh, he went on to get his liberal arts degree. It was a…his father called a 'worthless degree,' and you can believe me, that rankled Danny. His father…well, I guess we both hoped he would actually go into something like law. And what can you do with a liberal arts degree? His father said all you could do with it was teach. But that's what Danny really wanted to do."

"Teach?"

"Yes, yes. He got a job in some store while he was waiting for a permanent teaching job. Or waiting for the one he wanted." She shrugged with exasperation. "I don't know what he was waiting for. His father would have made a lot of that!"

"He was young," said Ransom with uncharacteristic gentleness, another memory prodding the back of his mind, "he had time."

"That's just what I said," Mrs. Lyman agreed quickly. "He was young."

She paused for a moment, the full impact of the words overwhelming her. Her eyes became watery, but for once the tears did not overflow. It was as if the gravity of the situation held them back.

"And what about outside work?"

"Reading," she said softly, "reading and friends. Reading mostly."

Ransom folded his hands on the desk and said cautiously, "Was he involved in any clubs or organizations?"

"Clubs? No…no."

"He wasn't into anything…out of the ordinary?"

"Out of the ordinary?" she replied, her brow furrowed and she looked almost as if he were implying something slightly unsavory.

In his mind's eye was the picture of the boy as his body had been found. Ransom had thought he would have looked pure and angelic were it not for the nasty holes that had been bored through his hands and feet. And those marks might have made the boy look saintly, if it weren't for the ugly gashes in his head. He felt almost as if he were further violating the boy by pursuing this line, but the marks were the outstanding feature in the case and had to be accounted for.

"Out of the ordinary?" she said again, drawing back in her chair. "No. What do you mean? No, he wasn't into anything out of the ordinary. Not…"

"Not that you know of?"

She dropped her hands defiantly in her lap. "I would have known."

Ransom sat back in his chair, folded his hands, and rested them on the desk.

"You said that your son was a good boy. Did he ever go to church?"

The woman's eyes widened. "Church? Church?" She looked at her hands and started to pick at the flakes of tissue. "My husband died about six years ago."

Ransom's right eyebrow elevated half an inch.

"We always went to church. I mean, we brought him up in the church…I mean…but when his father died…when his father died…" Tears welled up again and dripped over her lower lashes.

"Your son stopped going to church when his father died."

Mrs. Lyman nodded. "That sort of thing happens all the time, I suppose." She took a deep breath. "He stopped going to church, but he never stopped fighting for what he believed in...it's just..."

"Yes?"

"After that I wasn't exactly sure *what* he believed in."

She stopped and gave a little tug on the hem of her light brown dress, which was as nondescript as the woman herself.

"It was the church, I think, that finally caused our relationship...that finally ruined our family...what was left of it."

"In what way?"

She seemed to be of two minds about how to answer this, as if she either wasn't sure of the answer, or didn't like the answer.

"Well I don't know that I...I don't know."

"If you think that the church harmed your relationship with your son, you must have some idea of how."

She looked down at her hands. "I'm not sure what I meant."

Ransom sighed. "Did you argue about his falling away from the church?"

Mrs. Lyman sniffed noisily and swallowed hard.

"Oh, no. We argued about his going back."

At last, thought Ransom, we're getting to it.

"You objected to his going back to church? I would think most mothers would be glad."

"I didn't..." She twisted her hands together as if she had something she was trying to straighten out, and her plump face puckered with consternation. "I didn't actually...*object*. I just didn't like it."

Ransom tilted his head and raised his eyebrow.

"I'm afraid I don't understand. Why didn't you like his going back to your church?"

Mrs. Lyman's eyes darted up to Ransom's face.

"Oh, I wouldn't have objected to that. He didn't go back to our church. He went to some…church that one of his friends introduced him to. It wasn't…it wasn't like our family church. It was much more…religious."

Gerald looked up from his notes, his eyebrows knit in a way that Ransom found particularly amusing. Ransom had often said that that expression made his partner's face look like a question mark. At the moment, however, Ransom didn't notice the look. He was much too intent on the woman before him. He thought they just might be reaching the crux of the matter.

"Excuse me," said Ransom, "more religious?"

Mrs. Lyman nodded her head, her pudding-colored cheeks shaking with the motion.

"More religious. More holy. At least…Danny was not the kind to become 'holier than thou,' but he came close. Because, you see, he was so serious about everything he got involved in."

"So his personality changed?"

She seemed to consider this for a moment. "Not…really. Well, yes. I mean, he went to this church at least twice a week, and he started quoting the Bible all the time, not that that's a bad thing."

"Only tiresome," said Ransom, half under his breath.

Mrs. Lyman looked almost relieved that he understood. "Yes, yes, exactly. He just suddenly seemed to have all the answers."

Gerald looked up at the woman, his expression conveying that he could sympathize with the situation.

"And not that that's a bad thing, either. I mean, it shouldn't be a bad thing, it's just…" Tears welled up in her eyes once again, "It's just that it—that church—took up so much of his time." Her hands twisted in her lap again. "You see, he used to take care of me. He spent more and more time with the church, and things got more strained."

"Yes, yes," said Ransom, growing impatient, "I understand that. Now, can you tell us, when did you last see your son?"

Her wide eyes blinked at him. "Two years ago," she said with a sniff.

Both Ransom and Gerald snapped to attention. Gerald looked at his partner with a puzzled frown, while Ransom, his brow deeply furrowed, stared at the woman in amazement.

"Two years?" he said in loud disbelief. "Don't you think you waited rather a long time to report it?"

RANSOM WAS SOMETIMES known to his peers (though not generally to his face) as having an acid tongue. But even the worst of his detractors would admit that he had a healthy understanding of when and where to use it. His fellow detectives were occasionally the recipients of his barbs, and even Sergeant Newman was not immune: but with the subjects of an investigation Ransom was usually careful to curb his tongue until an appropriate moment.

He knew he'd made a mistake the minute he'd opened his mouth, although in this case he knew he couldn't help himself. What they had on their hands was a murdered boy who had definitely not been dead for more than five days, and his mother, who was reporting him missing after two years. Sometimes, thought Ransom, it really was simply more than one could bear.

Unfortunately, the result of his remark was to reduce Mrs. Lyman to a blubbering mess. She sputtered something about how good a mother she was, and how good a child she raised, and that even in the best of families children will go astray and fall out of communication with their parents.

It was with a renewed effort that Ransom continued to refrain from drumming his fingers on the desk, having lost patience with himself and the woman.

"I'm sorry, Mrs. Lyman," said Ransom, "but you must understand that your son has only been dead since this past weekend. You say he's been missing for two years. Surely you must see the discrepancy."

"No, I didn't," said Mrs. Lyman with rather watery defiance, "I didn't say he was missing, I said I hadn't seen him for two years. You see, he moved into that Community."

"Community?"

"The church! They call themselves 'The Community of the Lord.' I didn't see him, but I heard from him. He calls. He called."

"How often did he call you?"

"Once or twice a month."

Ransom spread his hands and shook his head. "Then how did you know he was missing?"

Mrs. Lyman leaned forward a little and whispered, "Somebody called me. Last night. Somebody from the church."

SEVEN

"AFTER ALL, JER, she just learned her son was dead. For God's sake, she just identified his body."

"I know that," replied Ransom testily.

"I'm just saying you could've gone a little easier on her," said Gerald, realizing too late that any amount of correction was too much for his partner.

"On the contrary, I thought I was patient above and beyond."

"Yeah," said Gerald, deciding that acquiescence was the better part of avoidance.

"My dear Gerald, given the fact that the woman, a good mother by her own estimation, was telling us that the beloved boy who'd been dead for a few days had been missing for two years, I think my restraint was admirable."

"She explained that," said Gerald, "and I don't think her story was that unusual. There must be a thousand parents in Chicago who don't always see their kids. It's a big city."

"Thank you for that explanation."

Actually, in the normal course of events Ransom would have found that situation perfectly understandable, too, his own parents being long since deceased and no longer lamented. He himself had spent years not exactly being in contact with anyone in particular during his off-duty hours. It was only over the past year that his filial devotion had been reborn, and that for the elderly Emily. But now that devotion had taken hold, his years of veritable seclusion had slipped away and he had even less patience for people with a biological bond who failed to exercise it.

After Gerald had ushered Mrs. Lyman into the arms of a duty officer who would explain the procedures for having her son's body released, he returned to Ransom's office to find his partner rapidly thumbing through the phone book. He quickly located the address and phone number of Nicholas Bremmen, the man whom Mrs. Lyman said had called to let her know her son was missing. Ransom tried the number, letting it ring several times before hanging up. He glanced at his watch and saw that it was not yet five o'clock, so it was not so surprising that the man wasn't home, presuming he had a job. He could only hope that it was a nine-to-five job.

Gerald suggested trying the church. Ransom flipped back to the ''Cs'' and found the listing for the Community of the Lord. He was almost surprised to find it listed in such an ordinary fashion. He'd half expected it to ominously glow in the dark.

He dialed the number and was taken aback to find the phone was not to a church, but rather to the residence of the minister (although Ransom wasn't sure which moniker this church would use for its leader). Having been raised a Presbyterian, 'minister' was the first term that came to mind. If memory served, 'pastor' seemed to apply to smaller churches, 'father' to Catholic churches, 'brother' to monasteries, and 'reverend' was the sole domain of televangelists. But it had been a long time.

The phone was answered by a silvery-voiced woman who introduced herself as Carla, Rev. Sam's wife.

Ah, thought Ransom, it's reverend. Her tone gave Ransom the vague impression that she was the first lady of something. Of what remained to be seen.

Carla Draper received the news of Ransom's identity as if it were an everyday occurrence to hear from the police, and said that her husband was unavailable at the moment. She assured him, however, that the reverend would be available briefly by the time they arrived, if they would come right away. She said this quite simply, but still managed to convey that she found the matter a minor annoyance, something to be brushed away like a fly buzzing around her ear at a picnic. Whatever her attitude really was,

Ransom found it irritating, at the same time feeling guilty for thinking that the good reverend's wife didn't quite understand that one doesn't adopt a cavalier attitude with homicide detectives.

As he hung up the phone, he thought that perhaps it was a by-product of having stopped smoking that he found this seemingly pleasant woman so irritating. After all, there was nothing overtly patronizing in her tone or in her words. But he couldn't help thinking there was definitely something patronizing in her intent. He shook his head at his own suspicions. Perhaps that was simply the attitude she had developed after years of the demands made upon her as the reverend's wife. He made a mental note to keep an open mind.

The address that Carla Draper had given Ransom was in Albany Park, one of the older areas of Chicago on the northwest side of the city. It is one of the most difficult areas to access by car, due to its lack of proximity to the local expressways. It can only be approached by the city streets.

Gerald pulled off the Kennedy Expressway at Kimball Avenue and started the two-mile trek north. When they reached Lawrence Avenue, the center of Albany Park, Ransom began to wonder anew at the depth of history embodied in the city of Chicago. While the downtown and near-north areas of the city are a rich combination of the old and the new, with new architecture spiraling up next to historical sites, this area seemed virtually unchanged for almost a hundred years. True, a new strip mall had sprouted up, and a new bank branch had been built, but instead of blending with the surrounding area (the way they do in the central city), these new buildings seemed like cancerous growths on the wrinkled skin of the elderly neighborhood.

The only major change was a proliferation of Korean shop owners so thorough that Lawrence Avenue had become known as Seoul Drive.

To Ransom, the neighborhood was oppressive, so old that it almost reeked with age, and so close that it was claustrophobic. Though Chicago's Gold Coast was from approximately the same period, it turned a glittering face to the lakefront; Albany Park was its less affluent sister: the one who had married badly and couldn't afford a face-lift.

Kimball is lined with huge, overpowering courtyard apartment buildings that had wrought-iron fences and gates in various stages of disuse. The buildings were built so close together that they seemed to have gelled to each other with age. The hundreds of windows were filled with ve-netian blinds and window shades that probably managed to look old the moment they were hung. And every single building, regardless of size or state of repair, sported a 'for rent' sign, ranging in design from handprinted to Wool-worth's specials.

Gerald hung a right at Ainsle, drove a couple of blocks east and turned left on Spaulding. They passed a large grammar school and proceeded to a block of close-knit houses. The address that the reverend's wife had given them was a few doors from the end of the block, which was cut off by a bend in the north branch of the Chicago River.

The houses on this street were so closely sandwiched that they looked as if they couldn't breathe. They were of every shape, size, and architectural design. They looked so un-natural together, it was as if they'd been shaken in a Yaht-zee cup and strewn on a board.

The Drapers' house was a two-story wood-frame struc-ture with a new coat of bright blue paint that made it look like an elderly woman wearing too much makeup to hide her age.

The detectives quickly found a parking space and went up the narrow cement walk. The front door was painted a dark blue to accent the rest of the house, and to resist show-ing the effects of everyday traffic. Gerald stepped forward and knocked, then fell back in line with Ransom, feeling not for the first time like his partner's valet. After a mo-ment, the door was opened by a woman whose plumpish face might have been pleasant if she had smiled, and whose mud-colored curls were tied up in a scarf. She was clad in rather obviously color-coordinated, middle-aged knits. Though her expression was generally agreeable, it was belied by her hard, amber eyes. Ransom felt that looking into them was like approaching the gates of Eden, only to find the drawbridge up. He placed her in her late thirties or early forties.

"You must be the detectives who phoned," she said before they had a chance to speak. "I'm Carla Draper, the reverend's wife. Come in."

They followed her into the dark hallway and then the living room. Mrs. Draper motioned for them to sit on the maroon couch, but the detectives remained standing.

"Thank you," said Ransom dismissively.

"You didn't say what this visit is about."

"No," said Ransom. There was something about this woman that made Ransom not want to budge an inch.

Mrs. Draper's stance slackened imperceptibly. "I'll tell my husband you're here."

After a beat she started from the room, pausing in the doorway.

"I've been waiting dinner for your business to be taken care of. I'd appreciate it if your meeting could be brief."

With this she disappeared down the hallway toward the back of the house, making a slight swishing noise as she walked.

Ransom surveyed the room with a practiced eye. The furniture all appeared to be first-rate secondhand, as if the owners liked the best of things but were unwilling to pay the best of prices. Ransom mentally chastised himself for allowing the word "unwilling" to come so quickly to mind. After all, this was a clergyman's house and they were not known for being able to afford the best. Unless, of course, they hit it big on television.

Both Ransom and Gerald examined the mantelpiece. Amidst the bric-a-brac was a picture of a man who stood with his right arm chastely around the waist of Mrs. Draper.

"You wished to see me?"

The original of the man in the picture stood in the doorway. His arrival had been silent, and to Ransom's mind the reverend was working at giving the impression that he'd been spirited into their presence. Ransom wondered if he'd accidentally rubbed a lamp while surveying the room.

"You're Reverend Draper?" asked Ransom.

"Yes."

"Yes, we wanted to talk to you in connection with an investigation in which we're involved."

The reverend came into the room, his hand extending toward the couch. Ransom took this as an invitation and sat on the couch while Gerald slipped into the chair that Michael Franklin had occupied two nights earlier.

His hand still extended, the reverend turned his head toward Gerald and examined him as if he were a specimen of undetermined origin.

"Wouldn't you be more comfortable on the couch?" he said with no noticeable emotion.

"I'm fine," said Gerald.

Ransom smiled engagingly. "My partner dislikes being the center of attention."

The corners of the reverend's mouth slid upward. "I'm so sorry."

As if putting an end to the first portion of their meeting, without another word the reverend sat in a chair beside the couch. This positioned him facing Ransom from about three feet away, his back purposefully turned to Gerald. Gerald accepted the slight with a half smile as he pulled his little spiral notebook and pencil from his pocket.

"As I was saying," Ransom continued as if there'd been no interruption, "we are involved in an investigation concerning one of your...is parishioners the word?"

"Members," said the reverend.

"We understand that one of your members has disappeared."

"Really."

"A young man named Danny Lyman."

Rev. Sam's smile remained unchanged. He didn't move. "Danny hasn't disappeared."

Though he would have liked to match the reverend's immobility, Ransom couldn't help raising an eyebrow at this. And he was in no mood to play dueling statues.

"Indeed?"

The reverend offered no further response, other than the challenge of silence. Ransom crossed his legs.

"Do you mean that you haven't noticed him missing?"

"I am aware that he hasn't been around for a few days."

Ransom made a little sound in his throat as if clearing it, then said, "Yes, I believe that constitutes missing, unless he told someone where he was going."

Though Ransom had offered this as a statement, Rev. Sam responded to the implied question with:

"Not that I know of."

Ransom smiled. "I realize that you are only his...minister, so we can't expect that you'd know all of Danny's movements, but we thought—"

"I'm a little more than his minister."

Ransom intertwined his fingers and rested his hands on his knees. "Oh?"

The reverend warmed to the subject. "We aren't just a church, we're a Community of Christians. Following, we hope, the precepts of the Bible. Like the apostles and the other early Christians, we have formed a family, and hold ourselves accountable, as Christians, to one another."

Ransom paused for a moment to let this statement hang in the air, then said, "With you as the leader?"

The reverend shrugged. "I am the spiritual head of the church, just like any minister should be. But I am equally accountable to the membership, which is a situation you don't generally find in the world—in ordinary churches."

"That being the case," said Ransom, "one would think you'd be even more aware of the comings and goings of your members."

The reverend smiled in a way that made Ransom feel as if he were being found a bit tiresome, and continued expansively, "Ordinarily, I would say yes to that. Except that doesn't mean I watch their every move. I don't know what each of our members is having for dinner and the like. That would be...silly, to say the least, and not in the best interests of anyone concerned. Our aim is to develop close, individual relationships to God—and as a Community we foster that and are accountable to one another—but we try not to get in the way of the relationship to God." The reverend paused as if he'd just delivered the Apostle's Creed and was waiting for his next cue. After a moment he continued, "Having said that, I would say that what would be closer to the truth—about my leadership—is that I am more involved in the lives of our Community members than most 'ministers' would be. But that is by mutual agreement."

Ransom looked at the reverend for a moment. After a suitable pause, he said, "Then you are aware that Danny hasn't been around for a few days."

"Oh, yes."

"But you didn't find that cause for concern?"

"Oh, no. As I said, I'm involved in the lives of our members. I know them pretty well."

He had said this matter-of-factly, but his expression had intensified just enough to imply a depth of knowledge that Ransom was sure would have made him squirm had he been a member of the reverend's flock.

"Why aren't you concerned?"

"Because I know Danny, probably better than anyone else. It isn't all that unusual for him to go away for a few days without telling anyone—although, I'll admit he hasn't done it for a while."

"Why?"

"Why what?"

"Why would he go away like that?"

The reverend shrugged again, as if to say that one could never tell with children.

"Because he's young. Because he doesn't think. Maybe because he wants attention."

Ransom leaned in a little. "But he gets enough attention from you, doesn't he?"

"I don't know…" he replied with what Ransom felt was practiced self-effacement, "I try to give the right kind of attention. I sometimes think it's important to let people know that you won't respond with the wrong kind of attention."

Ransom looked puzzled by this.

"What do you mean?"

"For example, a young child who feels neglected will sometimes misbehave so that his parents will yell at him, because negative attention is better than no attention at all."

"I see," said Ransom, "and you feel that that's what Danny does by disappearing?"

"It wouldn't surprise me."

"And what do you think the 'wrong kind of attention' would be, under the circumstances?"

Rev. Sam opened his hands nonchalantly. "To overreact."

Ransom considered him for a moment, and Gerald took the opportunity to quietly shake his writing hand. For Rev. Sam's part, he remained motionless, staring fixedly at Ransom's face. Finally, Ransom said, "I'm sorry, Reverend, but I would find overreacting an entirely proper response when someone's been missing for five days."

"Of course. You're a policeman."

"I would think that even if you weren't concerned, you'd at least be curious. But you don't find this situation unusual at all."

The reverend shrugged again, a movement that Ransom was beginning to find annoying.

"As I said, I know Danny."

They seemed to have reached an impasse, and Ransom was deciding how to proceed when the reverend surprised him with a question.

"There is one thing I'm curious about, though."

"Hmm?"

"How did the police get involved in this?"

"What do you mean?"

"Well, since I don't think anything of Danny having gone away, I can't imagine who thought to call the police."

In the ordinary course of an investigation, Ransom was loathe to divulge any information to the parties involved: It was *his* job to ask the questions. And since you never knew where a bit of leaked information might run to, it was better to say nothing at all. Ordinarily. In this case, Ransom felt an even more pressing importance to refrain from revealing that the real source of the Missing Person's report had been one of the reverend's flock. In fact, Ransom found this feeling perfectly ominous. He opted for the exact truth.

"Danny's mother contacted us."

"His mother?"

The reverend looked genuinely surprised, and if his next natural question was "And who told her?" he did his best not to show it.

Once the reverend had been caught even slightly off guard, Ransom gladly pressed the advantage.

"She reported her son missing yesterday, and came in to identify his body today."

"His body?"

Rev. Sam didn't look surprised this time, or even upset at the news of the death. But Ransom thought he detected a slight pulsation in the lower lid of his right eye.

"Danny's dead?"

Ransom nodded.

"I would think you would have told me that to begin with."

Ransom shrugged in a not-completely-conscious imitation of the reverend's own movement. "I wondered if you already knew."

"If I..." the reverend began, then realization seemed to come to him. "...I see."

"This is, you understand, a murder investigation."

"Murder?" said Rev. Sam, with no more emotion than he would have displayed had he been present when someone made an unusual dinner selection. "Danny was murdered?"

"Yes."

"Where did this happen?"

"His body was found in the Loop," Ransom replied, making the evasion as obvious as possible.

"Hmm. I'll have to make arrangements for a memorial service."

Ransom held his chin between his thumb and forefinger for a moment as he considered the reverend. He could not exactly put a word to the man he saw before him. "Slick" was the one that came to mind, but that seemed to imply an overt underhandedness that could not be attributed to the reverend. The word that came the closest was "polished": polished and with an internal intensity that made it seem as if a kinetic power lurked beneath the surface. The detective's assessment of the reverend was that he was a diamond out of the rough: cool, smooth, and hard.

At last Ransom said, "Forgive me, Reverend, but you don't seem very upset by this."

"Upset?"

"Most people, when they hear of the death of a...friend, are upset by it. Especially in cases of murder. But you don't seem moved by this at all."

There was a pause. There was no visible change in the reverend's demeanor, but Ransom still got the impression that displeasure was being conveyed to him.

"I am a Christian, Detective Ransom."

He stopped as if these few words should explain everything to an intelligent man.

"I'm sorry, I don't understand."

"A Christian believes that this life is just a vale of tears, and that everything good, wonderful, and blessed awaits us in the next life—where mansions have been prepared for us. A good Christian believes that death is not something to be feared, but to be welcomed."

"Even if it comes too soon?"

Rev. Sam smiled indulgently. "There is no such thing

as 'too soon' in God's time. We die when we're supposed to.''

Dammit, thought Ransom, you're good. But there was something about the reverend's delivery that made the words ring hollow, like a bell with a broken clapper, as if the man had so completely disassociated himself from the world that he could sit back and dispassionately toe the party line without the meaning or impact of the words ever touching him. Ransom wondered if the reverend really believed the words as he said them, and silently vowed that before this case was over, he would break through the man's veneer and discover what was truly there. But for the moment, he knew it was time to put an end to any further philosophical discussion.

"Putting 'God's time' aside for the moment, when someone is murdered, it is our job to find the killer and bring him to justice."

The reverend shrugged. "Justice is something that will eventually come to all of us. It belongs to the Lord."

Ransom brushed this aside. "Do you know of anyone who would have wanted to kill Danny?"

"No."

"Did he have any enemies?"

"Not in this Community."

"Indeed?" said Ransom, raising an eyebrow.

"We're brothers and sisters here, Detective. We're not enemies."

"And yet, Danny Lyman is dead."

Rev. Sam shrugged. "You said he was found in the Loop. Are you sure he wasn't killed as part of some sort of...mugging, or robbery? Was anything missing?"

A picture of the naked body flashed through Ransom's mind, and a smile crept across his face despite himself as he thought that yes, *everything* was missing.

"We are relatively sure that it wasn't a robbery," said Ransom, then added more pointedly, "are you sure that he didn't have any enemies?"

"Not in this Community," repeated the reverend with finality.

"What about his relationship outside the Community?"

There was a fraction of a pause before he replied, "I don't know of any."

"Any enemies, you mean," said Ransom with a smile. "Yes."

"Let me ask you this," said Ransom, casually shifting in his chair, "can you tell me when you last saw Danny?"

"Last Friday."

"Where?"

"Here, as a matter of fact. He stopped by to speak with me."

"About what?"

The patronizing smile reappeared on the reverend's face. "I'm sure you know that as his 'minister' I can't discuss that with you."

"The boy is dead," Ransom replied with mock incredulity.

"That doesn't alter the case."

There was another silence during which Ransom and the reverend held each other's gaze, as if suddenly caught in some sort of silent battle. Gerald looked up from his notebook, and thought just briefly that it was as if a line had been drawn between two chickens, whose eyes would never again move until the line was broken. As it happened, the line was broken suddenly by a voice.

"Sam, you really have to come and eat. You'll be late for the meeting."

Mrs. Draper's approach had been soundless. She was just suddenly in the doorway, much in the way the reverend had appeared earlier, as if appearing on cue was a talent they practiced together. Though she'd spoken to her husband, it was clear that the meaning was directed at the detectives.

Rev. Sam rose, beaming at his wife. "I'm sorry, gentlemen, but I really have to be going. We have an early meeting tonight, and if I don't get to dinner, I'll be late."

Gerald had stood just after the reverend, and Ransom now rose slowly.

"I'm so sorry," he said, his voice fairly dripping, "I didn't mean to keep you."

The reverend extended his hand toward the doorway, and his wife stepped aside, a superior smile spread across her face. Ransom had an uncomfortable vision of the Red Sea smirking at the Israelites.

Ransom started toward the hallway, then stopped for a moment at the doorway and faced the reverend. He said, as if in afterthought, "Oh, by the way, I'd like your permission to speak to the members of your church."

Rev. Sam didn't lower his hand. "Permission? You don't need my permission. Everyone is free to talk as they please."

"Thank you," said Ransom with a smile.

"It does present a problem, though," said the reverend, dropping his hand to his side.

"Hmm?"

"There are over a hundred members in our Community."

My God, thought Ransom. But his face remained impassive.

"A hundred. Hmm. Well, maybe you could narrow it down for us."

"How do you mean?"

"Even in a community of your kind, some of the members must be closer than others."

"The Lord tells us that we are not to show favoritism."

Ransom closed his eyes for a moment and steeled his jaw. When his eyes popped open, he was staring pointedly into the reverend's. "Surely he did not give equal time to a hundred people. Is there any way you can narrow it down to the people he came in contact with the most?"

Without a word the reverend crossed to a small secretary that stood in a corner of the room. He rifled through a stack of papers in the center drawer, extracting one sheet, which he brought back with him and handed to Ransom with irritated grace. It was obvious that he felt the detective had taken up quite enough of his time.

"This is a list of Danny's small group. Saul Berne is the leader."

"Small group?" said Ransom, scanning the sheet.

Rev. Sam answered quickly, as if trying to speed their departure, "The Community is broken into seven small groups, each with a leader."

"Chosen by you?"

"Chosen by God. That way all our members can get individual attention from the leadership. If there are problems, they bring them to their small-group leader. If it can't be sorted out at that level, it's brought to me."

"Hmm," said Ransom thoughtfully, "sort of like a small corporation."

There was the briefest pause before the reverend replied, "You might say that. All of the small-group members should be available except the Beckmans. They left on vacation Sunday morning."

"Sunday morning? Not Friday night or Saturday?"

"The Beckmans are good Christians. They wanted to attend the Saturday night meeting."

"Ah."

"Sam, please," said Carla Draper, her displeased expression directed toward the detectives.

"Now you'll really have to excuse me, gentlemen," he said with an apologetic shrug that Ransom felt was meant to imply "What can I do, she's the boss."

But as Ransom glanced back over his shoulder at the picture formed by the reverend and his wife, he was reminded instead that all tableaus are staged, and therefore not to be trusted.

Gerald passed through the front door, and Ransom stopped long enough to say, "We will be speaking to you again, Reverend Draper."

The door closed quietly behind him as he joined his partner. A sly smile crept across Ransom's face. When he noticed Gerald's questioning glance, he said, "The situation called for a dramatic exit line."

"That's the first time I've ever heard you ask permission to talk to suspects."

Ransom's smile broadened. "I just wanted to hear his reaction."

The detectives decided to walk back to Nicholas Bremmen's apartment on the corner of Kimball and Ainsle. If pressed for an explanation, Ransom would have said that they walked simply because it was too much trouble to drive the car the three blocks and park again in the congested neighborhood during rush hour. But somehow Ransom wasn't comfortable with the idea of positioning their car in front of Bremmen's apartment, drawing attention to their visit. It was a feeling that Ransom was at a loss to understand at the moment, but it was a feeling he decided to heed.

"What do you think of Draper?" Gerald asked.

Ransom smiled. "A good Presbyterian doesn't speak ill of the clergy."

"What does a bad one do?"

"Hedges his bets. I hate to disappoint you, Gerald, but I don't know what to make of the good reverend."

"Really?" said Gerald, with genuine surprise.

"Forgive me," said Ransom, his voice taking on a rather sharp edge, "my radar must be broken. But actually, I think many things of Reverend Draper."

"Like what?"

"I wouldn't want to accuse the man of lying, but no matter how firmly he holds his beliefs about life and death and the hereafter, it's difficult to believe that he could be so completely devoid of emotion on learning of the death of someone he cared for."

"Yeah?"

Ransom glanced at his partner, "So I suspect he didn't care for the boy. Either that or he already knew he was dead."

"Yeah," said Gerald slowly, "He wasn't too broken up about it."

"That, my dear Gerald, is an understatement. For the rest of it, whatever Draper's beliefs may be, and whatever he may have thought of Danny Lyman, one would expect that the clergy would be a bit more forthcoming in the matter of murder."

Gerald rolled his eyes so decidedly that his pupils almost disappeared into his head, a motion that did not go unnoticed by Ransom. An indulgent smile played about his lips. "You'd think he'd help us find a murderer."

"Thank you," said Gerald wryly.

"Tell me, what did *you* think of the good reverend?"

"He has a nice back," he replied with a cough, "and he sits up straight."

Ransom chuckled.

"But I think the same as you. He seemed awfully reserved."

"I wish I could think that's all it is."

"What do you mean?"

"Two things. One is that Draper is so reserved it leads me to believe that he has something to hide."

He fell silent, and Gerald finally found it necessary to prompt him to continue.

"And the other?"

Ransom sighed so heavily it seemed almost as if he were trying to get the world to roll off his shoulders.

"Well, given Emily's precarious condition, I'd like to think I could trust the clergy."

They arrived at Nicholas Bremmen's apartment building, a large, rambling, dusty-yellow bricked structure that seemed to have solidified with age.

Ransom tried the knob on the outer door and found it locked. A small metal box hung on the left side of the door frame, with a row of ludicrously small white buttons that served as doorbells. Gerald stepped up and squinted at the names, then pressed the little button marked "Bremmen."

The door unlocked itself with the sound of a loud buzz.

Ransom popped it open and headed up the stairs, which were narrow and carpeted with a very dirty, very old dark blue pseudo-shag rug. Gerald was close behind. At the first bend in the stairs, Ransom paused and was about to call out, but was interrupted by the sound of a door opening somewhere overhead, and a melodic male voice calling out, "Come on up, honey!"

Ransom glanced down at Gerald, who was smiling up at him from a couple of steps back. Ransom said "Pah!" and continued up the stairs. They found the open door on the second floor, and Ransom tapped lightly on it as he pushed it the rest of the way open. The apartment was small and clean, and had the same blue carpeting as the hallway, though it was obvious that a brazen attempt had been made to clean it. The room was furnished in the best that friends could donate. There was an old sofa bed and two chairs in the room, but no table. Gerald peeked around the corner into the kitchen, and saw a small glass table pushed up against the nearest wall, and a bare wooden chair placed beneath it. Long, light yellow sheers rustled noiselessly in the tepid wind that flowed through the open windows on two of the walls. Ransom thought that the room would seem a good deal dingier in another month or so, when the windows would have to be closed against the winter.

"Mr. Bremmen?" Ransom called into the apartment.

There was a moment's silence, then Nicholas called out in a surprised, questioning tone, "Yes?"

"May we speak with you a moment?"

"Just a minute." His voice sounded muffled and harried now.

After a second, Nicholas hurried out of the bathroom, which was through a walk-in closet to the left of the front door. He was running a comb through his hair, which was as dry as a towel could get it. He stopped when he saw the detectives, as if he hadn't known what he'd been expecting, but this certainly wasn't it.

"Can I help you?" he said, furrowing his brow in a way

that made his words sound more like "Who the hell are you?"

"I am Detective Ransom, this is my partner, Detective White."

"Detectives?" said Nicholas, his brow smoothing out as his eyes widened.

"Yes," said Ransom, proceeding cautiously, "I understand that you contacted Danny Lyman's mother. You had some concerns about Danny?"

"Oh, yes," said Nicholas, looking relieved to know the purpose of their visit, "we haven't seen him for days. I thought maybe she had." He paused for a moment, then said, "Did she call you?"

"Yes, she did."

Nicholas flushed a little. "Oh, I didn't mean for her to do that. I hope I didn't do anything wrong. I didn't want to upset Mrs. Lyman or anything, it's just that Danny's been gone so long."

"Mr. Bremmen, do you think we could sit down for a moment?"

Without moving, Nicholas replied, "What's the matter?"

Ransom assessed the young man. To the detective, he looked like a reasonably intelligent, well-grounded individual, maybe a bit full of himself (as anyone would seem, thought Ransom, if you met them while they were grooming), but he gave the impression of reliability.

"Mr. Bremmen, Danny Lyman was found dead on Monday morning."

The black comb that Nicholas had been clutching tightly fell to the floor. His face went white and he said "Oh, God," several times, his voice faint and breathless.

"Yeah, I think we'd better sit down."

This last seemed a bit redundant, as Nick had already sunk into the chair on the right side of the sofa. The detectives sat on opposite ends of the couch, with Ransom sitting by Nicholas.

"Oh, God," said Nicholas again, "I wish I could keep Pam out of this."

"Excuse me?" said Ransom.

"Pam. Pam is my girlfriend. Fiancée. She's on her way over here. That's who I thought you were when you buzzed. We're going out. I wish I could stop her."

"If she knew Danny, we'd like to talk to her."

"I suppose she's in it anyway," said Nicholas vacantly, his face a mask of confusion. After a moment he shook his head and seemed to pull himself together somewhat. He said, "I'm sorry, it's just a shock. I guess I never really believed anything was wrong."

They were interrupted by a tentative tapping at the door, which neither of the detectives had thought to close. Pamela stood with her right hand on the doorknob. She had apparently heard Nicholas's last few words.

"I'm sorry I didn't ring the bell," she said. "Somebody was going out when I was coming in, so I just came up. Is something wrong?"

All three men were on their feet in unison. Nicholas rushed to Pamela, drew her a few steps into the apartment, and closed the door. He faced her and put his hands on her shoulders.

"Pam, Danny is dead."

"Danny Lyman?" she said in disbelief.

He released her shoulders and his eyes traveled down to the carpet as if he were slightly embarrassed to be performing introductions under the circumstances.

"Pam, these are detectives. They're here about Danny. This is my fiancée, the one I was telling you about," he said, not realizing this made it sound as if he had others to choose from.

"Your name is?" said Ransom.

"I'm sorry, this is Pamela Frazier," said Nicholas, reddening slightly. He was beginning to feel as if he were host at a party in a nightmare.

"Detectives?" said Pamela, looking to Ransom and Gerald for explanation. She then turned to Nicholas for help. "There's something more, isn't there?"

"I don't...we didn't talk...they just got here."

"There is something more, isn't there?" said Pam, growing more agitated. "There wouldn't be detectives if there wasn't something wrong."

"Please," said Ransom, indicating the couch.

Pamela and Nicholas sat on the couch this time, and the detectives took the chairs at opposite ends of it. It was as if the music had stopped and they'd all found seats. Gerald flipped open his tiny notebook, and the couple's eyes turned to Ransom as if they already knew that he was conducting the interview.

"I said that Danny was found dead, but I'm afraid that was a bit misleading. He was found murdered."

Tears silently stole down Pamela's cheeks, in a way that Ransom found an attractive contrast to Mrs. Lyman's. Nicholas gently took his fiancée's hand.

"Do you have any idea who did it?" asked Pamela.

"That's what we're trying to find out."

"It was just some...he was...was he robbed or something?"

"The circumstances would indicate that it wasn't a random killing."

Pamela stared at him vacantly through watery eyes, as if she wished she could think of something else to ask him, some question she could put to the detective that would elicit an explanation that would make sense of the tragedy. But her mind took on the blackness of grief.

Ransom turned to Nicholas and said, "Mr. Bremmen, you said a moment ago that you didn't really think anything was wrong. Could you explain that?"

"What do you mean?"

"Well, I assume that since you were the one who called Mrs. Lyman, you *did* think something was wrong."

Nicholas thought about this for a moment, his brow furrowed, and he looked rather disgusted with himself. He said, "Yes, I know. It's just that...you don't like to think that something's wrong, even if you know it is. I've known Danny for a couple of years..."

"Since you joined this Community?"

Ransom was surprised to see that Nicholas's face seemed to harden at the mention of the Community.

"No. I've only been here about a year. Danny was the one who introduced me to it. We worked together before that, at a camera store downtown."

"Did he leave there?"

Nicholas nodded. "A few months ago he took a job running a computer for a small manufacturing company out in Skokie. I haven't seen him as much since then."

"Hmm," said Ransom, leaning back in his chair.

"Anyway, what I started to say was I've known Danny for a couple of years, and he didn't seem like the type of person who'd just disappear. He was pretty steady."

Nicholas stopped and a cloud seemed to pass over his face at the memory of his friend. Then he looked back up at Ransom. "But even so, I didn't like to think anything was wrong."

Ransom's eyes narrowed. "Then why did you?"

Nicholas looked at him quizzically.

"I mean, if you didn't see him that often anymore, why did you think he was missing?"

"Oh, my God," said Pamela, her right hand going up to her mouth. She looked sadly at Nicholas. "He was right. He was right, and I didn't believe him."

Nicholas tightened his hold on her left hand, transmitting his care to her.

"It's all right," he said quietly, "we couldn't know."

"But you believed him," she said plaintively, her tears flowing more freely.

"Not entirely," he said, "but I thought maybe..." His voice trailed off and he put his other hand around hers, cradling it gently as if it were a wounded sparrow.

"Mr. Bremmen?" said Ransom, his tone gently but firmly calling the young man back to attention.

"Michael told us that Danny was missing. Michael Franklin, Danny's roommate."

Gerald jotted down the name.

"I didn't realize that Danny had a roommate," said Ransom.

"We are all encouraged to have roommates, to…I'm not sure why, I guess it has something to do with brotherhood. Pam has one. Sarah Bennett. I don't."

"So," said Ransom, "why did he do that?"

"What?"

"Tell you."

Nicholas released Pamela's hand and turned to face Ransom. "Because I knew Danny from before I came into the Community. He thought I might know something more about his life outside."

"Outside?" Ransom repeated, his interest sparked by the choice of words.

"I mean about his family. And I did. I remembered him saying where his mother lived, so I looked her up and called her."

"That's very interesting," said Ransom slowly. "I would have thought from the way this Community is set up that Michael would have gone to Reverend Draper."

"Rev. Sam?" said Nicholas with a snort. "He did."

This brought both of the detectives up short. Gerald looked up from his notebook and tapped his pencil against his knee. Ransom frowned.

"Did he?"

Nicholas nodded. "He talked to him on Monday night." He made a sound like "harumph," then added half under his breath, "Rev. Sam didn't think there was anything to worry about."

"Yes?"

"But Michael still did."

"And so did you."

Nicholas seemed to wait a long time before answering this, then replied with a gloomy "Yes."

"He came and talked to us last night," said Pamela. "Oh Nick, if only we'd listened to him!"

Ransom considered Pamela for a moment. Though he was not the kind of man who liked to see a woman cry, he had been a homicide detective long enough to have developed a deep appreciation for true emotion. In the course of an investigation it was not uncommon to find people who—either because they didn't care for the deceased or out of fear for themselves—don't seem to give a damn about the dear departed. On more than one occasion, Ransom had found himself touched when happening upon someone who *did* care. He didn't feel he could leave this attractive young woman with a sense of useless remorse.

"Miss Frazier, Danny has been dead since last weekend. There's nothing you could have done to help him, especially if you weren't told he was missing until last night."

"But I…" she started, then stopped. Her mind went back to the moment when they'd run into Michael on Saturday night after the meeting. No, there was nothing there that could have told them this would happen. "I guess you're right," she said at last. She seemed to manage a very tentative smile to thank him.

"Can you tell me if Danny had any friends? I mean anyone in particular?"

Both Nicholas and Pamela started to speak at once, albeit hesitantly. Nicholas deferred to her.

"Well, there's Michael. They were friends."

Ransom seemed to consider this, then Nicholas said, "Everybody liked him. I mean, all of *us*." He laid stress on the word "us" as if there was an unspoken "them." Then he added quietly, "I like to think I was his friend."

Ransom said, "Hmm," then the party fell silent for a moment.

"I think that will be all for now," said Ransom, rising suddenly from his chair.

The men rose, Gerald slipping the notebook and pencil into the pocket of his blazer. Pamela got up from the couch more slowly.

"Thank you," said Ransom as he and Gerald headed for the door.

Though it was hardly necessary in a room of such diminutive proportions, Nicholas followed them, his arm wrapped protectively around Pamela's waist.

"If you have any more questions—if we can help—let us know."

Ransom turned and looked at Nicholas as if assessing whether he could be trusted for an opinion. Then he said, "There is one thing. What did you think of Danny Lyman?"

Nicholas lowered his eyes for a moment. When he raised them, a warm, sad smile had spread across his face. "I liked him. He was the type of guy who'd stick up for you. He was 'causey,' if you know what I mean."

Pamela smiled at a private memory.

Nicholas added, "If I was in trouble, I'd want him on my side."

AN ARGUMENT DID not exactly ensue immediately. It would be more accurate to say that Ransom began an argument with himself, and Gerald was reluctantly drawn into it.

"I suppose we should talk to him now," said Ransom as they walked toward Michael Franklin's apartment.

"I guess," said Gerald.

"It's getting late. I have to get to the hospital."

"We can wait till tomorrow."

"No we can't. Given what we know, we need to talk to Michael Franklin as soon as possible."

"What we know? What do we know?"

"We know that Michael Franklin thought something was wrong with Danny being gone before anybody else did."

"Uh-huh," said Gerald, prompting his partner to continue.

"And we know that that bastard lied."

At this, Gerald looked quite confused. "I thought the two of them were telling the truth."

"Not them! That bastard, the good Reverend Draper! He said he didn't know Danny was missing."

"But Jer, what he said still makes sense."

Ransom stopped angrily in his tracks, his right hand clenched in a fist and jabbed into his hip.

"Would you please explain to me how lying to the police makes sense?"

"He didn't lie," said Gerald with exasperation, "he said he noticed he wasn't there—he said he didn't think anything of Danny going away for a few days. That might not be a lie."

"He knew, Gerald, that *someone* was worried about the disappearance."

"But that doesn't make Draper's reaction any more suspicious. All he said was he didn't think it was unusual."

"He seems to be alone in that," said Ransom hotly, starting down the street again. "Bremmen thought it was unusual."

"Well, yeah," said Gerald, "but the Frazier woman said she didn't think it was—at first, and Bremmen admitted he hadn't seen Danny a lot lately. Maybe he'd changed. Maybe Reverend Draper knew him better."

"Better than his mother?" Ransom snapped.

Gerald shrugged. "She hasn't seen him a lot lately, either."

Ransom managed a smile at this. "Oh, Gerald, Gerald—you are here to keep me levelheaded, aren't you?"

"Nobody could do that."

"It seems his roommate was the first to think there was something wrong when Danny disappeared. I'll be interested to hear why."

They reached the red brick building and found that the front door opened into a vestibule. Gerald pushed the doorbell marked "Franklin" and they waited. There was dead silence. You could almost hear the motes floating in the air.

"Damn," said Ransom.

"We don't know how late he works."

"I suppose," said Ransom, glancing at his watch, "that it'll have to be tomorrow."

With this, the detectives departed.

The silence hung ominously in their wake.

EIGHT

IT WASN'T UNTIL about six-thirty that Ransom arrived at the hospital. He made a brief stop at the nurses' station, where Nurse Carter flashed her large brown eyes, wrapped her arms in her omnipresent cardigan, and informed the detective that Emily was a little better. Or, as she put it, "Miss Emily is getting back some of her spice." Even after the discouragement he'd felt at Emily's lack of progress the past couple of days, he was surprised at the intensity of the relief he experienced at Carter's words.

As Ransom greeted Emily, he did a quick survey of the room. A half-eaten dinner lay partially covered by a paper napkin on her table, which had been pushed aside. Good, he thought, she's eating. An enormous volume of the complete works of Shakespeare lay open on the nightstand. And Emily's appearance had improved. An attempt had been made to brush her hair into place, though from the amount of strands currently escaping from her bun it was evident that she hadn't done the work herself. Her eyes seemed to be in the process of making the transition from the dusty gray of the past few days, to their usual dusty blue.

"I understand you're getting better."

"You've been gossiping with the nurses again, haven't you."

"Hmm."

"It's a rumor that I hope will turn out to be true," she said, eyeing him playfully.

"Um-hmm," said Ransom, rubbing his chin as if considering her thoughtfully. "You're getting back to your old self."

Emily heaved a weary sigh. "My old self, I'm afraid, is going to be all I *can* manage."

"You'll be fine," said Ransom, taking a more peremptory approach, which he thought might be advisable under the circumstances. "And you'll be out of here soon."

"That would be nice," she replied wistfully, "to be back in my own house, and taking care of Tam. You have been looking in on her, haven't you?"

Tam was the cat that Ransom had given Emily not long after the death of her elderly tabby, Fedora, to fill the feline void in her life. Tam would be classified as a calico, though she was mostly white. Emily had so named her because of the one spot of color she sported: a perfectly formed circle, half black, half orange, in the center of her head that made her look as if she were wearing a rather jaunty little hat. That was Emily's explanation. Ransom wasn't too sure that she didn't just enjoy naming animals after her former headgear.

"Yes," said Ransom, "I've been feeding her. But she's not getting the attention she normally gets. She misses you."

It was a sorry attempt to instill in Emily the fact that she was needed. That she was important to Ransom was an understanding that remained tacit between them. Even now it would be something that Ransom would find difficult to put into words. But Emily was from an age in which such things often remained unspoken, but were no less understood for that.

"It's nice to know I'm needed," said Emily. "There's something about being old and in a hospital that makes one feel decidedly superfluous."

Ransom was uncomfortably reminded of what Nurse Carter had told him the other day: that sometimes after an operation the elderly felt they had nothing to live for. At the time he'd thought the warning was unnecessary, because the Emily he knew would never feel that way. The last few days had left him unsure. He drew the chair up beside her bed and said nonchalantly, "I'm working on a very interesting case at the moment. I hadn't wanted to bother you with it because you haven't been well..."

Emily managed a disparaging glance and smiled. "Tell me about it."

When Ransom had finished telling her about how and where the body had been found, Emily sat back against her pillows.

"There's something so...cruel about disposing of a body in that fashion," she said with a slight shudder. "Not that there's any nice way to do it—but I think it shows a profound disrespect for life. As if a human life was just so much refuse."

Oh, God, thought Ransom, this is not the train of thought I wanted to start.

"Anyway," he said in a tone that implied that they needed to move on, "someone reported him missing. Someone...well, indirectly, someone from his church."

Emily's forehead wrinkled. "His church?"

"Um-hmm."

"Well, now, that's very interesting. You wouldn't think that in this day and age, anyone from his church would notice. Or at least, not right away. It's not all that unusual for someone to miss a Sunday at my church."

Ransom raised an eyebrow. "I didn't know you went to church."

"I do a great many things, Jeremy. A good Methodist upbringing is not easily left behind. I don't attend as regularly as I used to, but then I don't do anything as regularly as I used to."

"You're a mass of surprises."

"But the point is, I suppose I'd *notice* if one of the regular churchgoers wasn't there, but I don't think I'd think anything of it."

"Well, this isn't exactly a Methodist church."

"Indeed?" said Emily, and Ransom was pleased to note a bit of the old sparkle returning to her eyes.

"We've only scratched the surface so far, but the surface seems to go pretty deep. The members we've met refer to the church as a Community, with a capital 'C'."

"Oh dear," said Emily warily, "that doesn't sound very promising. Is it some sort of cult?"

"It's too early to say. The leader of the Community...the minister assures me that the members are free to talk to us as they please."

"Didn't you believe him?"

"He said it in such a way that made me think that if I were one of his flock and heard him, I would immediately clam up. It seems that either he has nothing to hide, or he has nothing to fear."

"I'm not sure I know what you mean by that, Jeremy."

"I mean that none of his flock would say anything incriminating."

In her improving condition, Emily was able to discern that Ransom meant this in more ways than one. She nodded her understanding.

"So you've met the minister."

"The Reverend Draper, yes."

"And what do you think of him?"

"Too closemouthed by half for a murder investigation. Not inclined to be helpful, but quite suave in his presentation. I get the impression that he doesn't feel the police belong in his Community, no matter what the cause may be." He added wryly, "I'm sure he's very charismatic in the pulpit, assuming they have one."

Emily said "tsk" and her eyes wandered out the window to the darkened view of the lake. Moonlight shimmered off the water.

"Anyway," Ransom continued, "the point is that *these* church members are in far more contact with each other than the usual churchgoers."

"You said that the report of the missing boy came indirectly from the church?"

"Yes," said Ransom with a smile, feeling like a suspect in his own investigation. He often felt that Emily would be much more effective at interrogation than the most hardened detective on the force. Himself excluded, of course. "We had to work backward from that one. The mother reported him missing this morning. She hadn't seen him for two years.''

"How curious."

"She received a call from someone from the church."

"Now that's even more curious," said Emily with interest. "If the situation is as you suspect in this...community, isn't it surprising that one of the members would go outside of it?"

"Yes, well that's another story. I have a feeling that not all of the members are as committed as others. But at the moment that's only a feeling. At any rate, the beginning of the chain is the dead boy's roommate, whom we haven't been able to interview yet. He told the reverend that the boy had disappeared, but the reverend didn't exactly believe him—or think it was anything to worry about. Then this roommate told another couple, who didn't *exactly* believe him either."

"Like Cassandra," said Emily with another "tsk."

"I beg your pardon?"

"My dear Jeremy, it never ceases to amaze me that someone with your vast education does not know his Shakespeare better."

Ransom tried to retain his patience, the effort only betrayed by his gently drumming his fingers on the arm of his chair as he waited for her to get to the point.

"*Troilus and Cressida*, Jeremy. Which, of course, goes back a good deal farther than Shakespeare, but it's with his version that I'm most familiar. Cassandra is a character who was given a blessing and a curse. The blessing was the 'gift' of prophecy, if you can call it that in her case. And the curse was that nobody would believe her. This sounds like this roommate of yours. He seems to have known the truth, but couldn't get anyone to believe him."

"Except that the second person he told believed him enough to call the boy's mother."

"Perhaps that is a step up from Greek tragedy," said Emily, a twinkle in her eye.

"And she called us."

Emily folded her thin, veined hands on top of the tan hospital blanket that was pulled up to her waist, and looked at the detective.

"So, what do you do next?"

With a little laugh Ransom replied, "You really are wasted here, you should be a sergeant. Tomorrow we'll be trying to contact the dead boy's roommate, as well as whatever other friends he might have had—although the reverend tells us that the Lord doesn't allow them to play favorites enough to have friends."

"I hate to disagree with a man of the cloth," said Emily primly, "but I hardly think they could be quite normal if they didn't form friendships."

Ransom nodded and added wryly, "Let alone the fact that most of them are married. Of course, I have no personal experience, but I've heard that one is closer to one's spouse than to other people. Anyway, I think we'll have another try at the good reverend himself. Perhaps he'll be a bit more forthcoming once he's had a day to think about it."

"I wouldn't count on that," said Emily pointedly.

"The really odd thing is that you would think he wanted us to believe that he knew more that he was saying."

Emily nodded. "Many clergymen, both the regular varieties and the more irregular ones, believe that to be close-mouthed is to appear ethereal. It's a hard thing to shake them of. After all, the easiest way to appear to be intelligent is to keep your mouth shut. But then again, I'm sure there are clergymen who speak as little as possible out of respect for the secrets of the confessional—for fear of inadvertently giving something away."

"I wish I could believe that's all it is. But I really think there's something more to it with Reverend Draper. He seems to make a very...visible point of holding back. I feel I'm being challenged. If that's the way he acts with his members, I can see why they think he's some sort of oracle."

"They may see more than there is to see," said Emily.

They sat in silence for a moment, each contemplating the situation in their own ways. Finally, Emily said, "You know, Jeremy, when I was a little girl there were traveling preachers—yes, who even stopped in places like Chicago. Revivalists, they were called. They would come into town and run up their tents and hold revival meetings, and get people all stirred up in general. I suppose it was all very exciting, especially for people who didn't have the more everyday excitements in their lives. But then the preachers would go on their way—move on to the next town. The good thing about it was—well, I suppose this might sound blasphemous, but the good thing is that people don't generally stay revived. They usually settle back down soon enough and get back to believing in God and getting about their business. These days...unfortunately...these days, the revivalists put up their tents and stay. I'm not sure that's at all a good thing."

Ransom nodded, and then he and his adopted grandmother fell back into their silent contemplations.

A CHORUS OF deep male voices rang together in a disharmony of broken syllables. The leadership of the Community, eight men, stood in a circle in the living room of Greg Kirk's humble bungalow. Their heads were raised, their eyes were closed; they mumbled loudly through smiling lips in a language they believed was only understood by God.

Little by little, their voices rose in volume, until the discord became a loud chantlike noise that joined on one tone, then dissipated like a siren fading off into the distance. All eyes remained closed, all ears cocked in anxious expectation. Finally a loud, clear, melodic voice sang out in what the uninitiated would have described as an otherworldly, unchained melody:

Behold, I am your provider!
Behold, I am your protector!
As long as you are Mine,
As long as you walk in My light,

Your way will be clear,
And you will be blessed
All the days of your life!

The voice stopped suddenly but not unexpectedly, like the last blast of reveille. There was a satisfied silence, during which all of the smiles broadened and "amens" were volunteered. Tonight there had been a manifestation. Then the men started to repeat "praise the Lord," at first softly, then building to a joyous yell.

When the voices finally died down, Rev. Sam sat down in an overstuffed armchair by the ornamental fireplace and invited the men to take their seats. Saul sat on a hard wooden chair in his usual place at the reverend's right, and the rest of the men took their choices of the remainder of the tatty furniture, which had been arranged in a ragged circle around a large, secondhand braided rug.

Present for the meeting (besides the reverend and Saul Berne) were James Keller and James Hartwick, known affectionately in the Community as the James brothers, who along with their leadership duties shared an internal medicine practice on Lawrence Avenue; Terrance Foote, owner of the tenor voice that had provided the vessel for the Lord, who taught English at Von Steuben High School; Peter White, a graphic artist who worked for a large technical publishing company, mostly designing drab covers for drab volumes; Barry Stanton, an editor for the same publishing company; and Greg Kirk, foreman for a construction company and in whose house the meeting was being held.

Besides being the only Jewish convert among the leadership, Saul Berne was the only one to experience the occasional twinge of inferiority about his chosen profession: He was a lawyer. Rev. Sam had once explained to him that this feeling of inferiority was not actually due to being a lawyer, but because Saul had taken so much pride in his profession before he found the Lord and learned about the sin of pride. Saul had instantly recognized the profundity of this revelation.

Each of these men had earned a respected place in the

Community; each was in his mid to late thirties; each had married the woman that the Lord had chosen for him, and had varying numbers of children, depending on how they'd been blessed. Their wives were not present at leaders' meetings.

It was just as Ransom began his discussion of the case with Emily that Rev. Sam called the special Wednesday evening leaders' meeting to order with a wave of his hand.

"The Lord," said Rev. Sam, opening the meeting the way he opened all their meetings, "has been putting several concerns on my heart that I feel He's been wanting me to share with you. So I'm very happy that you could all get together with me on relatively short notice."

The men each nodded and murmured various modes of assent.

"We thought it was important when we had to cancel the work party," said James Keller jovially.

The reverend beamed his elder statesman's smile. "The church basement, though important, can wait. We can reschedule it for next Wednesday."

"Then we'll go two weeks without our small-group meetings."

"No," said the reverend patiently, "I think you should each try to hold a small-group meeting as soon as possible—tomorrow, if possible—to discuss the matters I will put before you tonight."

"What's on your heart, Sam?" said Terrance.

Rev. Sam scanned the faces of the upright men who looked to him for guidance, then cleared his throat. "First, I need to tell you about something that was just brought to my attention. It appears that one of our members has been killed."

There was a stunned silence that wasn't broken until Greg bleated out, "What?"

James Hartwick, his face a mask of seriousness, laid both hands on his knees and said, "Who was it, Sam?"

"Danny Lyman."

"What?" said Saul, his eyes bulging behind his thick lenses.

"Yes, I'm sorry I didn't get to tell you before the others, Saul, but I was just informed."

"How did you hear about this?" asked Peter.

Rev. Sam's expression became his most enigmatic, "I was informed by the police. Danny's death was not without its complications. His body was found in the Loop."

"The Loop?" said Peter. "What was he doing there?"

"I don't know," Rev. Sam replied solemnly. "Whatever his reason for being there, I would think that the fact that he was found dead there would indicate he was the victim of some sort of random violence—a mugging or robbery that became violent. The police, for reasons they do not choose to share with me, seem to feel differently."

"Why?" said Saul, knitting his bushy eyebrows.

"I have no idea. I assume they have their reasons." He said this with a smirk that more than implied he felt the police were getting above themselves.

"Wait," said James Keller, "they came here? What led them to our Community? I mean, it's not like we have membership cards or anything."

There was a little nervous, halfhearted laughter at this that didn't disguise the fact that they were all interested in the answer.

"I'm not sure. It was directly through his mother. She, of course, knew that he'd joined the Community. But I believe she was contacted by someone here."

"Michael Franklin," said Saul, rolling his eyes and resting his scraggly beard in his hands.

"It's a possibility," said the reverend, his tone indicating that he thought it was more than just a possibility, "but I don't know."

"Do they think someone from our Community is involved?" asked Greg.

"They give that impression, but I don't know that for sure, either. All I do know is that they seem to think Danny was killed by someone who knew him. They will be wanting to speak with some of us. I don't know exactly who they'll speak to, but I assume they'll talk to you, Saul, and most likely the others in your small group."

"What for?" said Saul.

"Because they want to talk to the people who were closest to Danny," replied the reverend, then he surveyed the rest of the leaders. "I don't know who else they'll want to speak with, but you should all be prepared."

"Prepared?" said James Hartwick.

Rev. Sam smiled sheepishly. "I meant that you shouldn't be surprised. If the police talk to you, I expect you to answer them directly and honestly, as the Lord leads you. Of course, you are all upstanding men—leaders—so I expect that of you at all times. But..." he paused and looked at each one of them in turn, "...I think it's particularly important that we make sure that we are not passing along...extraneous information."

Peter smiled and said, "What do you mean, Sam?"

"Gossip. I don't think that any of you would, but...I think it's important to remember under the circumstances, and to answer the questions that are asked of you."

They all mumbled their assent. This muffled affirmation might have sounded unsure to the interested onlooker, but it was merely the natural stumbling of any group of people facing a new and unexpected situation. Their loyalty was not in question.

"Good. Then I'll consider the matter closed for now."

Rev. Sam had a unique talent for telegraphing a change in subject without benefit of altered tone or body movement. He sat unmoving, enthroned in the armchair, and continued on to a new subject.

"As I said earlier, I felt led to call this meeting because I felt the Lord has been putting something very important on my heart."

If any of the men felt the least bit disconcerted by the shift in subject matter, or the implication that there could be something more important than the murder of one of their members, they didn't show it.

"What I feel the Lord is telling me is that we are falling away from our true calling, to be shepherds."

Once again he looked at each man in turn, almost as if daring them to interrupt and simultaneously challenging them to do so. He was met with seven very confused expressions.

"All of the people who make a commitment to our Community know that you serve as their shepherds, and I serve as yours. They know that when a problem arises, they are to bring it to you and you'll share with them and pray with them. And if it absolutely needs to go beyond that, then they can come to me, along with their small-group leader, and we will all pray and commiserate together. I believe that, as the Bible says, when two or three are joined together in prayer, the Lord hears us and answers us. In other words, it is the Lord who provides the answers. But of course, as the leadership, it's up to you...and me...to provide discernment. People will too often—especially new Christians—mistake their own thoughts and feelings for the Lord's. It's up to us to provide the clarity they need."

"But..." said James Hartwick tentatively, "isn't that the way it's been working? I thought that's how it's been."

Rev. Sam pursed his lips and nodded. "Yes, *most* of the time. But quite often—especially lately—there have been too many times when your small-group members have come directly to me, instead of going to you first." His expression transformed from admonishment to very self-effacing. "I'll admit that I'm to blame for that. What I should do when one of them brings a problem to me is first ask if they've discussed it with their small-group leader. If not, I should tell them to do that first and perhaps they won't need to see me. But..." he shrugged as if to say "what can you do?" "I've always tried to follow the Lord when he said 'Suffer the children to come unto me and forbid them not.' It's hard to say no."

"I didn't know that sort of thing has been happening," said Terrance.

"Just a few days ago Michael Franklin came to me, all

worried and upset about something minor," here the reverend offered an indulgent smile, "without first speaking to Saul. And I didn't tell him anything Saul couldn't have told him. But, of course, Michael's always been rather high-strung and not exactly obedient."

They all smiled and made noises of agreement. They all knew all about Michael.

"So what I'm saying to you, what I believe God is saying to me, is that you need to stress the structure of our Community to your small groups. We need a stronger respect for leadership and structure, and we need to stress that through learning to obey the leadership of the church, we learn true obedience to the Lord."

With this benediction, the invisible bonds of the Community silently tightened.

WHEN RANSOM LEFT the hospital, it was with the confidence that Emily was on the mend. Nurse Carter had been correct: Emily needed to know she was useful, and a murder investigation was a fitting tonic. But Ransom still found it hard to understand how Emily could ever have lost sight of her importance. After all, she had proven to be a great help to him on his more obscure cases, with her vast knowledge of human nature, gleaned from seventy-odd years of observation.

He stopped off briefly at Emily's house to take in the mail, feed the cat and generally make sure that everything was in order in her absence. He was greeted at the door by Tam, who looked clearly disappointed that he was not the mistress of the house, but suffered her ears to be scratched by the visiting detective since nobody else was available. She purred loudly, and rubbed her arched side against Ransom's leg. He poured the cat's food into its stainless-steel bowl and freshened its water. After which, Tam no longer had time for him.

As he passed back through the house, he noticed the thickening layer of dust forming on all of the horizontal surfaces throughout the house. He would have to see about finding someone to help Emily out around the house when she returned home.

It was almost eleven when he reached his apartment, more tired than hungry. But mostly he was feeling starved for literature, having had to forsake Dickens due to his extended work and hospital schedules. He checked his ancient wooden bookshelves, cocking his head sideways and scanning the titles. His eyes came to rest on one volume that appeared to be much less worn that the others: *Barnaby Rudge*, Dickens's fictional account of the Gordon Riots of the late seventeen hundreds, in which thousands of Protestants raged through the streets, rioting against Catholics. It was the least worn of his collection because it was his least favorite of his favorite author. Though he commonly examined the scenes of violent crimes with no problem, Ransom found even the idea of mob rule unsettling.

He knew that if he were to complete his rereading of the collected works of Dickens, he would eventually get around to reading this, and in the present circumstances, this might be the right time. After all, *Barnaby Rudge* was basically about the chaos started by religious fervor. He smiled at the one vivid memory he had of the book: the description of Barnaby, a clinical idiot, leading a storming Protestant mob through the streets without knowing what he was doing.

No, he thought, sliding the book back into its empty place on the shelf, this was not the time to reread it. He had entertained enough thoughts of chaos for one week.

He retrieved a snifter from one of the kitchen cabinets and filled its bowl with some of the inexpensive brandy he kept on hand. He swished the deep amber liquid around in the glass, lifted it to his nose and sniffed. Its heady aroma filled his mind with peace, and one sip seemed to ease his tired muscles into a state of soothing tranquility. A few more sips and he felt that all would be right with the world. No wonder they used this for medicinal purposes, he thought.

He stripped, letting his clothes fall where they may as

he passed through the living room, and took the glass to bed with him.

As Ransom slid between his comfortable powder blue sheets, there was another man, also naked, who had just found a different kind of repose. All of his cares had fallen away, all of his worries were now forgotten. No more troubles would haunt him in his newfound oblivion. Like Ransom, he was a seeker of truth, and he had found it. The truth had not set him free.

The hammer's claw dug into his lifeless hand, trying to grip the long nail that had been driven so far into it that it had disappeared. The claw caught hold, and the wood creaked as the nail was resurrected.

Ransom was wrong. All was not right with the world.

NINE

Thursday dawned like any other fall day in Chicago: with hazy sun and questionable weather. Typically, the temperature can range anywhere from thirty to eighty degrees, which makes dressing for the weather in Chicago a matter of hoping for the best but preparing for the worst. Like many, Ransom kept a heavy jacket in his car. Fortunately, it was mild enough that he wouldn't need it.

In his office, he fingered the list that Draper had given him. It contained the names, addresses, and home and work phone numbers for the members of Saul Berne's small group. Besides Saul and his wife, Bernice, there was Nicholas Bremmen and Pamela Frazier, to whom the detectives had already spoken; Michael Franklin, Howard and Stephanie Beckman, Sarah Bennet, Barbara Searly, and William and Janet Clayton. Oh, God, thought Ransom, it's going to be a very long day.

Gerald sat on the couch looking over a photocopy of the list.

"Who should we start with?" he asked.

"We might as well start at the top."

Ransom picked up the phone and dialed a number. It was answered by a female voice that chirped, "Leonard, Packard and Berne."

Low man on the totem pole, thought Ransom. He identified himself and asked to be connected with Mr. Berne. After a brief stint with a Muzaked version of "Like a Virgin," Saul Berne came on the line, and it was obvious from his tone that he was not pleased to hear from them.

From his place on the couch, Gerald could hear the belligerent bleat of the lawyer. After a brief consultation, Ransom said, "We'll be there directly," and hung up, smiling at his partner.

"Mr. Berne does not sound happy to make my acquaintance. Let's go."

The offices of Leonard, Packard and Berne were located on the second floor of a two-story walk-up on north Halsted street. It was flanked by a dentist's office and a psychologist's office. The thick smell of curry emanated from the first-floor Thai restaurant. Thai restaurants, thought Ransom with dismay, are becoming as prevalent in Chicago as McDonald's.

As they mounted the stairs to the second floor, he reflected that Berne's law firm was either new and couldn't afford to be downtown in the more pricey "lawyers row," as LaSalle Street is affectionately termed, or they were the type of altruistic lawyers who fight for the underdogs, who routinely do not have money for lawyers. Or, they were just not very successful. Ransom plumped for the last choice as they opened the door to the suite of offices. There was nothing overtly dingy about the place, but you would have thought that the rooms were decorated in early failure, as if an attempt had been made at respectability, but the result fell short. Though it was mid-morning, there was an air of afternoon slump about the place, which Ransom suspected it held all day long.

The receptionist, who owned the chirpy voice that had earlier answered the phone, was one of those rare people whose looks so perfectly match their voices. She was a small, young, bleached blond who fluttered her eyelashes when she wasn't talking, and fluttered her hands when she was. She was wearing a light gray suit that didn't fit her correctly, apparently in an attempt to appear businesslike. And if that is the case, thought Ransom, she needs to use decidedly less makeup. In what he thought was an anomaly in a young woman these days, she had on a thick layer of base, eyeliner that ran into the corners of her eyes, and an over-ample amount of mascara.

"Can I help you?"

"Detectives Ransom and White to see Saul Berne."

The woman perked up, as if she thought this might finally lead to the excitement she'd always thought she'd find by going to work in a law office. She fluttered her eyelids and a single lash, heavily laden with mascara, dropped down onto her lapel.

"Oh yes, yes. He's expecting you."

She pressed a button twice, never taking her eager eyes off the detectives.

"Would you like some coffee? Tea?" She waved a hand in the general direction of an ancient warmer on which sat two pots, one full of dark brown liquid and one full of water.

"No thank you," said Ransom.

Gerald shook his head.

A buzzer on the side of the desk sounded loudly, and the woman started as if she'd just heard a shot, clasping a hand to her heart and closing her eyes.

"Oh, Jeez!" she said. Her eyes popped open, and her lashes seemed even more globbed than before. "Mr. Berne will see you now."

Ransom thought with an inward chuckle that if he hadn't heard the buzzer, he would have thought she'd received this message by telepathy while her eyes were closed.

"He's right back there," she said, waving a hand at the hallway behind her desk, "at the end of the hall."

The detectives headed off in the direction she'd indicated. At the end of the hallway was a old wooden door with a large window of thick opaque glass. The door was about half a foot open, the space occupied by Saul Berne. He stared at them, unmoving, as they approached.

Ransom used the opportunity to appraise the man. Like the receptionist, Berne looked like his voice: intense, nervous, and belligerent. In fact, Ransom guessed that even at his most amicable, Berne couldn't help but look belligerent, with his shortish stature, plump legs, uncontrollable hair, and those thick glasses that made you feel as if you were looking at his eyes through binoculars.

Without a word, Berne pushed the door open for them and retreated into the office, seating himself behind his desk. There were two chairs set in front of it.

Both detectives noticed that the office was sparsely furnished with old but not shabby office furniture. There was a medium-sized window on the west wall that looked out into a narrow alley, the building on the other side just a few feet away. This allowed for only minimal reflected sunlight, and no direct sunlight at all, which lent to the effect of the office's dinginess, though it appeared to be clean enough. An 8×10 print of Jesus praying hung on the east wall.

"Saul Berne," he said by way of introduction. "Like I told you on the phone, I don't have a whole lot of time. I have a lot of work to do."

"We'll try not to keep you," said Ransom.

"What can I do for you?"

Gerald White sighed inwardly as he pulled his notebook and pencil out of his pocket. This was exactly the type of mousy little man who could bring out the cat in Ransom.

Ransom was thinking much the same thing himself. But it wasn't through sheer perversity that he toyed with suspects, it was much more to catch them off guard. And the best way to do that with someone who was obviously rushing you was to purposefully slow down. If his first impression was accurate, they'd have to conduct this interview at full brake.

"You know why we're here?" said Ransom, moderating his voice.

"Of course I do. You said on the phone, and Rev. Sam told us last night."

"Did he?"

"Yes," said Saul, his voice taking on an archness, "why shouldn't he?"

"No reason. I'm just surprised he got word out so quickly."

Saul looked affronted that there was some sort of implied criticism in the wording of this reply.

"We had a leaders' meeting scheduled last night. It was only natural that he should tell us."

"I quite understand. Now, what can you tell me about Danny Lyman?"

"What do you mean?" said Saul, looking more surprised than Ransom would have expected from someone who already knew the purpose of their visit.

"Danny Lyman. The dead boy."

"He wasn't a boy," said Saul, "he was in his twenties."

"I'm sorry," said Ransom with a coy smile, "you have to remember that I didn't see him when he was alive. He looked very young to me dead."

"Well," said Saul, looking as if he wasn't too clear on how he should respond to this, "he wasn't. He was an adult."

"What makes you say that?"

"What?" said Saul, looking startled again. Ransom was a little disappointed that the little man wasn't more of a challenge.

"What makes you say he was an adult?"

"I'm...I'm...I don't understand."

Ransom leaned forward in his chair. "We are looking into the murder of a young man whom we know nothing about. In order to find out who killed him, we need to find out as much as we can about him."

"That's what I don't understand. Sam said he was killed downtown. Why do you think it has anything to do with us?"

Ransom paused for a moment, his expression unchanged. "I didn't say it did."

Saul's hands trembled just a little. He clasped them together. "I just...you don't think he was killed by a stranger? I mean, downtown?"

"We have reason to believe that he was not killed by a stranger."

"What's that?"

Ransom sat back and crossed his legs. "Mr. Berne, let's pretend for a moment that I'm conducting this interview."

Saul looked momentarily stunned. His eyes widened behind his thick glasses, which gave him the look of something out of a Tex Avery cartoon. After a second, he pushed his chair back a few inches, unclasped his hands, and laid them palms down on the edge of his desk.

"I'm sorry. I'm sorry. I'm very upset about this."

"I'm glad to hear it."

"What?" said Saul, completely at a loss.

"Well, Reverend Draper didn't seem very upset."

Saul stiffened. "Rev. Sam is a better Christian than I am. He believes with all his heart that a better world awaits."

"Don't you?"

"Of course I do," Saul snapped, "but he's a better Christian than I am. I'm weaker. I get upset. Danny was in my small group, you know."

"That's why we've come to you," said Ransom easily. "We assumed you would know him better than most. And apparently you do."

"What do you mean by that?"

"You've said a couple of times, rather forcefully, that Danny was an adult."

"He was."

"But why do you say that? Was there something particularly 'adult' about him, other than his age?"

Saul appeared to consider this for a moment, then said, "Just that he was mature...in the world. He had a mind of his own."

"You say that as if it's a bad thing."

Gerald smiled to himself and flipped over the page in his notebook, then continued scratching his notes.

"You *would* think that, as a wordly man. But in God's world, nothing is your own, not even your mind."

With an effort, Ransom controlled his facial expression to remain as blank as possible in answer to this. However, he couldn't help but raise an eyebrow.

"I beg your pardon?"

Saul snorted and said, "You're not a churchgoing man, are you?"

"On occasion."

"That's what I thought. Well, in the Lord's world, to become a Christian, you give yourself over to the Lord. Your whole self. Having a 'mind of your own,' as the world puts it, is not a good thing. It's a sin."

It is my fervent hope, thought Ransom, that all of these people do not resort to religious tracts when I question them.

"But surely," he said, "even the people in your Community are expected to make up their minds—make their own decisions."

"You don't understand," said Saul, shaking his head disgustedly. "The Bible says that to follow the Lord, we are to become as little children. Little children might make decisions, but they have to check them out with their elders. That's the way it is in our Community. People make decisions, but they check them out with their elders."

"Didn't Danny do that?"

"He didn't respect authority. He always questioned authority."

"How?"

"It doesn't matter how," barked the little man, his bushy eyebrows turning up at the ends. "The Bible tells us that we are not to question why the Lord chooses to do one thing or another."

Christ, I really hate it when people hide behind the Bible, thought Ransom.

He maintained his calm demeanor and said, "That's not what I meant. If it was an important part of the boy's character, we need to know how he questioned authority."

Saul paused for a moment, like the temporary sputter of a motor before it catches hold, then said, "Danny was the type of person who always thought he knew better than anyone else."

"An example, please."

Saul exhaled sharply and flexed his hands several times on the edge of his desk, apparently trying to think of an example. Ransom waited him out, resting his hands on his knees. Gerald laid the notebook on his lap, crossed his arms, and tapped the end of his pencil against his lips.

"I can't..." Saul started, and then took another road. "Our Community is sort of like a small town. Things get around pretty fast. And Danny would sometimes hear about decisions that had been made concerning other people. And if he disagreed with it, he would go talk to Rev. Sam."

"Decisions made by the reverend?"

Saul flushed red, and glared at Ransom. "Decisions made by the Lord—with prayer. The way they're supposed to be made. That's the way it works. And like I told you, we are not supposed to question the Lord."

"Decisions made *with* the reverend, then," said Ransom, pressing the point.

"With his guidance. In prayer with the concerned party. And Rev. Sam will, if he feels he should, tell them what he thinks the Lord is saying in the situation. After all— after all—Rev. Sam is ultimately responsible for the Community."

"Hmm?"

"To the Lord," Saul explained irritably. "Just like parents are ultimately responsible for their children."

"I see," said Ransom.

Gerald smiled inwardly once again. He often marveled at the talent his partner had for infusing those two words with so much meaning.

Ransom cleared his throat and recrossed his legs. "Now, tell me, when did you last see Danny?"

"Me?" Saul replied, as if there were anyone else to choose from.

"Um-hmm."

"Well, I guess that would have been Friday night."

"Oh, really?" said Ransom with a renewed interest that was meant to throw the stubby little man off guard.

"Yes," said Saul with a questioning glance. "Why do you..."

"He must've had a busy evening."

"What do you mean?"

"We understood that Danny had a consultation with Reverend Draper on Friday night. Did he have one with you, also?"

"Oh. No. I was there. I was there when he came."

"I see."

"And he didn't have a consultation," Saul added, "he just came over, like he always did."

"What did the three of you talk about?"

"Well…well, that was a discussion with his spiritual leader. I really can't tell you about that." He had sputtered this out almost as if it were just occurring to him. "You can ask Rev. Sam. If he thinks it's proper, he'll discuss it with you."

I'll just bet he will, thought Ransom.

"When did Danny arrive?"

"About seven."

"And when did he leave?"

"I don't know, about seven-thirty."

Ransom gazed at Saul for a moment, then said nonchalantly, "Short consultation."

Both detectives were surprised when Saul suddenly blurted out, as if they'd gone back to an earlier part of their conversation, "And I told Rev. Sam at the time that I didn't think Danny really respected authority."

This statement hung awkwardly between them for a moment, then Ransom followed it up with, "And what did he say to that?"

Saul knitted his bushy brows together, an action that almost made them join in the middle. He responded with a derisive snort. "He said that Danny was just…"

Ransom smiled and said, "Yes?"

"He said Danny was just young."

"WHAT AN IRRITATING little man," said Ransom as he climbed into the car.

"What did you think of all that? I mean, besides thinking he's irritating?"

Ransom rolled down his window, rested his arm on the

sill, and drummed his fingers on the side of the door as he
answered, ''I think...that it's going to get very tiresome
very fast if we continually have to slog through the scriptures to get to the truth.''

''God, these people know the Bible, don't they.''

''They quote it, at least.''

''All these years me and Sherry've been going to church,
I can't remember any more of the Bible than the usual.''

Ransom slowly turned his head to face his partner.

''You go to church?''

''Yeah. We take the kids—Sherry takes them when I'm
on duty, but yeah.'' Gerald laid his hands on the steering
wheel and glanced at his partner, noting his expression.
''You look surprised.''

''You always surprise me, Gerald.''

''Where to now?''

Ransom pulled the list out of his pocket and ran his
finger down it, stopping at the name he'd been seeking.

''Michael Franklin. The dead boy's roommate. He's the
one who was so worried about Danny—and he doesn't
work far away. Betty's Bookstore, twenty-three hundred
block of north Clark.''

Gerald turned the key in the ignition, threw the car into
gear, pulled away from the curb, and headed north. Gerald's hands clenched and unclenched on the steering wheel
as he drove, he rolled his eyes once or twice, sighed, then
gritted his teeth. When he could stand it no longer, he said
much less calmly than was his nature, ''Jer, I wish to God
you would start smoking again, you're driving me nuts!''

''Why, Gerald, whatever are you talking about?''

''Would you please stop drumming your fingers?''

Ransom smiled and stopped the movement, but left his
hand where it was. He looked almost as if, without something to occupy his hands, he needed something to hold on
to.

''Sorry, Gerald, I was just thinking...'' He let his voice
trail off in the infuriating way that let Gerald know he was
supposed to serve as his partner's prompter.

Gerald heaved a sigh and said, "Yes?" He made the word three syllables long.

"I was just thinking that it's very interesting that both the reverend and his minion seem more curious about how we connected Danny Lyman to the Community than they are about how he died."

"His minion?" said Gerald with a short laugh.

"The good Reverend Samuel Draper and the good lawyer Saul Berne. Don't you think it's interesting that neither of them asked us how the boy died?"

"Well," said Gerald noncommittally. He would have liked to come up with some possible explanation for this, but found himself at a loss. Instead, he said, "I think it's interesting that you keep referring to Danny Lyman as 'the dead boy.'"

"I keep hoping to drive the situation home with these people. I don't seem to have been successful," Ransom replied, shaking his head. Then he added, "There's another thing I'm curious about."

"The consultation?"

"Yes, we need to find out what went on in the meeting between the reverend and Danny on Friday night."

Gerald pulled the car into the no-parking zone at the end of the block on which Betty's Bookstore was located. Betty's was something of a Chicago institution, a venerable old establishment that had managed to survive the invasion of "book superstores" that had recently caused a stir in the city. It was in the center of the block, in a small storefront that was crammed from floor to ceiling with books, all shapes and sizes sharing the same shelves. It looked like total chaos, but Betty was said to be on intimate terms with every book on her shelves and could lay her hands on any requested title within minutes.

A small bell tinkled as the detectives passed through the door to the shop. To Ransom, entering this store was like entering Heaven. The room was thick with the musty scent of accumulated knowledge, amassed in the collected volumes of fine literature.

"Be there in a minute," called a husky female voice from somewhere in the back reaches of the store. The voice was echoless, swallowed by the millions of printed pages closepacked on the shelves.

After a moment, Betty herself emerged. She was dressed in a knee-length, black jersey dress. Her hair was dyed black and flowed down to her shoulders like silky ink. She had a perfectly formed black dot on her right cheek—the kind that in Ransom's youth had been called a "beauty mark." The dot looked darker than it actually was because of the extreme pallor of her skin. The only things that betrayed Betty's age, which was somewhere in the mid-fifties, were the severely deep, long lines—"laugh lines"—that extended from her eyes, as if someone had carved an extra, deep set of eyelashes that ran east and west on the map of her face.

"What are you looking for?" she said cheerfully, her eyes running the full length of Ransom's physique in a way that made him feel like an after-dinner mint. She seemed to be sizing him up for something unmentionable. The right corner of her mouth twisted upward, and she said with a note of triumph, "Victorian."

"Excuse me?" said Ransom.

"Vic-to-ri-an, my dear," she drawled at him. "I would say you are Victorian."

Ransom glanced at Gerald, then back to Betty. With a laugh, he said, "I'm sorry, I don't..."

"Your period, my dear. I would say you're strictly Victorian."

"I would say you're amazingly perceptive," said Ransom. "I'm a Dickens fan." He choked on the word "fan," but he didn't know how else to put it.

She ran her hands through her hair and said, "I consider that a very lush period." She leaned her face close to Ransom's and added, "I have a new edition of *Sketches by Boz* you might find interesting." The huskiness in her voice had increased, making it sound like an obscene proposition.

"Actually, we're more interested in your staff today."

"My staff?" she said, pulling away from him. Her black eyes widened.

"Yes. We're here to see Michael Franklin."

"Michael? He's not in today."

"His day off?"

"No, he called in sick, and he sounded *terrible*. He could barely speak above a whisper. I hardly recognized his voice." She stopped and ran her eyes up and down the detective again. "Are you police?"

"Yes."

Her eyes narrowed. "This is about his roommate, isn't it? You've found him?"

"He told you his roommate was missing?"

"Young men aren't good at hiding their feelings, Mr. Policeman."

"Ransom."

"Okay. He's been a basket case the past few days. I asked him what the hell was wrong—ha! Wrong term to use with a Bible boy, eh? He told me. Is the kid all right?"

"The kid?"

"Michael's roommate."

Ransom glanced down at the floor and then back up into the woman's hungry eyes. "He was found dead."

"Crap," said Betty, the word sounding foreign coming from her. "No wonder Michael sounded so bad."

Ransom glanced at Gerald and said, "Well, I suppose we'll find Michael at home."

"Yes," she said, then added halfheartedly, "you'd better. I don't like being lied to." She smiled, somewhat embarrassed. "But he'll be there. Michael is a good boy."

The same term, thought Ransom, that Mrs. Lyman had used to describe her son, Danny. Ransom started for the door, followed by Gerald. He stopped by the door and looked back at the woman. "Um, is this the first day Michael's been out this week? He was here yesterday?"

"Oh yeah, he was here, for all the good he was. He was all nervous and upset. Like I told you, he's been a basket case."

"But he's usually a good worker? Reliable?"

Betty perked up. "He's very reliable. He's never given me any trouble—in any way." She gave him a wink.

"WHAT THE HELL was that last bit about?" asked Gerald as they walked back to the car.

"Who knows?" said Ransom wearily. "Betty seems to be on the warm-blooded side. Perhaps she tried something with him and he quoted the Bible at her."

"I'm surprised someone from that Community would work with someone all in black," said Gerald. It was impossible to tell from his expression whether or not he was serious about this. Ransom decided to give him some credit.

"Very good, Gerald."

Once in the car, they drove over to Lincoln Avenue and headed north to Lawrence.

"I saw that look you gave me when she said 'no wonder he sounded so bad.' What was that for?"

"Because she assumed that Michael already knows that his roommate's dead."

"Safe bet," said Gerald, "the way news travels around this bunch, it's a good bet he's heard."

"Yes. If he didn't know already."

The drive west on Lawrence wasn't quite as slow as it normally was, but it wasn't far to Kimball anyway. They pulled up in front of Michael Franklin's building. Ransom had no qualms about parking in front of it today, since their inquiry was by now common knowledge.

This time the vestibule of the red brick building was not empty. Barbara Searly stood by the mailboxes, her finger pressed against Michael's doorbell as if it were a boil she would dearly love to pop. She had light brown, shortish hair that was mostly covered by a stiff scarf tied so that it formed an inverted triangle on the back of her head. It made her look, thought Ransom, like a self-induced nun. When the detectives opened the door, she turned her colorless, lifeless eyes on them—or rather, on their feet. Ransom had the vague feeling that their appearance had somehow disappointed her.

Ransom glanced at her hand, which still pressed the doorbell. "You're here to see Michael Franklin?"

"I don't think he's here," she answered dully.

"Hmm," said Ransom, "he should be. He called in sick today."

He made a gesture at Gerald, who nodded, glanced at the apartment number, and left the vestibule. Ransom then showed his identification to Barbara.

"I am Detective Ransom. We're here to talk to Michael. And you are?"

"Barbara Searly. Michael's fiancée."

"Ah, yes, you're a member of the same small group."

"I don't think you'll get to talk to Michael today. I don't think he's talking to anyone." Each word fell like lead dripping from her lips, as if a heavy burden was pouring out of her, drop by drop.

Ransom frowned. "What do you mean, Miss Searly?"

"This is just like him. He broods, you know. And he doesn't want to talk to me—anybody. So he doesn't answer his phone. He unplugs it."

"Then why are you here?"

"I thought he might answer his door if I kept ringing at it. He can't unplug his doorbell, you know." She averted her eyes from him as she finished this statement. Ransom suspected that this move was made so that he couldn't see what he'd heard: that her despondency held a touch of malice.

Gerald reappeared in the doorway.

"I went to the back—he's first floor, right?"

Barbara nodded.

"I looked in. From what I could see, it doesn't look like there's anyone home. And it doesn't look like there's anything wrong."

Ransom thought about this for a moment, looking as if he longed for the days before civil rights, when the police could, theoretically, go crashing in anywhere they pleased in the name of justice. At last he turned to Barbara Searly.

"Is there somewhere we could go to talk with you?"

"With me?" she said with an unsuccessful attempt at modesty.

"You know why we're here?"

"Because Danny's dead. I know. I heard. It's been a shock to us all." Her voice was hollow and betrayed none of the emotion that should have accompanied her words.

"We'd like to speak with you about him."

She didn't speak, but her head gave a single nod in assent. She walked past them out of the vestibule, her head tilted downward and her eyes glued to the pavement, as if at her tender age—which Ransom took to be about twenty-five—she had been bent by an early onset of osteoporosis. Ransom wondered if her nose would get closer and closer to the sidewalk as time went by.

"I have a room on the third floor—it's their attic, really, converted to a little apartment—in the Claytons' house."

Ah, thought Ransom, that would be William and Janet Clayton, also members of the small group.

Barbara seemed content to lead them to her home in silence, but Ransom decided to use the time.

"Excuse me, Miss Searly, but do you have a job?"

Barbara's ashen cheeks turned pink. She once again turned her head away from them, which gave her the appearance of being intensely interested in something on the opposite side of the street.

"Yes. Yes, I do. I work in a dress shop. I'm sick today, though. All the upset. I called in sick."

"Indeed?" said Ransom, raising his right eyebrow. Gerald often envied his partner's talent for activating one eyebrow at a time. Ransom added, "A lot of people seem to be sick today." His tone conveyed surprise, though Gerald wasn't sure whether it was supposed to be surprise at the idea that "good Christians" would call in sick if they weren't, or the idea that they would get sick at all. Barbara seemed oblivious to everything except the sidewalk.

"How did you know Michael was supposed to be home?"

"I tried him at work. I thought he'd have to talk to me there. That woman...that woman he works for told me he was sick."

"Why was it so important that you talk to him today?"

She seemed to hesitate in her stride for barely a moment. "I'm his fiancée."

"So you said. So I'd assume you talk to him on a regular basis."

Ransom thought he heard her emit a sharp, high-pitched noise. But he couldn't be sure.

"We haven't set the date yet," she said, as if they would only talk on a regular basis after they'd married. But she didn't sound too sure about anything.

Ransom tried again. "So, why was it so important that you talk to him today that you got out of your sickbed and went over to his apartment and ran the risk of driving him crazy with the doorbell?"

"Because of Danny, of course," she said sadly, "because I thought Michael might need me now."

They had reached the house on Spaulding, which was about a block and a half south of the reverend's. This house was wood-framed and painted dark tan, with four wide concrete steps leading up to the front door.

Barbara looked in Ransom's general direction, careful to not catch his eye, and said, "I can't talk to you inside. Nobody's home."

"This is fine," said Ransom, indicating the steps.

Barbara cautiously swept the back of her peach-colored skirt with her right hand as she took a seat on the bottom step. Ransom sat on the step above her, and Gerald remained standing, leaning against the house and appearing to be surveying the neighborhood lawns and gardens as he surreptitiously scrawled notes of the conversation.

"I'm sorry," said Ransom, "but I didn't understand what you meant when you said Michael might need you now."

Barbara kept a firm grasp on the hem of her dress, as if she were afraid some nonexistent wind might whip it coquettishly over her knees.

"Michael and Danny were very close. I thought Michael might need me now..." Ransom thought he caught a note of bitterness in her voice, and was sure when she added "...now that Danny's dead."

Ransom stared at her for a moment, wondering whether or not this young woman was, in some perverse way, about to impart some important information to him.

"Are you implying that there was some sort of relationship between them?"

She looked at him directly for the first time. She seemed more irritated than shocked.

"What? No. No. Danny would never do anything like that."

Danny, Ransom noted, not Michael. As if reading his thoughts, she added impotently, "Neither would Michael."

Spoken like an unsure fiancée, thought Ransom.

"They were like brothers. Brothers in the Lord. They were deeply devoted to each other. I know Michael will be really hurting now that Danny's dead, and I thought I could maybe be there for him."

"Isn't that what a wife is for?" said Ransom, baiting her.

Missing the sarcasm, Barbara nodded. "But it doesn't matter. He just shuts me out. Like always. I should be there for him, and he just shuts me out." Her eyes became moist. She sniffed a couple of times and rubbed her nose with her index finger.

Ransom thought it best to go on to the matter at hand.

"Can you remember when you last saw Danny?"

"Last Wednesday, at the small-group meeting. I usually only see him on Wednesdays." Her tone implied that that was one day too many. "I haven't seen Michael since Saturday."

Ransom had a sudden surge of panic, until he reminded himself that Michael had been seen by others since Saturday: the reverend on Monday night, and Nicholas and Pamela on Tuesday night. Nobody had seen him today, but at least Betty, his employer, had spoken to him.

"Tell me about Danny."

Ransom could feel the young woman stiffen, the way some women do when their husbands mention having bumped into an old flame.

"Danny was…a very nice guy, I suppose. Opinionated, but nice, I guess. He was one of those people that're always on some soapbox, you know?"

"It gets tired," Ransom prompted.

"Yeah. Always saying this is wrong and that's wrong. Thinks he knows everything." She seemed to relent a little. "But I think he really loved the Lord, and he was a pain, but he…I'll admit, he was a pain for the right reasons." She sounded like she dearly hated to admit it.

"Can you think of anything specific? Any example of how he was a pain?"

"He disagreed with leadership a lot." She blushed and then added quickly, "Well, not a lot, but sometimes."

"But can you give me a specific example?"

"Like, we're encouraged to get married."

"Hmm?"

"Yes, because the Bible says that a man should be the husband of one wife, and Rev. Sam says that tells us we should be married…" She trailed off in a way that telegraphed to Ransom that she felt she was approaching dangerous waters. But she simply gave a little shrug, unconsciously imitative of Rev. Sam, and said lightly, "There's other reasons to get married, too, but that's the main one."

"Other reasons, like falling in love?" Ransom couldn't help asking.

To his surprise, Barbara gave him a look of total disgust that he wouldn't have thought she had the energy to generate.

"No," she said.

Ransom considered this for a moment, but decided not to pursue that particular avenue with her. He thought perhaps he should ask the reverend later for his take on the various reasons people should marry. It had been a long time since Ransom had read the Bible, but he thought he already knew the answer. To Barbara he said, "And Danny disagreed with the idea that everybody should be married?"

Barbara nudged a pebble with her shoe, sending it bouncing into the lawn.

"He said that was only one interpretation of the scripture, and it didn't apply to everyone, especially if you 'took it in its historical context.'" She quoted this last phrase in an unpleasant, mocking voice. "He always said you had to take history into account."

"Um-hmm."

"Anyway, Michael just *adored* Danny. He thought Danny was great." Her voice degenerated into a whine as she added, "I don't think he even likes me...sometimes."

I can't imagine why, thought Ransom.

"Can you think of enemies Danny may have had? Anyone who might have wanted to kill him?"

Once again Barbara surprised him. When she answered, she did not seem shocked or even irritated; if anything, she sounded bitter.

"We are Christians, Mr. Ransom, we do not kill."

Ransom couldn't help thinking that Danny had been right: You do have to take history into account.

"WELL, THAT ANSWERS the question about whether or not Danny had any enemies. That mousy little number isn't doing a great job of hiding her dislike for him."

"Come on, Jer," said Gerald, at his most exasperated, "these people have all had a shock. What do you expect?"

"I expect Danny's Christian brothers and sisters to act like they care that he's dead," said Ransom hotly. "None of these people are upset about the right thing. Don't you find that the least bit peculiar?"

"I guess I do."

Ransom gave a sidelong glance to his partner as they walked up Spaulding to the reverend's house.

"I sometimes think you are purposely obtuse, Gerald. Draper and Berne aren't upset about the death, they're upset that we're investigating it. And Barbara Searly isn't the least bit upset that Danny Lyman is dead. She's upset that it hasn't driven her fiancée into her arms. Which makes one wonder about their relationship."

"Danny and Michael?"

Ransom curled his lips. "No, Michael and Barbara."

"Do you think she killed Danny?"

"I can see her wanting to, for whatever reason. But I don't think I can see her wielding enough force to do it the way it was done, can you? And as far as being a suspect, I think the whole damn lot of them are suspect."

They arrived at the reverend's house and Gerald pressed the doorbell, which rang out like a mini-version of a school bell. They waited for so long that both detectives were beginning to think that nobody was home. Ransom's impatience getting the best of him, he actually leaned forward himself and pressed the button the second time. After a few more moments, the door was opened by the reverend.

He was dressed today in casual early-middle-aged garb: a cream-colored shirt with medium brown strips and tan pants, both in blends of natural and unnatural fabrics. His hair was slicked back, but the attempt to straighten the waves had been less successful today than normal. The perennial smile was pasted on his face in such a way that he looked as if he were making it clear that it required a supreme effort to be polite: He smiled, but he wasn't glad to see them.

"Gentlemen?" he said, making it sound more as if he were questioning their social standing than greeting them.

"We have a few more questions we need to ask you."

"Gentlemen, this is the time of day that I pray. That's why it took me so long to answer the door. You are interrupting my meditations."

"And you, sir, are interrupting our investigation," said Ransom, smiling back at the man. "I am sure that God will understand if your prayers are a little late today."

"God knows where my heart is," said the reverend, standing aside to let them pass.

Why do I feel like Jonathan Harker, thought Ransom.

They went into the living room where they'd spoken the day before, but the reverend made a point of not offering them seats, and the detectives made a point of not taking them.

"Now, Reverend Draper, there are a few more details you should be able to give us. We'll try to be as brief as possible."

"I'd appreciate it," he replied, his smile remaining in place.

"We haven't been able to speak to all the small-group members as of yet, but the ones we've spoken to so far claim that they have not seen Danny since their small-group meeting last Wednesday night. Last week."

"Yes?"

"That would mean that as of now, you and Saul Berne are the last two people to see Danny alive."

"I wouldn't say that. Someone else must have seen him. I would think it probable that his roommate saw him after that."

"Michael Franklin has been quite vocal about the fact that the last time he saw Danny was before he came to this house Friday night."

Rev. Sam's eyebrows crept up on his forehead. He looked as if he'd just caught the proverbial cat with the canary. "So you did speak to Michael?"

"Oh, I didn't say that," Ransom replied. But though his expression was at its most coy, he felt once again the importance of not revealing to this man that Nicholas has been the source of information. "However, I *did* tell you we'd be speaking to all of Danny's small-group members."

"I'm sure as you continue with your investigation, you'll find someone who saw Danny after he left here, but as I said, I haven't seen him since he was here."

"Of course."

Gerald hadn't bothered taking notes this time, which he

would find hard to do while standing, anyway. But he really wished he had a video camera. There was something electric that seemed to crackle between Ransom and the reverend. Gerald pursed his lips. A camera probably wouldn't pick that up.

"Reverend Draper, I have gotten the impression from speaking to some of Danny's...acquaintances in the Community that he was something of a troublemaker."

"Really?" said the reverend in a tone so dispassionate it made Ransom want to strike him.

"Yes. Did you find Danny a troublemaker?"

"No. I don't think in those terms, and I don't have time to dwell on such things. As the Bible says, and as I'm sure you've found in your work, each day brings troubles of its own."

"And did each day bring Danny?"

"No."

Ransom felt his impatience grow. He wondered briefly what kind of bargain he would have to strike with God to be able to smoke again. And he wondered if God would grant him the miracle of being able to do it without Emily noticing.

"You don't feel that Danny was a troublemaker," he said, hoping at least to annoy the reverend by repetition.

"No."

"Well, let me put it another way. Do you feel, as Saul Berne does, that Danny failed to respect authority?"

"Danny was headstrong."

"And that didn't bother you?"

"If you mean, did I find it an irritant, no. I do not usually allow myself to be irritated."

Apparently not, thought Ransom. "You must be a very unusual man," he said in a tone oily enough to deep-fry Chicago. "Danny seems to have greatly irritated some other people."

"Danny was new in the Lord," the reverend replied smoothly. "It is not unusual for new Christians to be over-zealous."

"Ah, so he was overzealous?"

"No more, I think, than normal."

Ransom gazed at the reverend. Never before in his decade or so on the force had he come across anyone who was capable of looking you so steadily in the eye, and conveying nothing. He thought that if the eyes were indeed the windows of the soul (congratulating himself for recognizing this as a biblical reference), then the reverend's soul was a blank wall. It was what was behind this wall that intrigued him.

Ransom cocked his head a little to one side, and as if the thought had just occurred to him said, "There is one thing you could tell me about Danny."

"Yes?"

"Was he engaged?"

"Engaged?" The omnipresent smile dwindled a little, and for the first time in their acquaintance, the reverend looked totally off guard. "No, he wasn't engaged. Why would you ask that?"

"Marriage seems to be quite popular in your community. After all, there are two engaged couples in Danny's small group alone."

"Marriage is a godly state."

"A sacred institution."

The reverend did not miss Ransom's tone. He decided to adopt the tone of voice he would use for a naughty child. "Yes, it is."

"Do you encourage your people to get married?"

The reverend's smile returned to its normal size. "I do not encourage anything. It is the Lord who draws people together."

Ransom considered this for a moment, never removing his eyes from the reverend. It may be the Lord who draws them together, but he wouldn't put it past the reverend to point them in each other's direction and give a not-so-gentle push.

"But that hadn't happened with Danny?"

"The Lord had not seen fit to select anyone for him as of yet."

"Do you think he ever would have?"

"Maybe. Eventually."

"And how would Danny have felt about that?"

"What do you mean?"

"Would Danny have welcomed marriage?"

"Danny, whatever his flaws may have been, would have welcomed anything that came directly from the Lord."

Ransom eyed the reverend for a moment, then the right corner of his mouth curled upward. "Would Danny have welcomed marriage?"

Rev. Sam replied with elaborate patience. "I have already answered that. I have a feeling that you're really asking something quite different."

"Is it possible," said Ransom slowly, "that Danny was gay?"

Ransom was careful not to appear surprised when a slight chink was evidenced in Rev. Sam's usual armor. Though the reverend neither moved nor changed expressions, Ransom would have sworn he was relieved.

"No, Detective. Danny was not gay. Now, if you'll excuse me, I need to get back to my prayers."

"Yes, I'm sure you do," said Ransom as he and Gerald followed the reverend as he led them unceremoniously to the door.

Not to be hurried by anyone, Ransom stopped in the doorway and said, "I have to ask you again, Reverend Draper, what you and Danny talked about when he came here Friday night."

"I told you before," the reverend replied with a beleaguered sigh, "as a spiritual leader I will not repeat private matters discussed with one of my people."

Ransom's eyes narrowed. "Don't you want us to find out who killed one of your church members?"

"The Lord knows, and He will judge and punish as he sees fit in the next life."

Ransom's expression hardened. "It is my job to discover who the murderer is so he will be judged in *this* life."

The reverend shrugged. "You may find that you have to wait until the judgment day, when all will be revealed."

"And you, Reverend, may find that judgment day is sooner than you think."

The smile remained on the reverend's lips, and Ransom was seized with the burning desire to remove it very slowly with a pair of pinking shears. He was reminded of *The Black Cat,* the movie in which Boris Karloff plays the head of a bizarre religious cult, and Bela Lugosi punishes him for his sins by flaying him alive. As the reverend closed the door on them, Ransom felt he could sympathize with Bela.

TEN

"I FEEL WE'RE being led on a merry chase," said Ransom as they walked back to the car.

"What was all that about marriage?"

"I don't know. I'm not sure. But marriage seems to be very important in this group, and I can't help thinking that it figures in somehow."

Gerald's whole face pursed in a way that Ransom had said made him look like fresh dough pouring out of a food processor.

"But what gave you the idea that Danny was engaged? Nobody said anything like that."

They had reached the car. Ransom crossed his wrists and rested them on the roof, eyeing his partner across the top.

"No, nobody said anything like that." Ransom ruminated for a moment, then added, "But was it my imagination, or did the good reverend seem relieved when I asked if Danny was gay?"

"I thought I noticed that, too."

"It was as if he were relieved to get off the subject of marriage."

"But why?" said Gerald earnestly. "If Danny wasn't engaged, what difference could it make?"

"'That,' to quote Hamlet, 'is the question.'"

Something past Gerald's left ear seemed to catch Ransom's attention.

"And unless I miss my guess, some of the answers are coming our way."

Gerald turned and saw Pamela Frazier walking in their direction on the opposite side of the street. Today she was clad in a white blouse and blue plaid skirt, topped off by a light blue sweater hanging on her shoulders. She saw them and waved, and Ransom felt that she gave them the first genuine smile he'd seen all day.

"Don't tell me you called in sick today," he called as he crossed the street to join her. Gerald followed.

"What? Why would I do that?"

"Just a joke," said Ransom. "A couple of your small-group members weren't feeling well today, and called in sick. Barbara Searly and Michael Franklin."

"Poor Michael," said Pam with a glance toward his apartment, "he must be taking this very hard. He and Danny were good friends."

Not a word for Barbara, Ransom noticed.

"And no, I'm not sick. Actually I was running home for lunch. I work up the street at Northeastern—the university."

"Lunch this late?" said Ransom. "It's after two."

Pamela smiled ruefully. "I work in the administrative office, Mr. Ransom. The fall is our busiest time. I couldn't get away before now."

"We haven't had lunch yet, either. Could we take you?"

"Well, I don't have a lot of time. I have to get back." She sounded reluctant but not unwilling.

"It would be our pleasure. We won't take up much of your time, but we've got some more questions we'd like to ask you."

Pamela capitulated quickly. Although she didn't seem displeased, Ransom wasn't quite sure if she was happy about it, or if agreeing to lunch had just seemed expedient. She suggested a small sandwich shop on Lawrence Avenue that was only about a block from where the detectives were parked. When they had purchased their sandwiches and drinks, they sat in one of the three booths in the window.

"I really don't have much time," she said apologetically as she took a hefty bite of her turkey sandwich. A small dab of mayonnaise remained on her lip, and she whisked it away with the tip of her tongue. Ransom was surprised by just how pretty this young woman was. Not pretty in the fragile sense, but in the way the so-called lusty peasant classes might be if they knew how to dress well and take care of themselves. The fact that this reference sprang to mind was proof positive to him of the profound effect Emily and her love for Shakespeare had had on him.

Gerald forsook his note-taking in favor of a warm corned beef on rye, and Ransom's roast beef remained untouched as he questioned the young woman.

"That's all right, I only have a couple of questions to ask you."

Pamela raised her eyebrows over her sandwich as she took another bite, which Ransom took as his cue to proceed.

"Miss Frazier, do you want to get married?"

The sandwich dropped from her hand onto the plastic tray, and she stopped chewing for a moment, staring saucer-eyed at the detective.

"What?"

"I'm sorry, let me put that more clearly. Are you pleased that you're getting married?"

She looked confused for a few seconds, then finished chewing and swallowed.

"Of course I am," she said. "I love Nick. What a weird question!"

"Hmm. Perhaps. I just wondered. I have been questioning people this morning, and I somehow got the impression that maybe the members of this Community were... encouraged to get married—that they didn't necessarily have a lot of control over the matter."

"Well, for Pete's sake, we're not Moonies, you know!" This was said without rancor. But she seemed to think about what he'd said a little, and then adjusted her reply. "You make it sound like we're pushed into it, but we're not. Exactly. But the leadership takes male-female relationships very seriously here, so we don't date forever...or casually...without it going anywhere. I guess to an outsider it might look like we were...guided that way."

"Was Danny getting pushed in that direction?"

"Danny?" A momentary cloud passed over Pamela's

face, as if she'd just remembered that Danny was no longer with them. "No, Danny would never get pushed into anything."

Ransom sat back, as far as that was possible in the skimpy plastic booth, and folded his arms. "You liked Danny, didn't you?"

Pamela smiled. "Oh, yes, I did. Danny was always for the underdog. I like that. Nick is like that, too, only..." Her voice trailed off, and her face clouded over again.

"Yes?"

She laid the remains of her sandwich down, and it would not be touched again.

"I don't know that I should say." She seemed unable to look up at him.

"Please, Miss Frazier, this is a murder investigation. Whatever is going on here may be important."

She folded her hands on the table and finally drew her eyes up to him. She said sadly, "Nick has been pretty unhappy with the way things are going lately. He wants to leave the Community."

Ransom considered how to respond to this for a minute, then said, "Would that be so terrible?"

"I've been with the Community for five years. I've only been with Nick for one. If we were to be married and he decided to leave the Community, I'd have to go with him."

"Couldn't you do that?"

"Of course I could." She tried to sound firm, but at the same time Ransom sensed that she had some doubt.

"Miss Frazier, why did you join this Community?"

Pam dabbed at her lips with a paper napkin, her eyes fixed on the center of Ransom's chest. She seemed to be turning the question over in her mind. Then she replied tentatively, "I guess if you were looking for the spiritual reason, I'd say that the Lord led me to it." She looked up into Ransom's eyes, as if silently asking him if that would suffice. She could tell from his expression that he knew there was more. She sighed and seemed to deflate just a little. "If you were looking for another reason...my mother had cancer."

Ransom's brow furrowed, and he said softly, "Yes?"

"I took care of her the last two years of her life. It was very hard. She needed me night and day. And when she finally died I...I guess I just needed to be taken care of myself."

"And you are taken care of in the Community?"

Pam replied earnestly, "That doesn't mean that the spiritual reason isn't true, too, though—don't you see? The Lord could have led me to what I needed."

The words "could have" stood out to the detectives as a positive sign.

"Mr. Ransom, you haven't seen the Community at its best, the way I have. When I committed myself to it, it was a group of people—a big group—who were all seeking a closer relationship with God. But now, I'm not so sure anymore." She looked guilty the moment she said it, but she seemed to screw up her courage and went on, "Nick has shown me things about the Community that I can't deny."

"Such as?"

She seemed reluctant to answer this, but with a sigh she said, "Leadership has become more and more important. Checking everything you do with leadership. I mean, there's a biblical principle here—that I don't think I can explain, because I'm not sure I understand it myself. But there's been more and more emphasis on talking to the leadership before you do anything and getting..." She appeared to be trying to think of a word. Ransom decided to provide it.

"Permission?"

Pamela looked at him and smiled. "You sound like Nick. The word I was trying for was guidance."

"And are you pressured to follow that guidance?"

"Not really." She said this too quickly. "Not really. But Nick says he feels like he's being watched. And I can understand why. I mean, everybody seems to know what everybody else does."

That's not entirely true, thought Ransom. Nobody seemed to know what had happened to Danny.

"And things have gotten worse lately, especially since we've gotten involved moneywise."

This piqued both the detectives' interest.

"In what way?" said Ransom.

"Oh! Oh, no, I didn't mean we're being bilked or anything. You see, we used to hold our meetings in school auditoriums or in church basements—whatever was available. And about a year or so ago, the leadership started praying about whether or not we should purchase a permanent home. Rev. Sam said the Lord seemed to be saying yes, and a few months ago, we pooled what money we had and put the down payment on an abandoned church—an old Methodist church. It's right next door to the building I live in."

A Methodist church, Ransom repeated to himself. Emily would be appalled.

"It's silly, really, because now that we have it, we're redoing the inside to make it look less like a church. We've finished the sanctuary, and now we're working on the basement. Well, the men are, actually. They're converting it into some sort of recreation/reception room."

"That sounds like a lot of money and a lot of work."

"It is," Pamela replied ruefully, "and even that's been interrupted by this business with Danny."

"How so?"

"The men were supposed to work on the basement last night, but that was postponed for a special leaders' meeting." She stopped, then surprised Ransom with a little smile. "Actually, Danny would probably like that he's interrupted work on it. Danny wasn't in favor of buying the church."

Ransom smiled. He was beginning to like Danny. "Well, he *might* have been glad that the work was interrupted, but it wasn't on his account."

"It wasn't?" said Pam, her eyes becoming a bit more attractive as they widened.

"I'm afraid not," Ransom explained. "The reverend wasn't told of Danny's death until Wednesday afternoon—the meeting was already set before that."

Pam blinked and looked a little disappointed. "Oh, that's right. Oh well, Danny *would* have liked to have interrupted the work."

"Was he that causey?"

She nodded. "He never backed down."

"Who's that?" said Gerald, startling Pamela. Though he'd been there with them in the small booth, she'd forgotten he was there.

Ransom and Pamela looked in the direction that Gerald was indicating with his thumb.

On the opposite side of the street, a tall, thin man dressed in a neat suit was staring at them. He looked almost startled. He saw their heads turn in his direction, and he hurried on his way with an air of someone who's been caught staring, and trying to act as if he hadn't been.

Pamela sighed heavily and the corners of her mouth dropped. "That's James Keller, one of our leaders. He's a doctor. His office is in that building across the street." She glanced at her watch and added quickly, "I really have to get going."

"One more thing," said Ransom, gently staying her with his hand. "Can you tell me what Danny's relationship was with Michael Franklin?"

"They were brothers," she said. When she noticed Ransom's expression, she said, "I'm sorry. They were friends. They were good friends. Like I said, Danny was always for the underdog."

"Is Michael an underdog?"

She hesitated a moment, already sorry that she'd opened her mouth. But it was too late now.

"Yes," she said reluctantly, "I guess so."

"In what way?"

She removed her hand from under his and said, "You'll have to ask Michael that."

With this she hurried out of the shop.

"YOU'RE TAKING WAY too long on this case!" said Newman, his salt-and-pepper hair falling across his craggy forehead into his eyes.

Ransom remained calm behind his desk, although the intensity of his cool blue eyes betrayed the fact that he wasn't amused.

"Exactly how long is too long to find whoever it was that drove nails through that boy's hands and feet and then bashed in his head?"

"Don't you have any idea who killed him yet?"

Ransom spread his hands. "Not a clue."

"Not funny, Ransom. The bodies are piling up around Chicago—I need you on other cases. Now, what do you have?"

"I have a church full of people, very few of whom are exactly telling me the truth."

"You haven't been able to get *anything* out of them?"

Ransom smiled. "Vague rumblings of unrest. Nothing concrete. It appears that the deceased was something of a troublemaker."

"Oh!" said Newman, his face brightening. "Was he, now?"

"Not that kind of trouble, Newman. It seems that after he left home and joined 'the Community,' he didn't leave his old ways."

"What're you talking about?"

"He was something of an activist when he was younger, and he apparently stayed one. Even his detractors in the Community will admit that he stood up for the little guy. They say this with varying degrees of warmth. Some of them admired him for it, others—like the leaders of the church—felt that it showed he didn't respect authority." Ransom's lip curled as he finished this, and Newman wondered for a moment if he was being made fun of.

"So, who's lying to you?" said Newman.

"The Good Reverend Samuel Draper, for one."

"Oh, Christ, this is just what I need. Do you know what

we'll look like if we have to drag a minister in here without any concrete evidence?"

Ransom couldn't help allowing a little smirk to play about the corners of his mouth. "That's why we haven't done it. We have no reason to do it, yet."

If Newman's head were as empty as Ransom believed it to be, at this point steam would have been coming out of his ears. He slammed his fist down on Ransom's desk.

"Don't you have anything?"

Ransom seemed to take pity on him. "For one thing, the reverend isn't exactly lying to me, but he's not telling me what he knows. And he gives the impression that he knows plenty, although that may just be force of habit."

"What the hell does that mean?"

"Never mind, it would take too long to explain. Whatever the cause, I'll have a go at him again tomorrow. Maybe he'll 'see the light' and decide he should help us."

"He's not helping at all?"

"Hardly," said Ransom with a withering glance. "'Judgment is the Lord's,' saith the reverend, and he thinks we have no business interfering."

"Jesus."

Ransom's tone became positively acid, but it was not directed at Newman. "Maybe he'll pray about it and God will tell him he should help us. God is a regular chatterbox where the reverend is concerned."

"Ransom…"

"Sorry."

"He's a minister no matter what else he is. And unless you can prove otherwise, you'd better go softly on him or we'll have the whole city down on us."

"Yes, sir," said Ransom with a smile.

"No other leads?"

"Just one: Michael Franklin, the dead boy's roommate. I don't know how, but he seems to be the linchpin of the whole mess, somehow."

"What's he have to say?"

"Nothing so far. We haven't been able to locate him."

"Is that something to worry about?"

"I don't know," said Ransom reflectively. "We're told he has a habit of going incommunicado, so it may mean nothing. But according to the good reverend, Danny was in the habit of disappearing, too, so I don't know what we should believe. It is worrisome. We need to talk to Michael Franklin."

"Well, you better do it fast. We need some action on this case!"

Newman needn't have worried. By the next morning, there would be more action than he wanted.

RANSOM WAS STILL irritated from the encounter with Newman when he arrived at the hospital. He was so used to working on his own, with the help of his own personal Watson, Gerald White, that he tended to forget that he was part of a chain of command. And he didn't like to be reminded, especially by someone he felt to be intellectually one step behind.

His mood was due for an abrupt turnaround, as he stood waiting for the elevator, when a silky voice called to him from across the lobby.

"Mr. Ransom?"

Ransom turned to see the approaching figure of Lynn Francis, an attractive, tawny-haired woman he'd met while investigating the murder of her employer. Lynn was a prepossessing woman in her early thirties, who had at one time been a valued personal assistant to a very important executive. She delighted in catching people off guard by telling them that she'd left her important position to become "charwoman to the rich and famous." She had done this because it afforded her the time she needed to take care of her ailing companion, Maggie Walker. Lynn eschewed any hint of martyrdom, though. She was, perhaps, the most contented person Ransom had ever met. He wondered, though, after hearing how Pamela Frazier had become involved in the Community, if someone like Lynn would ever be pushed to the point of needing a group to take care of her.

He doubted it. He couldn't imagine Lynn putting up with anyone or any group trying to make her decisions for her. Ransom's pleasure at seeing her was dampened by the realization that her presence at St. Joseph's most assuredly meant bad news.

"Good evening, Miss Francis'."

"Lynn," she said, extending her hand.

"Good," replied Ransom, giving her hand a brief squeeze, "and you can drop the 'Mister.'"

"Thank you."

She pressed the elevator button even though it was already lit, stepped back, and smiled. "Well, as you can imagine, I'm not here for my health. Maggie isn't doing very well."

"Sorry to hear it."

"And at the moment she's the only woman on the AIDS floor. You can imagine how much she likes that!" She gave him a coy grin.

Ransom was at a loss for what to say. Lynn was as disarming as he remembered her. For all her straightforwardness, Ransom had never asked Lynn how her lover had contracted AIDS, and she had never offered an explanation. Both of them held the same silent understanding that the cause wasn't an issue, the effect was all that mattered. Finally, he asked, "How bad is it?"

"She has tuberculosis. Isn't that a kick in the ass? All that time on Pentamidine, and instead of pneumonia she gets something else wrong with her lungs. I've always found life ironic."

Ransom made conciliatory noises, but he was warmed by the way she appeared to be handling the situation.

"What brings you here?" she asked with a toss of her head, her eyes sparkling. "I assume you're not just sight-seeing."

"I'm visiting someone. An older woman who had a heart attack and a bypass."

"A relative?"

"Not by blood."

Lynn nodded and searched his face with deep brown eyes that reminded Ransom of an exceptionally rich cocoa. There was something in her expression that made him feel that from the few words he'd offered her, she could understand the whole of the importance of his relationship with Emily. Oddly enough, this didn't make him uncomfortable.

The elevator doors slid open. They stepped aside to let the passengers off, then entered it themselves. He pressed the button for the fifth floor, she pressed nine. Before they reached his floor, he asked Lynn for her card.

Ransom was surprised to find Emily propped up in her bed, delicately sipping tea as the television news chattered the latest national violent-crime statistics. She looked much better: like someone who has been through an ordeal and is fairly certain that it is now over. She looked so much more like herself sitting there sipping her tea and resting her tiny wrists on the roll-away table, that it was as if she had been dropped into the hospital by mistake, and would be calmly tolerant while waiting for the mistake to be rectified.

"Emily, you look wonderful."

"Thank you," she replied primly. "My doctor tells me I may be discharged tomorrow—which, I must admit, makes it sound as if they're intending to send me home by way of a large cannon."

"That's...great," said Ransom, the only reason for his hesitation being that it was not in his nature to betray emotion. "You don't have to worry about being shot home. I'll see you home myself."

Emily made a little "tut tut" sound as she lowered the cup into its saucer. "That's very nice of you, Jeremy, but I'm sure you have more important things to do."

There was no hint of self-effacement in her voice. If anything, Ransom felt he was being gently reminded that his duty lay elsewhere.

Born by pure exasperation, Ransom became more firm with her than he ever had before. "You can't possibly believe that I would leave you to your own devices under the circumstances.''

"A young man who had his whole life ahead of him has been brutally murdered. I think it's far more important that your time be spent finding the killer than seeing an old lady home.''

Ransom bristled. "I will see to it you are transported home gently and safely.''

In the relatively short time that Ransom and Emily had known each other, this was the closest they'd come to an argument. Ransom stood at his most erect at the side of her bed, while Emily's slender fingers gingerly touched the rim of her teacup, their eyes never leaving each other's. At last Emily blinked twice and the wrinkled corners of her mouth broke into a smile. She looked like someone who had won something in defeat.

"As you wish,'' she said, taking a sip of her tea. "Check-out time is eleven o'clock.''

Ransom felt a mass of conflicting emotions. He went almost limp with relief that she had relented, as well as for the fact that her being up to challenge him in the first place signaled a return to her usual feistiness. At the same time, he felt a little guilty for having challenged her to begin with. He dismissed these thoughts by pulling the chair up beside her bed as if it were time they got down to business.

"So, what have you learned?'' asked Emily, taking her cue, her eyes bright with interest.

"Some things, but not nearly enough. I really dislike the way we have to work at this case. I feel that I'm forever going backward.''

"Like the man who gazes out the back window of the bus so he has a clear view of where he's been.''

"Exactly.''

"Are you forsaking Dickens for Carroll?''

"Hmm?''

"Lewis Carroll. *Through the Looking Glass,* into a land where everything works backward.''

Ransom smiled. "I don't think it's as bad as all that, but

you're not far off. You know, murder is usually the end of something. A culmination. I think if I can only put my finger on where this all began, the rest would fall into place."

"What *did* you find out?"

"Some very vague things. Danny was a crusader—of the soapbox variety, not the religious. We've been told that he readily challenged the leadership of the church when he disagreed with them."

"How uncomfortable for them."

"His peers either found him annoying or admired him, depending, apparently, on which side of the soapbox they fell on. His small-group leader found him disrespectful, and seems to really resent it."

"But I wouldn't think that would be something you would kill for," said Emily.

"Neither would I. Now Reverend Draper, the leader of the unhappy clan, claims that nothing irritates him."

"Tsk," said Emily, "I find that very difficult to believe. I like to think I have a fairly equitable temperament, but even I become irritated now and then."

"No, not you."

"It's not nice to mock your elders," said Emily with a sly smile. "Is there anything else?"

Ransom sighed heavily. "Something that sounds so…odd, that I hazard to mention it."

"Hmm?" said Emily, her curiosity piqued.

"Well, it seems marriage is very important in this Community. Most of the members are either married or engaged. *All* of the ones in Danny's small group are either married or engaged."

"And this seems important?"

Ransom shrugged. "Only because it's important, if you know what I mean."

"Was the murdered boy engaged?"

"That's what's so strange. I asked Reverend Draper that very question, and he said no, but he seemed awfully relieved when we got off the subject. I know it seems insignificant, but it seems to me there's something wrong there. Only…'' his voice trailed off, and he looked as if he were in danger of lapsing into one of his reveries.

"Only," said Emily, taking up the train of thought, "you don't know why the reverend would lie about Danny being engaged, if he did."

"Exactly. But what possible difference could it make if Danny was engaged?"

"Well," said Emily thoughtfully, "it could make a difference if they were afraid his fiancée could be a suspect."

"Yes, but there are a couple of things wrong with that. One is that I have trouble believing that a woman committed the murder—it required a lot of strength to subdue a man…"

"If they're all engaged, these women must be more capable of that than you think," said Emily with a twinkle in her eye.

Ransom returned the smile. "I meant subdue him and nail him to a cross, or whatever it was he was nailed to."

"But are you sure that's what happened?"

"According to the medical examiner there were wood shavings in the wounds, but even without that, the implications of the wounds themselves are pretty obvious."

Emily shook her head. "I hardly think that he would have just lain there while someone drove nails into him."

"He was tied up. There were rope burns around the wrists and ankles. But I didn't mean to imply that he'd been subdued by being crucified. Most likely he was subdued by one of the blows to the head. That's also, according to the ME, what killed him."

Emily thought about this for a moment, then said, "But that means that a woman could easily have done it."

"Perhaps…" said Ransom slowly, "…but could she have then lifted and carried the body on her own and transported it to the Dumpster?"

Emily pursed her lips and raised an eyebrow, contemplating the possibilities. After a moment she shook away her own thoughts and turned back to Ransom.

"What was the other thing?"

"The other what?"

"We were discussing the possibility that the reverend had lied about Danny being engaged. I suggested he might have done that if he was afraid the fiancée would be a suspect. You said there were a couple of things wrong with that."

Ransom looked at her blankly for a moment, then smiled at Emily's renewed sharpness. "Oh, yes, the other thing is that Draper can't possibly believe that we wouldn't find out somehow that Danny was engaged. News travels extremely fast in the Community."

"He could if his influence is as strong as you seem to think it is."

Ransom considered this for a moment, then shook his head. "No, no, when it comes to that, there are a few weak links in the armor."

"You're mixing your metaphors, my dear."

"Sorry. Anyway, there is one couple whom I believe has told us the truth. They were the ones responsible for reporting the disappearance in the first place. They are also engaged, by the way—in their instance, happily—which is not the case with all of them. And the young woman admitted to us—reluctantly, but she did it nonetheless—that they are sort of pushed to get married." Ransom shook his head. "None of them seem to be willing to go into why they are 'encouraged' to get married."

"I would think there are as many reasons to get married as there are fish in the sea."

"So would I, but the only one they give me is because 'the Lord draws them together.'" His tone had become somewhat contemptuous, which caused Emily some concern.

"Now, Jeremy," she said in the manner of a caring schoolteacher, "I will admit that there are many religious charlatans in the world. And I personally think that one of the most despicable things one can do is to twist the words of scripture to suit one's ends, whether it be for money or power, but the fact that charlatans exist should not taint all of the clergy in your mind.''

"One bad apple, et cetera," he said wryly.

"That's exactly what I mean," Emily replied, using the prim voice that always managed to make Ransom feel as if he'd been misbehaving.

"Now about marriage," he said in an attempt to get back to the matter at hand.

"Ah, yes." Emily retrieved a pair of reading glasses from the nightstand and placed them on her nose. They were large and round and gave her an owlish appearance. She then took a book from the drawer of the stand and flipped it open.

"I asked Nurse Carter to find a Bible for me. She was so sweet about it, she acted as if I'd just found religion. I didn't have the heart to tell her that I needed it for a murder case.''

Ransom chuckled as Emily turned the pages of the well worn copy of the King James Version of the Bible with a touching degree of reverence.

"If I remember correctly," she said, "there is a chapter about marriage in First Corinthians. If they indeed view marriage with so much importance, I think we can assume they got their ideas from here.''

She continued to thumb through the Bible, pausing occasionally to glance down a column and smile. Finally she said, "Oh! Here it is. First Corinthians, chapter seven. Hmm...interesting," she said as she read through the verses.

"What?"

"Well, there's nothing here about marrying because God has brought you together. In fact, it seems to be quite the opposite. Listen to this:

'It is good for a man not to touch a woman, nevertheless, to avoid fornication, let every man have his own wife.'

"There's a good deal more here," she said, scanning the page. "I'm afraid the apostle Paul was a bit wordy, but...here's something. It seems to contradict what you see happening in the Community. In verses eight and nine it says:

> 'I say therefore to the unmarried and widows, it is good for them if they abide even as I. But if they cannot contain, let them marry for it is better to marry than to burn.'"

She closed the book gently and laid her hand on it. She seemed lost in thought. At last, she said, "So it would seem your Reverend Draper should be encouraging people *not* to marry."

"Unless they can't control their desires."

"Perhaps that's the answer," Emily speculated. "If Danny couldn't 'control himself,' and so was being pressured into marriage."

"Well, except there are two problems with *that,* Emily. First, there's Pamela, who assures me that Danny couldn't be pressed into anything. And I'm inclined to believe her. She seems to be one of the rare, believable Christians in this little scenario. The other thing is that the reverend denies that Danny was engaged."

"That doesn't mean that he wasn't being pressured to do so."

"True," said Ransom slowly.

They fell silent for a moment, both turning these matters over in their minds. Their meditations were broken by a disgusted snort from Ransom. "It still doesn't make any sense. Whether or not Danny was engaged, whether or not he was being pushed—why not tell us about it? What could it possibly have to do with his murder? I can't believe they'd murder him for that."

"The nettling thing is," said Emily, "that the reverend's reluctance to be perfectly frank about it may serve to make it seem more important than it really is." She paused for a moment of reflection, then said, "Have you spoken to the dead boy's roommate yet?"

"No. We haven't been able to find him."

Emily's eyes widened. "Oh, that doesn't sound promising at all."

"It may not be anything to worry about. His fiancée tells us that he has a habit of cutting himself off when he's upset—and murder has a way of upsetting people. Unfortunately, there's no law against refusing to answer the door—if there was, we'd all be besieged by unwanted relatives."

Emily thought for a moment. "Can't you get a search warrant or something so that you can go into his apartment? After all, the young man who was killed lived there, too."

"No. It's not as easy as all that to get a search warrant." Ransom said this as if he would rather it were otherwise, then added, "And besides, it's not a crime scene...that we know of."

Emily shook her head. "It's all very frustrating."

"Um-hmm. With every passing moment he seems more like the key to this whole thing. He lived with Danny, he sounded the alarm about his disappearance, and now we can't find him."

Emily's voice was edged with concern. "And Jeremy, it's imperative that you do."

"I know, Emily, I know," he said with an exasperated sigh. "And I feel more and more like that man looking out the back window of the bus!"

ELEVEN

AT SEVEN O'CLOCK on Friday morning, one of the men Ransom had referred to as "garbage connoisseurs," was making his usual run up a Wells Street alley. He was known to the locals as Crazy Ned. He had a balding crown with long, stringy, black hair that left traces of oil on the shoulders of his filthy khaki coat. He wore black pants, smudged from top to bottom with dirt, grime, and some other matter that is better left unreported.

He sang the half-remembered words of "The Sound of Music" as he picked through a large steel trash barrel behind a Dollar for Everything store. He found nothing suitable for sustenance in the barrel, then moved on to a mid-sized Dumpster behind a bar called The Golden Slipper. This was one of his favorite spots, as it usually would yield at least dregs from the bottoms of a variety of liquor bottles, as well as half-eaten sandwiches, half-eaten pizzas, and sundry food that had passed the point of being eaten.

Crazy Ned pushed the sleeve of his coat up to the elbow, in an entirely unnecessary attempt to save it from further soiling, and plunged his arm into the refuse like an arcade crane digging for a prize. His hand wriggled down through a panoply of plastic bags, things too wet to be retrieved in solid form, and various mounds of Styrofoam, until about halfway down he struck pay dirt: a solid piece of meat (at least, it felt like meat) that seemed fresh enough that something could be done with it. He gave it a tug, but it was apparently stuck on something that held it back. But Crazy Ned was not in a position to let go easily. He was hungry, and not about to give up a stubborn piece of food. He gave a strong pull on the object, and it jerked upward as if it were at least partially dislodging from whatever held it. In his semi-sodden state, he reeled backward with the effort, and was astonished to find himself holding a hand. A hand with a hole in it. He let go and the hand snapped back atop its arm, which poked up through the garbage. The hand flopped madly atop the arm like a fish on a pedestal.

Crazy Ned stopped singing.

IT WAS ALMOST two hours after Crazy Ned's close encounter that Ransom arrived at area headquarters. When he was called into Newman's office, he was expecting yet another session of not-so-thinly veiled recriminations about his lack of success, and other generally unhealthy banter. He was surprised to find the sergeant seated behind his desk, a grave expression frozen on his face. He looked like he didn't have enough energy for a sparring match.

"We've got another one," said Newman without preamble.

"Another what?"

"Body. Another dead...boy." The last word was accentuated with disgust at the thought of a wasted life.

"Where?" Ransom said sharply.

"Alley behind Wells and LaSalle. Off Goethe. Behind The Golden Slipper."

"The Golden Slipper," Ransom repeated as if something was beginning to click. "Damn!"

"Robinson and Carter are already there, as well as the crew, but you'd better get over to the scene," Newman called to Ransom's retreating figure.

"Gerald!" Ransom shouted as he plowed through the squad room. Gerald had fortunately been waiting nearby, and followed obediently without yet knowing what the problem was. Ransom filled him in on the ride over: a ride that Ransom found interminably long. At last they pulled onto Goethe, their tires squealing as they turned into the alley.

All of the crime scene impedimenta was already in evidence. Police tape was up in a wide band around the Dumpster, and men from the crime lab were working over the area. Detectives Robinson and Carter stood talking with two uniformed policemen, forming a group that seemed to be forcing casualness over intensity. Gerald stopped to speak quietly with the group as Ransom continued on.

Ransom was struck with a sickening sense of déjà vu as he approached the scene. Ferman, the police photographer, hovered over the body like an obscene paparrazo, his same mustard overcoat flapping in the breeze.

The body had already been moved so that more detailed photographs could be taken. It was lying at the foot of the Dumpster. It was a young man who looked not quite as angelic as the first victim, but they did have things in common: There were holes driven through the hands and feet, and the head had been severely battered. The boy's face looked like it reflected some of the agony it had suffered in passing, as if it had not achieved complete repose in death. Also like the first victim, this body was naked. Debris from the Dumpster clung to the body: bits of food and little bits of damp paper, and smears of something that looked like dried tomato sauce adhered to it like spatter paint. There was one major difference between this body and the first: Ransom felt fairly sure he knew who this was.

"Seems to be a trend, doesn't it?" said Ferman as he snapped happily away.

"You have your Polaroid?"

"Of course."

"I want a set in detail. Now."

THE DRIVE TO the reverend's house was performed at high speed in intense silence. Ransom was so obviously seething that Gerald thought he might be the first eyewitness to a spontaneous combustion. Gerald recognized his partner's barely subdued fury as something potentially dangerous— not recklessly dangerous, but dangerous nonetheless. Ransom's right hand drummed forcibly against the armrest.

"We couldn't have done anything to prevent this," said Gerald.

"We could have solved it sooner."

"Not with nothing to go on."

"We would have had something to go on," Ransom said hotly, "if these goddam Christians would have told us the truth!"

Gerald debated with himself for a moment whether or not he should continue, and decided that it was important to at least attempt to temper his partner's understandable rage. "That boy, he looked like he's been dead over twenty-four hours. That would put it back to at least Wednesday night."

"And we know from Miss Betty's bookstore that he was alive Wednesday until he left work."

"We didn't even know this group was connected to the first murder until Wednesday. Jer, we couldn't have prevented this."

There did seem to be a partial evening of Ransom's temper as he replied, "If we weren't forced to look at this backward...if this thing hadn't been allowed to start to begin with. But it started far too long ago."

"What do you mean?"

"It started with however these dead boys developed into the kind of people who would get involved in a group like this in the first place. But it has to stop now."

"You got that right," said Gerald, thinking of his own daughters and wondering if he might have already erred in a way that would lead them into a fatal mistake.

"The time has come..." said Ransom through gritted teeth.

"What?"

"If Reverend Draper insists on quoting the Bible at me again, I may be forced to quote something that Emily reminded me of last night. *Through the Looking Glass.* '"The time has come," the walrus said, "to talk of many things."' And none of them are in the Bible."

When they arrived at the reverend's house, Gerald almost couldn't keep up with Ransom as he marched up to the door and jabbed the doorbell. In the hazy morning light,

Albany Park looked darker and more oppressive than it had on any of their previous visits.

After a moment, the door was opened once again by Mrs. Draper. As before, she was dressed in her coordinated knits, this time in shades of brown. Unlike her husband, Mrs. Draper didn't even bother with a pretense of politeness.

"What do you want?" she said through thin lips.

Ransom was frankly in no mood for sparring with the woman. He said simply, "Your husband," as he walked past her into the house.

"Wait a minute! Wait a minute!" she said angrily. Gerald smiled and gave the woman a nod as he followed his partner.

"What is it, dear?" said Draper, appearing in the living-room doorway. His hair was slicked down but seemed to have gained another recalcitrant wave, as if the accumulated pressures of the past week were curling it before its time. When he saw the detectives, his usual tolerant smile froze on his face.

"Oh. Good morning, Detectives," he said as Ransom and Gerald brushed past him into the living room.

There they found Saul Berne, who leapt to his stubby legs as they entered. His uncontrollable hair seemed to flare upward in indignation.

"How dare you! How dare you barge in here like this! This isn't a police state, this is America!"

Ransom's withering smile beamed down on the steaming leader. "I shouldn't think that would bother you, Mr. Berne. You don't live in this world, you live in God's world, don't you?"

Saul responded with only the hateful glare of someone who's been bested in his own language by a tourist.

"I'm surprised to find you here this morning, Mr. Berne." In his present state of mind, even Ransom's most commonplace statements seemed to shoot from him like electrical arcs.

"I...I...don't have any clients today," Saul answered, redfaced, as if Ransom's statement had been an accusation.

"I was...just using the opportunity to meet with my leader."

"Hmm."

The reverend and his wife were holding a tense, hushed conference in the hallway that ended when the reverend started into the room.

"Sam," Carla protested in the doorway.

"It's all right, darling."

"But, Sam..."

He gave her his firm look.

"It's all right."

There was the briefest pause during which something seemed to be silently communicated between them. Without a word, Mrs. Draper acceded. She wasn't happy, but she left, disappearing down the hallway.

Rev. Sam came into the room. If it were possible to express displeasure with a smile, that is what he did now. His eyes were set on Ransom, and the vein beneath his right eye pulsated. He did not invite them to sit down, and though Gerald didn't like taking notes while standing, he realized that this was hardly the occasion for the polite conversation that a comfortable seat would imply. The four men stood in a tense grouping in the center of the room.

"Gentlemen," said Draper, directing himself to Ransom and ignoring Gerald, "I have tried to be patient with you, but I really can't have you upsetting my household in this fashion."

"Indeed?" said Ransom, returning the smile with one that had been dipped in acid. "That's a shame, because I have only begun to upset your household."

"This is outrageous," Saul blustered, "this man..."

Draper cut him off. "Saul, please. What is this all about, Mr. Ransom?"

"Murder, Mr. Draper, the same thing it's been about from the beginning."

"And as I told you from the beginning, I don't see why you think this Community has anything to do with a murder that took place in the Loop, even if it was one of our members.''

"If we weren't sure before, we are now.''

For the first time there seemed to be some hesitation in the reverend.

"Why?''

"Because it has gone beyond the murder of Danny Lyman.''

Ransom reached into his blazer pocket and withdrew a handful of Polaroids.

"This boy was found without any identification on him,'' he said as he handed the photos to the reverend, "as you can see. We don't know who he is. But I was sure you'd be able to identify him for us.''

The reverend looked at the top picture, which featured the head and shoulders of the body that had just been discovered. The reverend's smile faded, which Ransom considered a victory. But still the man showed no emotion.

"This boy was found this morning in a Dumpster, Mr. Draper. A Dumpster. Shoved in with the trash. You may notice that some of it has rubbed off on him. He was found just north of the Loop, not a mile from where Danny Lyman was found. In a Dumpster, Mr. Draper, behind a bar called The Golden Slipper. He had his head bashed in, among other things, and then he was thrown out like garbage. Perhaps you could tell us who he is?''

Draper stared at the photo as if he were trying to burn it with his eyes. At last he looked up at Ransom and without any trace of emotion said, "It's Michael Franklin.''

Ransom reached for the photos and said, "I thought it might be. Now, Mr. Draper...''

"*Reverend* Draper,'' Saul snapped.

Ransom ignored him. "Now, Mr. Draper, it seems more than a little coincidental to me that two members of your church have been found murdered this week.''

"But coincidences *do* happen,'' said the reverend, "and seeing as how Michael was also found downtown...''

"In Old Town, sir,'' Gerald corrected him.

"...so far from here," Draper continued as if he hadn't been interrupted, "it seems within the realm of possibility that it *is* a coincidence."

"I don't like to press you," said Ransom in a tone that clearly implied he would be happy to press the reverend flat, "but for someone who is supposedly so concerned and informed on the comings and goings of your flock, you seem inexcusably uninformed as your members slip away to be murdered."

"As I've told you before," said Draper smoothly, "I do not have the Community under constant surveillance. This is not a prison. Our members are free to come and go as they please."

Unhampered by steel bars, thought Ransom. Then aloud, "You've also told us that you know your members better than anyone else, better than they know themselves, apparently."

"That is uncalled for!" barked Saul.

"So perhaps you could explain to us what Michael Franklin would be doing in Old Town."

"I have no idea what he would be doing there now." There was the slightest emphasis on the last word.

"Now? Did he frequent it at one time?"

The reverend wandered over to the fireplace and leaned an elbow on the mantle. His expression hadn't changed, but his body moved more slowly. Ransom could have sworn he'd been affected in some way.

"Where did you say he was found?"

"Stuffed in a Dumpster," said Ransom, unrelenting, "behind a bar called The Golden Slipper."

"Isn't that...isn't that a gay bar?" sputtered Saul.

"Yes, it is," said Ransom, with a glance in his direction.

"Then it was worse than we thought," said Draper.

"What was?"

Draper sighed. "Before Michael came to the Lord, he was a homosexual."

"He *was*," said Ransom, his forehead wrinkling.

"He frequented places like that. Like that bar. But when

he became a Christian, he understood that homosexuality was unacceptable in the sight of the Lord. So he prayed for the Lord to heal him, and we prayed with him and for him.''

At this point the left corner of Draper's mouth sagged ruefully. "I don't know that he ever believed that the Lord would heal him.''

"Heal him?" Ransom repeated disdainfully.

"The Bible says you have to believe in order to receive," Saul explained with the attitude of someone forced to cast pearls before swine.

"So you tried to get Michael to believe that God would *cure* him of being gay."

"With God, all things are possible," said the reverend softly.

Good Christ, thought Ransom, if either one of these men quote the Bible at me again I will beat the holy shit out of them. Gerald was, with good reason, concerned about what was going through his partner's mind; at the moment he was finding it difficult enough to control his own temper.

"Forgive me," said Ransom with measured tolerance, "but I was under the impression that Michael was going to marry."

"He was."

"Was that after the cure, or part of it?"

"The Bible is very clear on such matters," said Draper, "and tells us that if someone is unable to control their desires, they should be married.''

So Emily was right, thought the detective.

"Marriage is the lesser of two evils?" said Ransom, unable or unwilling to hide the irony in his voice.

"I can't expect you to understand the depths of our belief.''

Ransom considered him for a moment, more for dramatic effect than in hope of learning anything. At last he said, "And how did his fiancée feel about this arrangement?"

"Barbara Searly is a devout Christian, and would do anything the Lord decreed."

"Through you," said Ransom, trying his best not to sneer. But Draper didn't take the bait. He merely repeated at length a description of how decisions were made within the group with prayer and guidance. Ransom refrained from expressing his thoughts on the subject. Instead, he decided to pursue another route.

"When we told you where Michael was found, you said 'It was worse than we thought.' Exactly what did you mean by that?"

Draper seemed reluctant to answer this, but Ransom held a firm stance and said, "The boy has been murdered, Mr. Draper. There is nobody for you to protect now except the murderer."

"Michael was backsliding," said the reverend evenly. "We've suspected it and I think our suspicions were right, given where his body was found."

"The way he was going," Saul cut in, "the way he was falling back, you would've expected him to end up in a gutter!"

Ransom slewed his eyes around to take in the squat man. "But not in a Dumpster, Mr. Berne."

"We tried to help him as much as we could," the reverend explained. "We tried to save him. And we prayed for him. Both alone and as a body. In Michael's case, apparently it didn't help. But Michael was a child of the Lord. And his death now…at this time…may be the Lord's way of stopping him before he was completely lost."

Ransom could take it no longer. He shuffled through the photos quickly, drew one out, and shoved it in the reverend's face.

"The Lord did not drive nails through this boy's hands and feet."

Draper took the photo from him, holding it by the bottom corners, and looked at it as if it were a sample of pornography that a child had given him to try to shock him. It was a full-length shot of Michael Franklin's body. His arms were laid at his sides with the palms up. Each palm was marred by a brownish-black stain, where a sharp object had been driven through. The fingers were curved like claws. Both feet bore similar markings.

Ransom studied Draper's face with growing disgust. There was something obscene about the dispassionate way he looked at the photo. And it seemed the very last indignity that Michael should be seen like this by this man.

Ransom snatched the photo from him and said, "This is the same condition in which we found Danny Lyman. I think you can see from the wounds on the body that it is fairly evident that your Community or one of its members is involved. We are going to rule out the Lord for the moment. Now, Mr. Draper, whether or not you want to believe it, you and the members of your little Community are subject to the laws of this state."

"I'm well aware of my legal responsibilities," said Draper, his voice displaying the tiniest crack in his veneer.

"I wouldn't have believed it from the way you've avoided answering my questions."

"I have not avoided them. I've answered you as I felt the Lord led me."

Ransom arched his left eyebrow and said, "Does the Lord lead you to lie?"

"How dare you! How dare you!" Saul sputtered again, going red in the face in a way that made him look like a particularly unlovely troll. Ransom was tempted to dispatch him to his place beneath a bridge.

"Saul!" said the reverend, quelling him with a calmly raised hand. Then he turned to Ransom and said, "I have not *lied* to you."

Ransom's face became a mixture of contempt and satisfaction. He didn't like semantical games, especially in the middle of an investigation. But he knew that by getting the reverend to say this, he had won a victory; the fact that it had to be said was proof that Draper knew he hadn't been straightforward, to say the least. And it was time to get down to cases. If Ransom hadn't been so enraged over the deaths of the two boys, he would have enjoyed this.

"You told us that Danny didn't have any enemies."

"That's true."

"Is it?" said Ransom. "And yet he's been described to me as a troublemaker. Troublemakers are hardly lovable types."

"If Heaven were to be populated only with lovable people, it would be a very lonely place."

Ransom made a silent vow not to get drawn into another theological round-robin. He chose his next words carefully.

"Can you tell me why Michael's fiancée, Barbara Searly, seems to have disliked Danny Lyman so intensely?"

"Did she say that?"

"It was evident."

The reverend glanced at one of his hands, as if checking his latest manicure, and replied, "Once again, Mr. Ransom, we are approaching matters which have been discussed with me in…"

"I know," Ransom cut in, "the 'secrets of the confessional.' Would you like to see the pictures again?"

Draper glanced at Ransom. Gerald noticed for the first time that the perpetual smile was gone, and wondered if it would ever return.

After a long pause, Draper replied reluctantly, "I would say, though, that Barbara didn't hate Danny. But it's true that she had her problems with him."

Ransom was curious as to where the word "hate" had come from: He hadn't used it, but he suspected that Barbara had at one time.

"A problem?" said Ransom, making the words sound ridiculous. "I would also say that Mr. Berne here had 'a problem' with Danny. Danny was forever challenging authority."

"He didn't challenge *my* authority!" Saul snapped.

Ransom glanced at him and then back at Draper.

"And then there's you. It must be very difficult to be in your position and have someone always questioning you."

"It is," said Draper in an attempt at irony.

"Did you have a problem with Danny, too?"

Draper responded with the weariness of a father whose

child insists on repeating a question. "I have already answered that—during one of your frequent visits."

The crack grows wider, thought Ransom with an inner smile.

"Yes. You would have us believe that constantly being challenged by your subordinates is not irritating. I think otherwise."

"You may think what you please," said Draper.

Ransom wondered if the reverend was silently kicking himself for having let that sharpness slip into his voice.

"And then there's Michael Franklin. We know that he visited you on Monday night."

Draper looked slightly surprised, Saul looked aghast.

Ransom added, "We told you we would be talking to all the parties involved. Michael visited you on Monday night, and expressed his concern over the disappearance of Danny."

Draper shook his head as if to dismiss the detective's idea. "Yes, he did, and I told him the same thing I told you on your first visit: that I saw no reason for concern."

"Despite the fact that Michael did?"

The reverend shrugged slightly. "Michael was flighty and very high-strung."

"He was also right," said Ransom pointedly. "And now he's dead. Odd, isn't it, that two different boys should be murdered after visiting you?" To his surprise, a ghost of the reverend's smile reappeared.

"Surely you're not going to suggest that Michael disappeared from this house. Since you know about his visit, it's obvious that he was seen after he was here."

Ransom furrowed his brow—something that only happened when he was disappointed with his own results.

"It doesn't really matter to me at this point when Michael went missing. We have a fairly good estimation of when he went dead."

There was not even a twitch from the reverend.

"Due to the condition of the body when it was found. It's a rough guess, at the moment, which will be confirmed by the coroner as soon as possible. Tell me, Mr. Draper, where were you between, say, late Wednesday afternoon and Thursday morning?"

"This is outrageous!" Saul bellowed. "This is a man of God and you're interrogating him as if he were…as if he were…" Rage and frustration robbed him of the words. Ransom filled them in for him.

"As if he were a suspect in a murder. He is. And so are you."

"Me?" Saul goggled, his thick glasses making him look more dumbfounded than normal.

"Where were you?" Ransom repeated to Draper.

The reverend answered him with the stiffness of someone who sees that he must submit to an indignity. "You were here in the late afternoon, so I spent that with you. As you know, I had dinner right after you left, then I went to our leaders' meeting. It was held at one of our small-group leader's houses."

"His name?" said Ransom, delighting in the fact that he could ask a question that demanded direct answers rather than the religious bumper stickers he'd gotten earlier.

"Greg Kirk."

Draper provided Greg Kirk's home and office addresses at Ransom's request, with a modicum of righteous indignation.

"And you?" said Ransom, turning to Saul.

Saul blustered for a moment, finally managing to get out, "I was at the same meeting…of course."

"And when did this meeting adjourn?"

Draper and Berne glanced at each other as if there might be some question about who should answer this.

Draper said, "Around nine o'clock."

Ransom's lips pursed for a moment, then formed a smile. "And can your wives verify when you got home?"

There was a sudden stiffness in the room—the startled silence one would expect from a deer who doesn't see the car until it's upon him.

With studied calm, the reverend said, "Well, that presents a bit of a problem."

Somehow I thought it would, thought Ransom.

"How so?"

"The sisters—I mean the leaders' wives—used our meeting as they often do for an opportunity to have a get-together of their own. They met at the Hartwicks' and had a little party. Unfortunately, when the sisters get together, they have a tendency to get carried away. I don't think Carla herself got home until eleven-thirty."

Somehow it didn't surprise the detective that he'd asked Draper for an alibi, and had been supplied with one for his wife instead; this showed an incredible talent for not answering the question that was asked. Ransom's smile became more malevolent. "Mr. Draper, for a man who apparently understands the seriousness of this situation, you don't seem to be trying very hard."

"I've done all I can."

"With or without your help, I'm going to find out who killed these boys. I should think you'd want to help."

Draper's eyes never left Ransom's. The reverend remained so still it was as if even his blood had ceased to circulate.

"I don't know anything about these deaths."

Ransom's eyes narrowed. He wasn't sure, but he thought he detected something peculiar in the way he'd said "know."

The detectives stayed just long enough to see Mrs. Draper and verify what her husband had told them. Under the circumstances it was an unnecessary gesture, since Ransom was sure she would not contradict her husband: It was simply a further indignity Ransom felt fully justified in inflicting on the good reverend. Mrs. Draper answered with a characteristic lack of graciousness that she and the sisters had enjoyed an evening of fellowship, and that she'd gotten home before midnight. And she affirmed that neither of them had gone out again that night.

AFTER THE DETECTIVES had gone, Reverend Draper returned to his place by the mantle. Saul was visibly fuming.

"I can't believe it! I just can't believe it! To treat me that way. To treat *you* that way! To subject you to that…inquisition! It's shameful!"

Draper said, "I don't know…I just don't know. There are things going on in this Community that I don't know about. Important things."

Saul looked a little hurt. "I discuss everything with you."

Draper turned his steadfast eyes on his subordinate and said, "Do you, Saul?"

Saul's expression transformed into one of concern. "Of course I do."

Draper held his gaze a few more moments before saying, "I hope you do. I would hate to think that any important matters, anything that needed prayer, would be withheld."

"I would never do that. None of the leaders would."

"I don't know," said Draper again, "the detectives seem to know—or at least think they do—things that have happened in our Community that I'm not aware of. I'd at least like to think I'm as informed as an outsider."

"They don't know anything," said Saul, his cheeks going red again.

Draper turned his eyes upon Saul and said, "Are you *sure* you tell me everything?"

Saul's face was a combination of hurt and confusion. His voice was hollow when he said "Yes."

"I wonder…" said Draper slowly, "who Michael spoke with about Monday night. Mr. Ransom seems to know all about it."

"You know," said Saul, his bushy eyebrows creeping upward like red caterpillars, "Pamela was seen talking to them yesterday."

"That means nothing. The detectives are planning to talk to everyone in your group. Still, I would like to know what Michael had to say about his visit here." He was silent for a moment, then added offhandedly, "You *did* contact your small-group members and remind them to be discreet, didn't you?''

"Of course I did!"

"Of course you did," said the reverend apologetically.

They fell silent. Saul fussed with some lint he found dangling from his right cuff, but the reverend remained still and quiet, as if the cosmos would provide an answer for him. At last, as if in answer to prayer, an idea came to him.

"You know, I don't think Pamela would have shared extraneous information with the detectives. She has been with us a long time. She's a good sister, and she understands our Community and what we're trying to achieve. Nicholas, on the other hand..."

Saul's face brightened. He was catching on. The reverend continued:

"...Nicholas hasn't been with us very long, and I'm unsure as to how committed he is to the Community."

"Yes, yes..." said Saul, getting excited, "and you remember, he was brought into the fold by Danny."

Draper glanced at him for a moment. He looked uncharacteristically hesitant, as if he couldn't decide whether or not some sort of rebuke was necessary.

"Um-hmm," said Draper finally. His eyes slowly slid shut, his face turned upward. He stood that way for fully two minutes while Saul looked on, waiting: then his eyes slid open.

"I really think we need to talk to Nicholas."

AFTER THEY LEFT the reverend's house, Ransom and Gerald had a discussion surprisingly similar to the one just recorded, only in more worldly terms.

"I think we have to have another talk with Nicholas Bremmen. I got the impression that there wasn't a lot of love lost between him and the Community, and he seems to have a good head on his shoulders. I think he might be able to shed a little more light on the relationship between Danny and Michael."

"You think there was a relationship?"

Ransom gave Gerald a withering glance. "Not *that* kind of relationship, Gerald. I mean that obviously there has to be some kind of connection between the two boys, since they had the same fate."

Gerald let out an exasperated sigh. "What's wrong with the obvious? They were lovers?"

"And so who killed them?" said Ransom in a tone that matched his earlier glance, both of which Gerald found infuriating.

"How about your favorite suspect?"

"Who would that be?"

"Reverend Draper."

"Heavens," said Ransom coyly, "I didn't realize I was being so transparent. All right, Gerald, why would Reverend Draper kill these boys now?"

"You heard him," said Gerald, warming to the idea, "he thought the Lord got rid of Michael because he was backsliding. Maybe he decided to help the Lord along."

To his credit, though Ransom had been toying with Gerald, he gave the idea some consideration. As a solution, it wasn't any worse than any of the others that came to mind, but he still didn't buy it.

"No, it has to be something else."

"How do you know that, Jer? How do you know one of these zealots didn't just spring a leak and kill Michael because he was gay?"

"Two reasons: One is entirely subjective. I just don't *feel* that that's it. I know that isn't scientific, but I don't believe it."

"And the other?"

"Much more practical, Gerald. It doesn't explain Danny Lyman's murder."

"Maybe he *was* gay. Maybe he just hid it better. Somebody found out and killed him for the same reason."

"This you'll like less," said Ransom. "I don't think that is why Danny was killed, because the reverend told us that he wasn't gay, and I believe him."

This really stopped Gerald in his tracks. His eyes opened

wide, looking like two large raisins floating in vanilla pudding.

"You're kidding!"

"No, I'm not," said Ransom, then he grumbled, "and nobody's more surprised than I am. But we have to look at the facts: His lies have been lies of evasion—not telling us what he knows. Even now, assuming he's not the killer himself, I could almost bet if he doesn't know who the killer is, he has some idea. But one of the few direct answers we've been able to get from him is that Danny was not gay. I think I believe him."

"All right," said Gerald, "but as far as Michael Franklin goes, Barbara Searly would be a good suspect. And she didn't like Danny, either."

"Yes, well she's another one I have two 'problems' with, to use the reverend's term. The first is one I discussed with Emily: I hate to sound like a sexist, but these murders seem a little brutal to have been performed by a woman. Aside from…" he shied away from using the word "subduing" again, "immobilizing the victims—there's the fact that the killer had to move the bodies after death, which couldn't have been any small task."

"And the second?" asked Gerald, once again submerging the twinge of resentment he felt when put in the position of sidekick.

"The second is that if I were Barbara Searly, I'd kill the reverend."

Gerald couldn't help but laugh at this.

"There's another fact we have to take into consideration here," said Ransom.

"What's that?"

"Even though I greatly enjoy the idea of the good reverend as the killer, we have to face the fact that it could be any of them."

"So where does that leave us?"

"It leaves you here, if you don't mind going on on foot."

"Well, okay," said Gerald, surprised, "what do you want me to do?"

"Check with Saul Berne's wife, verify the Wednesday night hen party—again. Make sure she was there. And then check out this Greg Kirk person, see if he can verify when the leaders' meeting broke up. And see if you can get hold of Nicholas Bremmen. Set up a time when we can meet him. Preferably as soon as possible."

"Where will you be?"

"I've got a date at the hospital."

TWELVE

RANSOM ARRIVED at the hospital at about eleven-thirty to find Emily ready and waiting, with the little floral overnight bag that had belied its name by having kept her for a week.

Nurse Carter was on hand to say her good-byes. Emily took the nurse's dark brown hand in her frail hands and gave it a little pat as if congratulating the nurse on a job well done. Carter flashed a broad, satisfied smile and said, "Now don't you come back too soon!"

On the way to Emily's house, Ransom filled her in on the case. He had been reluctant to discuss it with her as they traveled, thinking that the drive itself would be excitement enough under the circumstances, but his plans to help revive her sagging spirits by interesting her in the case had proven too successful. She was not to be detoured.

Ransom started with the fact that Michael had finally been located, dead, which elicited Emily's harshest condemnation: She clucked her tongue.

"Oh, Jeremy," she said, "you really shouldn't have taken the time to take me home. You simply *must* put all your energy into finding this killer."

"Not to worry, Emily," he replied, "Gerald is taking care of some necessary details at the moment. And when I have you safely settled, I'll rejoin him and we'll go from there."

"Exactly where will you be going?"

"Down the rest of the small-group list. There are a few we haven't spoken to yet."

"And then?"

Ransom sighed wearily. "And then we'll have to talk to the rest of them all over again. In a way, Michael's murder may be a big help to us."

Emily raised her thin gray eyebrows, and placed her hand on the armrest, as if the effort required support.

"How?"

"We've been hampered in investigating Danny Lyman's death because we're too vague on when he was killed. With apologies to television, a pathologist really can't pinpoint that accurately when the death took place. There are too many mitigating factors. But at the moment we can make an educated guess on when Michael was killed. We know that he worked Wednesday until late afternoon, early evening. So far as we've been able to find out, he hasn't been seen since. So he was killed sometime between when he left work Wednesday, and Thursday morning. He was found this morning, and even we could tell he'd been dead more than a day. At least that gives us something to go on. Unfortunately, it's still not a lot."

"Why is that?"

"Well, first of all, the leaders had a meeting that went on until about nine, and their wives had a 'little party' that went on until eleven-thirty. That leaves almost two and a half hours during which the leadership of the Community is unaccounted for. Second, that still leaves us with the rest of Wednesday night, overnight, I mean. Even if any of the small-group members could provide alibis for their whereabouts that could be corroborated, it wouldn't make a difference. If one of them didn't have an alibi, it would still only hint at opportunity. It comes nowhere near demonstrated concrete evidence."

Emily's already wrinkled forehead wrinkled further. "I wonder exactly how long it took to commit these crimes. Crucifixion is rather time-consuming, you know."

"Crucifixion was only the icing on the cake in these cases, remember. They were actually killed by the blows to the head. It's unlikely that either of them would have died from the nail wounds, anyway, if they'd been given time to. The wounds were too small for them to have bled to death."

"Most people who had the misfortune to be executed in

that fashion died of asphyxiation," said Emily, in the off-hand manner that served to disarm people who mistook her for a frail old woman. If she were frail at all, it was only physical.

"Indeed?" said Ransom, shaking his head. "Emily, you are a storehouse of the most amazing information."

"Many things can be learned from any sermon through which one can stay awake," she said simply. "That bit of information was from a sermon that I...believe was entitled, 'They Pierced His Side.' The minister—it was Reverend McCarthy at that time—endeavored to explain why the soldier had pierced Jesus's side with a spear after he'd been hung on the cross."

"A charming Sunday school lecture for the kiddies," Ransom grumbled.

Emily offered him a reproving glance. "In that sermon he explained that the soldier did it to make sure Jesus was dead, because they had taken him down early because...for reasons I can't quite remember. Anyway, victims of crucifixion usually died of asphyxiation—their lungs collapsed—which could take days."

"A highly inefficient way to go about killing someone," said Ransom.

"It was symbolic," said Emily.

"Hmm?" said Ransom, taking his eyes off the road for the first time and looking directly at her.

"They were hung up for everyone to see, Jeremy. As an example."

Ransom turned his attention back to the road, but now his eyes were narrowed.

"Symbolic..." he repeated softly.

Emily seemed to grow more attentive to her surroundings as they neared her house. Her eyes grew as wide as fine china saucers, and sparkled in the midday light. When he turned onto her street, her hand crept up to the neck of her dark blue dress, and when he pulled in front of the little house and turned off the motor, she sat for a moment and stared at her home as if it were a long-lost friend. For the first time in their acquaintance, Emily had tears in her eyes.

Ransom saw her into the house and tried to get her to go immediately to bed, but it was to no avail. What she wanted most was a hot cup of tea in her own cup, in her own kitchen. So he sat with her, mindless of the length of his lunch hour.

Tam had emerged, presumably from her regular space behind the stove, on hearing them enter. She stood in the hallway and stared at their approaching figures until sure of their identities, then turned her tail on them and strutted back into the kitchen.

Now, as they had their tea, the cat came to Emily and rubbed against her ankles, emitting little whining mews to express her displeasure at having been abandoned. After a few minutes, the cat rolled over on its side, covering Emily's left foot.

Emily sipped her tea in her usual ladylike manner, but Ransom couldn't help thinking that she did it as if it were her first square meal after a long incarceration. Despite the fact that she was obviously tired, Ransom was happy to note that now that she was out of the hospital she no longer looked old in a way that worried him; she looked old in the way all grandmothers do, as if they were born that way.

"It's good to be home," she said, a little catch in her throat. "The house is in desperate need of a good dusting."

"You will not clean house," said Ransom so firmly he almost startled her. "It will be taken care of."

"Very well," she said with a smile. "Now, you didn't finish telling me about your case. Have you been able to form any opinion of who might be involved?"

"I like the reverend as a suspect," he replied, "because I don't like him any other way. And he hasn't been exactly up front with us. But as far as suspects go, it could be any one of them: And so far, we're still only dealing with the boy's small-group members. The second murder points to someone in that group, and I certainly hope that's right because there are about ninety other members."

"Um-hmm," said Emily, sipping her tea.

"I suppose the most puzzling thing about these people is that they stay in the Community at all. None of them seem to be happy. There's Saul Berne—one of the small-group leaders—he's an intense little man who keeps telling us about breaches of authority—the reverend's authority, not his own. He's the type of man you'd expect to jump up in the middle of every business meeting and start spouting *Robert's Rules of Order.*"

"Hmm," said Emily, "his belief in God must be very tenuous. Many people cling to rules when they have nothing else."

"Michael Franklin, by all accounts, was suffering an intense inner struggle. The reverend was trying to get him to believe that God would cure him of his homosexuality."

Emily clucked her tongue. "As much as setting him up for a fall."

Ransom continued, "He was being pressured into a marriage to help him conquer his sexual desires." He smiled at the old woman. "So you were, of course, correct in your choice of scriptures."

Emily gave him a little nod. "And the object of Michael's lack of affection?"

"Barbara Searly. She's something of an unhappy—but not unwilling—sacrificial lamb about to be offered on the altar of Michael's sexuality. She was primed to be part of the cure."

"How unfortunate for her."

"Pamela Frazier and her fiancée, Nicholas Bremmen, seem to be the most well-adjusted of the lot. Pamela has been in the Community for several years. She told us that once the Community was something good, but now she doesn't know. Her confusion is in part due to Nicholas, who hasn't been in the group long enough to go completely blind."

"And Danny Lyman was a troublemaker," said Emily.

"He didn't respect authority," said Ransom with a nod. "I think I know how that figures in with what was going

on with these people, but not how it would get him murdered.''

"That's quite a collection," she said.

"Consider yourself fortunate you don't have to meet
them," said Ransom with an ironic laugh. "It's as I said
before, none of them seem happy, but they all seem devoted
to the Community—with the possible exceptions of Nicholas and Pamela.''

Emily set down her cup and gazed reflectively out the
window.

"Devotion can be a very dangerous thing," she said at
last.

"Hmm?"

"Well, just look at Shakespeare. Troilus and Cressida
were ruined by it, as were Romeo and Juliet."

"But that was devotion to people, Emily. These people
are supposed to be devoted to God.''

Emily continued to gaze out the window, looking as if
she hadn't heard him. After a while, it began to worry Ransom.

"Emily?"

She broke from her reverie and turned back to him. "I'm
sorry, my dear, I was just thinking. It's very important that
you find the motive for these murders right away."

He gave a little laugh and said, "Of course, but..."

"Because, you see, there's no way of knowing."

Ransom shifted in his chair and leaned in toward her. "I
don't understand.''

She shook her head as if she'd lost patience with herself
and said, "I know, my dear, I'm sorry to be such a muddle.
It's been a very trying week. What I mean to say is, I
believe the motive in this case is the most important thing.''

She paused for a moment as if collecting herself, then
raised her eyes to his. "Without knowing the motive for
these killings, there's no way of knowing if there'll be
more."

"How is Miss Emily doing?" asked Gerald.

Ransom dropped into the chair behind his desk.

"She's home, she's happy, and she's in imminent danger of cleaning house from top to bottom."

Gerald laughed, "Sounds like she's back to normal."

"Now, what did you find out?"

Gerald pulled out his small spiral notebook, flipped it open and cleared his throat.

"I found Greg Kirk at his office. He confirmed that their Wednesday night meeting broke up at about nine o'clock. They stood around as usual, talking after the meeting, but all of them were gone by nine-thirty. He's pretty sure of that. And he seemed pretty touchy about answering these kinds of questions."

"Hmm?"

"He's another one like the Berne guy—doesn't think we should be asking questions about a holy man."

Ransom raised an eyebrow. "Did he actually say that?"

"Yup," said Gerald.

"What about Berne's wife?"

Gerald let out a low whistle and rolled his eyes. "I gave up taking notes on her."

"Indeed?"

"The ones I tried are a jumble, and so is she. Berne has the kind of wife you'd expect."

"Apologetic?"

Gerald looked up, surprised. "Yes, how'd you know?"

"You said he had the kind of wife I'd expect."

"Yeah, well...she spent most of the time explaining to me that the 'sisters' don't meet that often, and that they meet just for fellowship and they really don't gossip."

Ransom smiled. "Did she tell you what they don't gossip about?"

"The other members. What they're doing, what they're saying, who they're seeing."

"You sound disgusted, Gerald."

"They talk about everybody who's not there, and excuse it by saying they're just 'sharing things that need prayer.'"

"Ah," said Ransom, swiveling around in his chair, "gossip by any other name would still smell bad."

"Yeah," said Gerald. "Anyway, Berne's wife—her name is Bernice, by the way—and it would be—did at least verify that they had their 'get-together' and then she apologized for not getting home till after eleven."

"Apologized to whom?"

"To me. I think it was the matinee performance of the one she'd given her husband."

"Your impression of her?"

"She's one of those women who apologize for everything. Her hair, her clothes, the weather. Oh, by the way. She said she was sorry she couldn't have been more help."

"Did you get hold of Nicholas Bremmen?"

"Yep. He works at Belden's Camera Shop on south Dearborn. He said he'd be glad to talk to us any time."

"Good," said Ransom, then with a glance at the phone added, "you'd better call Sherry. It looks like we'll be going on overtime again tonight. I have to make a call before we go."

Gerald nodded and headed for his own desk. Ransom pulled out his wallet, removed a business card from it, picked up the receiver, and dialed the number on the card.

As Ransom hung up the phone, his private business satisfactorily concluded, Detective Robinson poked his head in the door. Ransom refrained from grimacing, the reaction he usually had to suppress when confronted with one of his less talented associates. He was sure that Robinson would happily climb the police version of the corporate ladder, rising well beyond his own level of incompetence.

"Ransom?"

"Yes."

"We've got that kid's parents here."

"Which kid's?"

"The Franklin kid's. We tracked down the parents and had them identify the body."

"Very good," said Ransom, as if he were patting a puppy on the head.

"You wanna see 'em?"

"Why not?" said Ransom, spreading his hands and his smile at the same time.

Mr. and Mrs. Franklin were ushered into his office and seated on the wooden chairs in front of his desk. Gerald joined them, notebook in hand.

The Franklins had the shocked look of a middle-aged couple who had managed to get through life without a hint of tragedy. Ransom felt a twinge of pity for them. Although every right-minded person hopes to avoid troubles, Ransom firmly believed that the little bumps along the road of life helped to strengthen a person for the bigger bumps that are bound to come along sooner or later.

"Mr. and Mrs. Franklin, I want you to know I'm very sorry about your son."

"Thank you," said Mrs. Franklin, her ghostlike voice coming out in a puff of breath.

"I want to assure you that I intend to find out who did this to your son and bring him to justice."

Ransom was not sure the Franklins had heard him. The couple stared wide-eyed and unblinking at him, as if his statement rebounded around their heads but didn't go in. Mr. Franklin's hand crept up onto his wife's arm and rested there.

"We don't have much information about Michael, and we need all we can get in order to solve this crime."

The couple continued to stare at him.

"Can you tell us anything about his friends? Acquaintances?"

They stared a minute longer, then Mr. Franklin said in a halting voice that sounded foreign to him, "Well, we really didn't know many of his friends, other than what Michael told us. He never really brought people home."

"Did he ever say anything about girlfriends? Boyfriends?"

"Boyfriends!" said Mr. Franklin, his eye seeming to dilate, "what do you mean, boyfriends?"

Oh, God, thought Ransom, they didn't know. And he

didn't want to be the one to tell them. He proceeded carefully.

"We just have to explore all the possibilities," said Ransom without expression.

"Mikey wasn't queer," said Mr. Franklin with a little laugh. His wife's shock seemed to deepen. She shot a nervous glance at her husband.

Ransom had seen far too much of this sort of thing and what it could lead to to have any patience for it, but his purpose here was not to dispel myths or deepen the parents' grief. His purpose was to solve the murders.

"I'm sorry, Mr. Franklin, I didn't mean to imply anything. We need to ask because your son's body was found behind a certain type of bar."

"A fag bar?" asked the father, wrinkling his nose.

"Yes. However, we know that he wasn't killed there, he was only left there, which could mean absolutely nothing. We just needed to make sure."

"Well," said Mr. Franklin, his face becoming a bit more stern, "you don't have to worry about that. You know now. You go looking someplace else."

"So, Michael did have girlfriends?"

"Yeah, 'course," said Franklin, looking as if he were trying to remember their names, "in high school, like any normal kid."

"Anyone currently?"

"No…not that he told us."

So they didn't know about the impending marriage, either, thought Ransom. Perhaps it wasn't as impending as the reverend would like to think.

Franklin continued, "But the last…" he glanced at his wife, "…what was it honey, a year?"

"Almost," she replied in her hollow voice.

"…the last year, we haven't seen him all that much."

"But you did see him?" asked Ransom.

"Oh, yeah," said Franklin, "now and then."

"Did he ever talk to you about his church?"

"Not much, but it was good to see him going."

"Hmm?"

"We're a churchgoing family." He patted his wife's arm. "Mikey hadn't gone to church for a while. We were just glad he found one he liked."

"Then he did discuss it?"

Mr. Franklin knit his brows over his wide eyes. "Not really. Why? Was there something wrong with it?"

"No," said Ransom, cautiously, "we are just interested because it was an important part of his life at the moment."

"No," said Franklin, shaking his head, "he didn't say much about it, but he liked them enough to move up by them—the other church people. He lived with us at home up till then."

"I missed him," said Mrs. Franklin vacantly. Her husband squeezed her arm.

"He seemed to think the world of that pastor, though. I can't remember his name. But Mikey spoke pretty highly of him." There was a certain bitterness in his tone, as if he felt his son had spoken of the reverend in terms that should be reserved for a father.

"Is there anything else he said that might help? Any problems?"

Mr. Franklin shook his head again. "Mikey was a good kid. Never gave us much trouble."

A few more questions proved to Ransom that the grieving parents had no further pertinent information to offer. He released them with the assurance that he would do everything in his power to find the killer.

Mr. Franklin left the office first, apparently sure that his wife would be right behind him. Mrs. Franklin hesitated in the doorway just long enough to say, in a voice so meek it was barely audible, "If Michael had been gay, we would have accepted him." Then she spirited herself away in her husband's wake.

I'm sure, thought Ransom, shaking his head.

IT WAS AFTER two o'clock when the detectives pulled into a no-parking zone in front of Belden's Camera Shop on the two hundred block of south Dearborn. As they entered the long, narrow store, they were greeted by Morris Belden, a short, plump man who was bald except for two fringes of gray hair that arched like matching footbridges over his ears. His pate was speckled with age spots. He wore wire-rimmed glasses and gray slacks and vest over a tieless white shirt. He looked as if he carried the sum total of the world's knowledge of cameras in his head.

He greeted the detectives with a cheery, lightly accented "Hello," and gave a little salute. He asked if he could help them.

Ransom said, "We're here to see Nicholas Bremmen."

Belden's head rolled to the side in a kind of shoulderless shrug.

"Ah, the detectives," he said. "Terrible business, this. Young man being killed."

"Yes," said Ransom, "only now it's young *men.* Plural."

Belden clucked his tongue, then rolled it around the inside of his cheek.

"Terrible, terrible business. I've never liked the idea of that little group he belongs to."

"Sir?"

"That little church—that bunch of people. I don't like the idea."

"Why is that?"

The rotund man shook his head ruefully, an action that Ransom thought was probably common to him.

"Religion shouldn't float around on its own. It should be rooted in something. Strong, deep roots, like the church. It shouldn't stay off on its own. That's bound to cause trouble. Give me my religion straight, with lots of pomp and pageantry."

"I couldn't agree with you more," said Ransom.

"Nick!" Belden called to the back of the store.

Nicholas Bremmen appeared through the heavy half-length curtains that separated the storeroom in the back from the front of the store.

"Good afternoon," he said to the detectives.

A pair of customers came in through the front door, and Belden said quietly to Nick and the detectives, "You go back to the storeroom and talk, you won't be disturbed there."

"Thank you," said Gerald, speaking for the first time.

The storeroom was also long and narrow, though L-shaped. The walls were lined with gray industrial shelves filled with stacks of boxed camera equipment in perfect order.

Nick led the detectives to the foot of the L, where there was a metal desk and a couple of chairs. He sat at the desk and Ransom took the other chair. Gerald sat on a crate.

"I've received a royal summons," said Nick, the corner of his mouth sloping downward.

"Oh?" said Ransom.

"Yes. Saul called me a little while ago and told me Rev. Sam would like me to stop by on my way home from work."

Ransom didn't look happy. "For what reason?"

"Royalty doesn't need to explain itself."

Ransom sat back in his chair, folded his arms across his chest, and heaved a sigh.

"Mr. Bremmen, may I ask you a personal question?"

"You're the detective," Nick replied with a smile.

"Why are you in this group?"

Nick rested his left arm on the desk and his cheeks turned pinkish. He looked away from the detectives.

"No reason. I was sort of drifting. You know what I mean? I wasn't doing anything. I mean *anything*. Danny— he used to work here—suggested I come to his church with him. And I agreed—I mean, not because I thought God was the answer, but I didn't have anything else to do that day. Don't get me wrong, I believe in God, but not…well, forget it, it's not important."

"That's why you went, why do you stay?"

"Because I met Pam. And I…well, you know."

Ransom nodded.

"But the Community," said Nick, his face darkening, "the Community is...not my style. I've just started talking to Pam about leaving it. But you know, she's been with it for a long time, and it's hard to leave."

"Hard to leave?"

"Not physically," said Nick carefully, "but people only leave 'with the Lord's blessing' after a lot of prayer and guidance from the leadership. You can imagine how often 'God leads' the leadership to willingly release members."

Ransom's expression hardened. No physical restraints, just the assurance that the lowly member will be going against God Himself if he goes against the leadership. The same type of emotional abuse inflicted on battered woman, who stay because they're convinced there's nothing better for them.

Ransom drew a deep breath and said, "Maybe it's time you stepped up your efforts to get Pamela to leave."

Nick considered the detective gravely for a minute, then said, "Because of the murder?"

"I don't know if you've been told about this yet, but Michael Franklin was found dead this morning."

Nick's normally white skin went whiter, then flushed with anger. "No!"

"I'm afraid it's true. He was found in the same condition as Danny Lyman."

"The same condition?" said Nick, his face puckering in confusion.

"Let's just say they were found in a condition that indicates the murders had something to do with the Community."

"I'm a big boy, Mr. Ransom. Unless you can't tell me."

Ransom stared at him for a moment, deciding, then said, "It appears that nails were driven through their hands and feet. But they were killed by blows to the head."

"Jesus," said Nick softly.

"So we need to ask you a few questions."

Nick looked up at him quickly. "You don't think I had anything to do with this?"

"No, we'd just appreciate your help." Ransom realized that by rights Nicholas, merely by being a member of the group, should be considered a suspect. But Ransom also knew that he didn't consider the young man one.

"What can I do to help?" said Nick, his face such a mask of seriousness that his sincerity seemed unquestionable.

Ransom settled back and Gerald prepared to take his obligatory notes.

"You said that Danny brought you to the Community. What was your relationship to him?"

"Relationship? To Danny? We worked together. He was a friend. I liked him."

"That's all there was to it?"

Nick looked quite confused. "Of course it is. What more could there be?"

"Something deeper," said Ransom carefully. "We were wondering if Danny was gay."

"Oh," Nick replied, looking as if he didn't know whether or not he should be offended. "No, no, there was nothing like that. Danny was straight."

Ransom accepted this with a nod and said, "He seems to have been the only unattached male in your little group."

Nick laughed ruefully. "That's not for want of trying."

"Hmm?"

"I mean Rev. Sam's trying. It was a bone of contention between them. Danny had a kind of romantic vision of love and marriage. He thought you fell into it. Rev. Sam believes men should pray for a mate, then sort of choose from the herd and trust God to make your choice right. He called Danny's view 'worldly.'"

"*You* fell in love."

Nick smiled. "I was lucky. It happened before I was told any different."

"So, Danny wasn't gay. Were you aware that Michael Franklin was?"

"Of course, we all were. We prayed for him."

Ransom frowned. He wasn't happy hearing this from someone he considered rather levelheaded.

"You prayed for him to be cured?"

Nick smiled slyly. "No, I just prayed for him. I don't think you can turn straight, do you?"

"Not in the way your reverend means it, no. And I think in your Community you might be a minority. What were *you* praying for?"

Nick sobered. "For help. I thought Michael needed help. Rev. Sam and Saul had him pretty damn confused."

"And Danny?"

"Danny didn't think Michael was confused at all. He thought the whole thing was stupid."

"What whole thing?"

"Michael. He thought Michael should just be what he was."

"Danny sounds like he was very sensible."

"He was," said Nick, his mood clouding, "and very sensitive."

Ransom studied the young man for a moment, then asked, "Can you think of anything else Michael might have said to you on Tuesday night, when he came to ask about Danny? When we first spoke with you and your fiancée, you indicated that he was upset. Did he say anything else about Danny, or his conversation with the reverend?"

Nick thought, his forehead wrinkling in a way that Ransom was sure Pamela found endearing. After a couple of minutes, Nick said. "No...not that I can think of... except..."

"What?"

"Well, he was so upset I told him he should relax. And I said he was lucky we'd have a night off on Wednesday."

"A night off?"

"From working on the church—we were supposed to have a work party that night, before they decided to have a leaders' meeting."

"What did he say?"

"When I said he could get some rest Wednesday night,

he said something like, 'Not for me—there's no rest for the wicked.'"

"Do you know what he meant?"

Nick gave a little laugh. "No, sorry, I don't."

Ransom sighed and said casually, "So, what did you end up doing with your night off?"

Nicholas smiled coyly. The implication of the question was not lost on him. "I spent it with Pam. Just like any other night off. Do you need the details?"

Ransom shook his head, sat up in his chair, and said, "Mr. Bremmen, do you have any idea who killed these two boys?"

"No," said Nick. "I'm not crazy about these people, but it's hard to imagine them killing anybody—unless they prayed them to death."

There had been irony in his tone when he said this, but there was a touch of something else, too. Ransom thought it was just possible that Nick had his doubts. But then, under the circumstances, he'd be a fool not to.

Ransom was not much for giving advice, but he couldn't stop himself at this point.

"Think about what I said, Mr. Bremmen, and maybe have a talk with your fiancée about your future in the Community."

Nicholas seemed to harden with determination.

"We have a date tonight. It'll probably be a good time to bring it up."

ON THEIR WAY back to Albany Park, they made a quick stop at The Golden Slipper. The detectives met with the proprietor, a very congenial, slightly heavyset man named Barry Parks. Parks was quite willing to help, especially since the body had been found behind his establishment. As he put it, "This is a respectable place, where guys expect to be able to come without any trouble. I want this cleared up as much as you do."

Ransom showed Parks pictures of both victims. Parks identified Michael as someone who had frequented the bar regularly, but hadn't been in for several months. He said he had never seen Danny Lyman before.

Back in the car, Gerald asked Ransom why he had bothered with the bar at all, since they knew the murders were connected to the Community.

"Outside verification," said Ransom, beginning to lightly run his fingers on the armrest beside him. "I believed both Draper and Bremmen when they told us that Danny wasn't gay, but I wanted to make sure—not that the word of one bar owner is proof. But I at least wanted to attempt to make sure that you weren't right."

"Me?" said Gerald, so surprised he almost swerved into a parked car.

"Yes—when you said perhaps Danny just hid it better."

"But why does it matter at all?"

"Because I think Emily's right. She suggested that in this case the motive is the most important thing. There is so far nothing connecting these two boys except that they were roommates and in the same church. There has to be something similar that caused their murders. That's what we need to find."

THEIR NEXT STOP was Barbara Searly's attic apartment. They were greeted at the door by Janet Clayton, a brunette in her mid-twenties, who looked as if under normal conditions she would be rather pretty. Today she merely looked somber. News about Michael's death was getting around. Of course, his fiancée lived here, so Ransom quelled the touch of irritation he felt by reminding himself that it would be natural for them to know. Still, he was surprised that everyone in the Community hadn't developed a severe case of paranoia.

"Are you Mrs. Clayton?" asked Ransom.

"Yes?" she said, making it a question.

"We're Detectives Ransom and White. We're here to talk to Barbara Searly."

Janet didn't challenge this, though she looked as if she'd like to. She just stepped aside and said, "Come in."

The front door opened directly into the living room, which was furnished humbly, but in good taste.

William Clayton—Bill to his friends—was seated on the couch, which was covered in a nubby brown fabric that always reminded Ransom of burlap. Bill rose when he saw the strangers.

Janet said, "Bill, this is the police, Detectives Ransom and White."

Bill proved to be a tall, dark-blond man, also in his twenties, with good teeth and a broad smile that he could apparently adjust to the occasion. When he shook the detectives' hands, the smile was welcoming but sober, as if he was glad to meet them but at the same time knew this was a serious situation.

"We came home as soon as we heard," said Bill in answer to an unasked question. "We both work, but we thought Barbara needed someone to be here with her."

Janet nodded, without the smile. "It's a very difficult time for her." There seemed to be something of an accusation in her tone, as if she didn't think the detectives should be bothering them now.

"I understand that," said Ransom. "It must be a difficult time for all of you."

"But it's worse for Barb," said Janet, pressing the point. "After all, Michael was her fiancée. And their relationship..." She stopped herself and looked startled, her pupils widening and contracting in their brown irises, like a cat who's gone through a rapid change of lighting.

Ransom paused, looking from husband to wife, then said, "Could I have a word with the two of you before I speak to Barbara?"

Despite being phrased as a question, there was little doubt in the couple's minds that they had no choice, or that Barbara would be spared in her grief.

"Come in and sit," said Bill.

Gerald was pleased to note that although Bill Clayton always smiled, there was nothing questionable about the practice in his case: It appeared to be genuine.

The detectives came into the room and sat on the couch, Bill taking a seat nearby. Janet hung back for a moment as if she'd like to protest, but then shook her head and joined them.

Ransom crossed his legs and said, "Could you tell us a little about the relationship between Barbara and Michael?"

Bill replied, drawling the words out. "Oh, I don't know that we should do that. I don't like to talk about people."

One corner of Ransom's mouth crept upward.

"I'm afraid that's a disclaimer that simply won't work in this group, Mr. Clayton. Word seems to travel around the membership extremely fast."

Bill's smile became sheepish. With a little laugh, he said, "You got me there!"

"Bill!" said Janet, trying to look cross through loving eyes.

"Sorry, darling, but it's true. Word does travel."

"So," said Ransom, "what can you tell me about Michael and Barbara's relationship?"

Janet Clayton's features took on a sharpness.

"I don't think we should say anything, either," she said.

"But why?" said the detective, giving them his most ingratiating smile. "Was there a problem?"

"No, of course not!" said Janet.

"Now, sweetheart…"

"I mean it, Bill. I don't like this idea of talking to outsiders."

Ransom let that sit for a moment, then said, "Surely you don't want to protect a killer."

Janet looked shocked. "No."

"And you know that two of your members have been killed in the past week. It's entirely possible that someone else will be killed."

Janet glanced at her husband as if this had never occurred to her before, and he might be next. But she still wasn't sure.

"Well, the thing is…outsiders don't always understand the beliefs of the church."

Ransom raised an eyebrow. He had the sneaking suspicion that she had heard this recently, and he didn't think he'd have to look far for the source.

"Is that what Rev. Sam says?"

"It's the truth," she said, startled.

Ransom leaned forward, resting his arms on his knees.

"Mrs. Clayton, it has always been my understanding that Christians are an honest people—which has not exactly been my experience of the people in your Community."

"That's not fair!" Janet protested.

"Perhaps—but what I'm trying to get across to you is that this is hardly the time to develop scruples about passing on information. This is a murder investigation."

There was an affronted stiffness in the air. Bill Clayton still wore his smile—Ransom thought that under different circumstances he might like this young man—but he seemed to be silently deferring to his wife. Janet at first looked insulted, but after giving it some thought, she apparently decided there was some credence to what Ransom had said.

Ransom allowed her to work out her conflicting emotions, then tried again.

"Now, when we came in, you started to say something about their relationship. Will you tell us what it was?"

Janet absently swept her brown hair back behind her ear.

"Well, it's just that I don't think they were very happy. She prayed—we all prayed about it. Barbara was sure in her heart that Michael was her chosen mate, but Michael wasn't."

"What wasn't Michael sure about?"

Janet looked confused and a little wary. "He just wasn't sure."

Ransom gave a slight nod. "We know that Michael was gay."

"Not anymore," said Bill confidently. "We prayed for him."

"I don't know," said Janet. The detectives weren't exactly clear about which part she was referring to, but she clarified. "I don't think he was sure about getting married. He was so wishy-washy about it."

"How did Barbara feel about that?"

"Well…" said Janet slowly, "she said she thought the Lord would work it all out…but…"

"What?"

"I don't know…I don't know that she really believed it. It's a terrible thing to say. I mean, I can't really judge what was going on inside another person. It's just what I thought."

"I appreciate that," said Ransom, in a tone that assured her that he would accept what she said with the proper grain of salt.

"Barbara's been hit pretty hard by this. She's been in the Community longer than…well, about five or six years, I think. And it's been hard on her, because she's had to watch while all her friends got married, and there wasn't anybody for her. There aren't a lot of single men left in the Community."

Fewer every day, thought Ransom.

"I can vouch for that!" said Bill with a chuckle. "Boy, when I joined the church, it was like I was a sitting duck!"

"Oh, Bill!" said Janet, giving him a playful slap on the shoulder, then immediately looking guilty for having experienced pleasure in this situation.

"It's true! There's, like, two or three women for every man in this bunch!"

"Bill!"

"But I was lucky. The Lord led me right to Janet here." He gave her a pat on the hand and she blushed attractively. "We've been married six months next Tuesday."

Yes, thought Ransom, it probably was very hard on Barbara Searly.

"You see, marriage and having a family are big things here. They keep it a secret before you join," said Bill with a conspiratorial wink, "then after you're in, *wham!*"

The couple laughed and Bill squeezed Janet's hand. After a moment, she grew more serious. "Anyhow, it wasn't until

Michael that Barbara had anyone. Special, I mean, because she always has the Community. So whether or not the way was rocky for them, it's been a big blow, losing him.''

"I can imagine,'' said Ransom. It was time to interview Barbara Searly. Ransom reflected irrelevantly that society had not provided a term for a fiancée who had lost her intended. Widow was close, but still inappropriate. However, Ransom was sure that most people who had the misfortune to find themselves in Barbara Searly's position would feel like a widow.

Janet had speculated that she didn't know whether or not it was proper for the detectives to see Barbara alone in her "apartment,'' but Ransom had nixed the idea of having her join them in the living room. Somehow he was certain that their discussion would go much better unchaperoned. Bill offered that it would be all right for the detectives to go upstairs, as long as he and Janet were in the house.

"Oh, by the way,'' said Ransom as he approached the foot of the stairs, "is Miss Searly feeling better?''

Both Bill and Janet looked confused and shocked. With a gruff edge to his usual joviality, Bill said, "Well, her fiancé's been killed, you know. That's not something she'd be feeling better about soon.''

Without changing expression, Ransom replied, "Oh, I'm sorry, I didn't mean that. We ran into her yesterday and she told us that she'd called in sick from work.''

The Claytons seemed to exhale in unison, releasing whatever tension the question had caused.

"Oh, that,'' said Janet, her voice tinged with disdain, which surprised Ransom, given the subject's present circumstance. "Yes, she's better. I suppose.''

"Was she sick on Wednesday night?''

"She was...'' Janet began, sounding exactly as if she were about to break her own rule and say more than she thought should be said to someone outside the Community.

"She wasn't feeling well,'' said Bill, heading her off. He then leaned in a little toward the detectives and added in a tone that implied it was something only the men could understand, "All the upset, you know! Barbara's stomach gets fluttery when she's upset."

If he winks, thought Ransom, I'll strike him.

"The first night off we'd had in quite a while," said Janet, who was unable to keep the tinge of bitterness out of her voice, "and that had to happen. We had to stay home with her all night."

Bill's cheeks colored slightly. He put an arm around his wife's shoulders' and gave her a little shake. "Oh, well, praise the Lord, right, honey?"

"Right."

Ransom and Gerald climbed the shag-carpeted stairs to the second-floor hallway. At the end of the hall there were three steps up to a blue door that had a small metal bracket in which was placed a card with "Barbara Searly" written in black ink, as if it were an apartment door in a large building. The detectives exchanged glances, and Gerald smiled as he stepped up and knocked on the door.

After a moment, the door was opened by Barbara Searly. Her eyes were not as dull now: They were enlivened by red streaks, and were shining with tears. Her hair was not sporting the scarf she'd worn when they'd first met, and it looked somehow damp. Her face was pale and had several pink blotches. Her nose was running, and she held a cheap handkerchief balled up in her right hand. She pressed it to her nose and sniffed.

"Oh, it's you," she said without disappointment. She didn't sound as if she were expecting someone else: She sounded more as if she didn't want anyone she might expect.

"May we speak with you?" said Ransom.

Her shoulders went up and down in a quick, slight movement. She turned and walked up the five stairs on the inside of the door. The detectives followed her, thinking that it hardly constituted a third floor. Gerald closed the door behind them. They found themselves in a small, finished attic, and were surprised that it wasn't the garret that Barbara's earlier reference to it had implied.

The ceilings sloped downward in accordance with the roof, so that the actual walls were only about four feet high, with small latticed windows on each side. There were bright yellow curtains peppered with small white flowers on each window. The severely angled ceilings gave one the feeling of being in a small dome. She had set up a miniature kitchen: There was a tiny refrigerator in one corner, on which had been placed a blue ceramic vase that held some slightly stale cut flowers, and an electric hot plate and toaster oven sat on a small stand to one side. The floor was covered with a large oval multicolored braided rug.

A small drop-leaf table and three chairs were positioned by the front window. Barbara led them there, and they each took a seat. Ransom had the uncomfortable feeling of being at a tea party in a doll's house.

"Miss Searly, let me start by saying that I'm terribly sorry for your loss."

"Thank you," she replied, her voice thin and colorless.

"We'll do everything we can to find the killer."

She pressed the handkerchief to her nose again, but said nothing.

"Do you think you can help us?"

She sniffed and said, "It doesn't matter anymore."

"I'm sorry, what doesn't matter?"

"Any of it," she said, with an awkward wave of her hand. Tears rolled over her lower lashes and fell in large drops, staining her tan blouse. "Rev. Sam tells me that it's all God's will, and that we can't know why the Lord has allowed this to happen, and we can only believe that He has a purpose in all this, a purpose we can't see right now, but we'll probably be able to see it some time in the future. But we may never know. We may have to wait till the next life." She leaned forward, resting her elbows on the table and jabbed her right fist into her forehead. Her tears dropped onto the table in silent splashes.

"I'm sorry, I'm sorry," she said through choked sobs.

"Don't be," said Ransom.

"It's just it's been such a long time. And it's all been so hard."

Gerald rested the notebook and pencil in his lap, and sat staring at the polished surface of the table. Ransom's eyes never left Barbara. She was trembling, but not simply from crying. Something stronger and more deep-seated seemed to be shaking her at the core.

"With Michael...it was never right, from the beginning. But I thought he was the one the Lord had chosen for me."

"The Lord, or Reverend Draper?" said Ransom.

"The Lord," she replied with an edge. "But it was never right. At first I thought it was him, then I thought it was me."

"You thought what was you?"

She looked up at him and said, "That was wrong...that was making it so hard. But it wasn't. Now Rev. Sam tells me it was the Lord. All of this happened because of Him."

"Miss Searly," said Ransom, trying to modulate his voice to be as calming as possible, "two young men are dead, and there are some things we need to know that I think you can help us with. I have a feeling that Michael is somehow the center of what's happening here, but I don't know how. Can you help us? Can you answer a few questions?"

She unclenched her fist and dropped her hand onto the table. Her pale cheeks were a little more blotched and streaked with tears. She swallowed hard a couple of times, then nodded.

"Tell us about Danny and Michael."

"Michael..." she said, turning her face to the window "...Michael started coming to the meetings a little over a year ago. I don't know...I don't remember how he knew about us. I thought he was...not handsome, but he was cute. And he was shy. And nervous. He made his commitment to the Community a couple of months later."

"His commitment?"

"People come here to the meetings. Strangers. Sometimes they come a few times and realize it's not for them.

Sometimes they realize they belong here and then they make a commitment to God and the Community at one of the meetings.''

"Publicly."

She nodded her head. "At one of the meetings. And Rev. Sam prays over them, and asks God to solidify their commitment.''

Ransom's eyes narrowed. "And you got involved with him.''

"I felt drawn to him. He was funny and sweet to me. At first. And Rev. Sam and Saul, they noticed. And Saul told me that the leaders had prayed about it, and they thought the Lord was drawing me and Michael together. But he told me Michael had special problems, and I needed to be patient and understanding and trust in the Lord.''

"Michael was gay."

Barbara turned her streaming eyes to Ransom. "But he was praying for release. And with God, all things are possible.''

Ransom found himself once again suppressing a grimace. He thought it best to ask another question quickly.

"What if it wasn't God's will for him to change?''

"How could it not be?" said Barbara, but her expression was vacant and she seemed to be responding by rote.

Ransom decided to try a different approach.

"Tell me, how does Danny enter into this?''

Barbara's head lolled backward and she closed her eyes, squeezing a couple of more tears from them.

"For a while I blamed Danny, but Rev. Sam says it was all God's plan, and who are we to question God?''

"Miss Searly," said Ransom, trying to remain patient, "Barbara, what happened with Danny and Michael?''

"The leadership felt that prayer wasn't all that Michael should do for himself. That he should take practical steps as well. So he did things like—he did a lot of work on our new home.''

"Your home?''

"Our church. The men are renovating the insides. Mi-

chael was never excused from the work parties, and he was
asked to help a lot when one of the other brothers was
working on it on their own. It was man-type work, and it
was important for him to do.''

''And Danny?''

''Michael wanted to move away from home—his parents. And Rev. Sam was all for it. He thinks everybody in
the Community should live in the neighborhood. So we can
be close. So we can be a family. So they asked Danny to
let Michael move in.''

''Why Danny?''

Barbara's gaze wandered back out the window.

''Because he's the one the Lord chose.''

Ransom heaved an exasperated sigh. He decided to re-
phrase the question in her terms.

''Do you have any idea why the Lord chose Danny?
Why not someone like Nicholas Bremmen?''

''Nicholas and Pamela were already going strong, and it
looked like it wouldn't be long till they got engaged.''

So the Lord was being very practical, thought Ransom.

Barbara choked back a sob. ''Danny was very straight—
I mean, like they used to say, 'a straight arrow,' very much
a man. And he wasn't easy to influence. They thought he
would serve as a positive role model in Michael's life.''
She once again pressed her balled-up fist against her forehead, her voice taking on a whining note. ''Some model!''

''You mean all of the prayer, and manly work, and mas-
culine example didn't change Michael?'' said Ransom, unable to hide his disgust at the whole procedure.

''It was Danny's fault,'' she said loudly, turning back to
Ransom. ''All he did was confuse Michael!''

''How?''

''By telling him he should be what he was.''

Ransom's previous high opinion of Danny rose a few
more notches.

Barbara added, ''He told Michael if God had made him
gay, it was silly to try to change. He told him that the Lord
loves gay people, too. But how could He?''

She was crying more freely now. Ransom was surprised to find himself feeling a little sorry for her. She was, like so many people, caught up in a morass of beliefs—both her own and those imposed upon her—that didn't mesh with her own reality.

"Miss Searly, did you see Michael Wednesday night?"

She shook her head. "No, I thought I might when they called off the work party, and I asked him, but he said he had to work."

"At the store?"

"Probably. I don't know. I didn't ask. Michael always told me he didn't like me to hound him. I spent the evening with the Claytons."

"And you never left the house?"

She shook her head. There was a long silence while tears ran down her face and neck. Her collar had uneven damp stains. After a couple of minutes, she pressed the handkerchief to her eyes and said, "I don't blame Danny anymore, really. Or Michael, either. It wasn't his fault. Even *he* couldn't know."

"Know what?" said Ransom.

"It was all in God's plan...it was God's plan...it was God's plan..." she repeated as she turned her face back to the window.

"THAT WAS INFORMATIVE," said Ransom as they left the Claytons' house.

"I don't see that we know anything we didn't know before."

"Ah, but we do, my dear Gerald. We know what Danny's latest cause was: Michael. I would be willing to bet that was what he went to talk to the reverend about."

"So?"

"So, indeed," said Ransom.

"So what if he did?"

"I knew what you meant, Gerald, and I fully agree. If he did go to talk to Draper about the pressure being brought to bear on Michael to marry—and to straighten out—what difference would that make?''

''I don't see how that would get him killed.''

''Neither do I.''

Ransom patted the pocket in which his cigars were normally kept. When he realized there were none there, he had the guilty thought that now that Emily was out of the hospital, he had no reason to continue his abstinence—other than his health and the fact that in or out of the hospital, Emily greatly disapproved of his habit. He dismissed this internal debate with a shake of his head, and turned to Gerald.

''Who's left on the small-group list?''

Gerald withdrew the paper from his pocket and consulted it.

''The Beckmans, who are out of town, and Sarah Bennett, Pam Frazier's roommate.''

''We might as well tackle Miss Bennett,'' said Ransom, heading for her apartment building.

His attitude would have been much less cavalier had he known the piece of the puzzle she held.

THIRTEEN

As THE DETECTIVES headed for the apartment shared by Pamela Frazier and Sarah Bennett, Nicholas was arriving for his command performance at the reverend's house. He rang the bell and waited.

The door was opened by Saul, who looked as if the day had not worn well on him since Ransom's visit. His unruly hair seemed to have curled out a couple of inches, and his eyes bugged behind his glasses. Small beads of sweat had formed on his forehead and hung there like condensation on a rusty pipe.

"Saul," said Nick, "I didn't expect to see you."

"We both want to see you," said the little leader as he ushered Nick into the living room.

Somewhere in the back of Nick's mind was a half-remembered rhyme about a spider and a fly. He thought that if he could recall the whole verse at this moment, he wouldn't find it comforting. Rev. Sam was waiting for them in his usual chair by the couch. He didn't rise when they entered, but motioned for Nick to sit on the couch. Saul pulled a chair up to the opposite end of the couch, which put Nick at the disadvantage of having to turn back and forth to speak to the two of them.

"Thank you for coming, Nicholas," said Rev. Sam benevolently.

"Why did you want to see me?" asked Nick, his voice rather hard.

Rev. Sam smiled in a way that, given the circumstances of the last few days, Nick found almost chilling. "We were just wondering how you've been doing."

"How *I've* been doing?" said Nick, knitting his eyebrows.

Rev. Sam inclined his head. "I'm afraid I've been a little out of touch lately. Of course, I've been keeping up on things through the small-group leaders, but that's not the same thing. I feel that it's time we get back to the basics in the Community, and I start trying to be more in touch with all our brothers and sisters."

Nick didn't move, and it was only with an effort that he kept the skepticism out of his voice when he said, "So you're going to be doing this with everyone?"

There was the slightest hesitation before he replied, "Eventually. I feel, especially with all the unpleasantness that has come our way recently, that the Lord has been showing me that I simply haven't been the shepherd that I should be. A shepherd doesn't delegate his flock, a good shepherd keeps his own eye on them."

Several things went through Nick's mind in rapid succession: The first was that he was right to feel paranoid; the second was that he was going to have to be firmer than he originally intended tonight when he spoke to Pam about leaving the Community; the third and most unsettling was that there was something going on here, and he didn't know what it was. He knew the reverend would get around to it eventually. However, his immediate problem was that the reverend had stopped speaking, and seemed to be waiting for some kind of response.

"I wouldn't say that," said Nick, running a hand over his hair.

"But it's true, it's true," said the reverend, raising his palms in protest, "that's what the Lord's been telling me, and I can't disagree with Him."

Rev. Sam and Saul chuckled at this. Nick smiled unwillingly and glanced at Saul, then turned back to the reverend.

"I can't ignore the conviction of the Lord," said Rev. Sam. "Anyway, that's the reason I've asked you to stop by. I thought we might as well start with you."

"I'm to be the first?" said Nick. "I suppose I should feel honored."

There was the faintest flicker beneath Rev. Sam's right eye, as if under ordinary conditions he would not have let anything approaching insubordination pass by unchecked. But he said nothing directly in the way of rebuke.

"I know, I know," he said, his smile still in place and his tone self-effacing, "you are probably skeptical and have every right to be."

Nick looked down at the floor. He was uncomfortable that the reverend had come so close to reading his mind.

"And I'll admit," he continued, "that I haven't been hearing the Lord clearly lately. Of course, that isn't His fault. The Lord always speaks clearly, but sometimes even I don't listen."

Nick shuffled his feet. The reverend had stopped again, and some form of rebuttal seemed to be called for. But Nick was damned if he'd disagree with him on this point, and he couldn't think of any other appropriate response. He was more curious than ever about the object of this meeting.

Saul's eyebrows sloped inward, almost meeting in the middle. He was evidently displeased with Nick's silence.

"You're being too hard on yourself, Sam," Saul interjected, still looking at Nick.

"No, no," said Rev. Sam, palms up again, "I'm willing to admit when I've been wrong. And it would be hard for me to deny, the way things have been going. The Lord has been showing me I had to take full responsibility."

"For what?" said Nick despite himself.

"For our recent deaths. I blame myself. I blame myself most severely."

Nick experienced a sudden and intense surge of revulsion at the possibility that the reverend was about to turn the tragic death of two of his friends into a simple lesson to be learned on the road to the Lord—as if these two violent acts could be reduced to harmless Sunday school anecdotes. It was at this moment, after all that had gone before, their scrutiny of his relationship with Pamela and the recent tragedies, that Nicholas realized something for the first time: He didn't like the reverend.

"How are you responsible?" said Nick, his face hardening.

"I should have kept a firmer hand on things."

"You could hardly do that," said Nick, trying to keep the irony out of his voice.

Rev. Sam decided to let that pass, too. "If I'd kept a firmer hand on things, if I'd kept more in touch and informed, perhaps their deaths could have been avoided."

"How?" said Nick, dreading this more every minute.

"By intervening before it came to this point."

"I don't understand."

"Let me see if I can explain it to you," said the reverend, trying to be inoffensive while at the same time implying that Nick might be a bit slow. "If I'd kept a closer eye on Danny and Michael, I might have seen them going wrong and could have done something to stop it. I have to admit that I did see Michael backsliding, and Saul did keep me on top of it, but I can't help feeling that if I'd been more directly involved, I could have helped turn him around in time."

Now Nick was sure: He hated this. In a brave attempt to hold his temper, he said, "Do you mean you think Michael was killed because he was backsliding?"

Rev. Sam shrugged. "Perhaps. Indirectly."

"What makes you think he was backsliding?"

Saul said, "It's obvious. He was found outside a gay bar."

Nick turned to him at the sound of his voice, but Nick's mind silently repeated the details of the murders that the detectives had related to him. He turned away without saying anything.

"But Danny is more of a puzzle. I knew he was headstrong, but I didn't stay close enough to the situation to see that there was something terribly wrong."

The reverend paused for a moment. This time he didn't seem to be waiting for a reply. After a moment, he said matter-of-factly, "I suppose you could help me understand where I went wrong with Danny."

Nick looked up from the floor, his expression one of confusion. "Me? How?"

"Well, I understand that Michael came to see you Tuesday night, about Danny."

So we've come to it at last, thought Nick with disgust. His eyes narrowed and he said, "Yes?"

"I was just wondering if he'd shared anything with you that would shed a little light on what was going on with Danny."

Nick straightened himself in his seat and said evenly, "The only thing he said was that he was worried about Danny being gone...and he didn't think you were. Either of you." He added this last with a glance at Saul.

"He didn't say anything else?"

"No..." said Nick slowly.

The reverend cleared his throat and said, "So you didn't say anything more to the police?"

Nick tried to remember exactly what he *had* said to the police, and drew one of the infuriating blanks that sometimes happens when under pressure. He replied with barely suppressed anger, "There was nothing more to tell. What's this all about?"

"Nick!" said Saul sternly. "It is only what Rev. Sam told you. He's trying to be more informed about the brothers and sisters."

Nick turned back to the reverend.

"And I'm to be the informant?"

The reverend's smile became more pronounced, and his face glazed over as if frosting it into place. His eyes were hard and staring.

"No, Nicholas, I'm not looking for you to be an informant. I am just concerned about the serious matters that have come into this Community. I would think you would understand that."

"I do," said Nick with a noticeable lack of conviction.

The reverend's torso inclined slightly toward him. Nick found the action unsettling, as it didn't seem to require any movement.

"I don't know that you do. I'm just as concerned about you as I was about Danny and Michael."

"About me?" said Nick, a pang of doubt serving as evidence that he feared he may have been mistaken about the real purpose of this meeting. "Why?"

"The attitude I've been observing in you lately—this evening, your tone of voice—tells me that you are not as mature in the Lord as we may have thought."

Nick felt his cheeks burn with anger. "That's not true. And it's not for you to say! You don't know my heart."

"I am your spiritual leader," said Rev. Sam, unruffled. "It is my responsibility to make these assessments."

"Your responsibility." Nick spat the words back at him.

"You will control yourself," said the reverend evenly. He paused for effect, staring at Nick. Energy crackled among the men, forming a triangle of tension.

"I realize," the reverend continued, "that you are relatively new to the Lord..."

"That's not true," said Nick warmly, "I'm just relatively new to this Community."

Rev. Sam closed his eyes for a moment, letting Nick know that his patience was being tried, and that he needed to draw strength from the Lord. As he opened his eyes, he continued:

"I realize you are relatively new to a deep and abiding commitment to the Lord. And it takes time to grow and mature. We have been patient with you..." he raised a palm to stop the protest that Nick moved to offer "...as we would be with any babe in the Lord. If it were merely a matter of your spiritual growth, that wouldn't be a problem. But your development—or your immaturity in the Lord—affects others."

Nick would have chosen to remain silent, forcing the reverend into an unprompted monologue that might make what he was saying sound faintly ridiculous. But his curiosity and his anger were beginning to get the best of him.

"How?" he asked.

"There has, for some time, been a sort of understanding between you and Pamela Frazier."

This is it, Nick said to himself, I haven't given him the respect he thinks he deserves, and now he intends to use Pam to hurt me.

"Ordinarily we would not have allowed such a relationship to develop with someone so new...to the Community. But we thought that with a lot of prayer and a lot of guidance, it would be all right. It looks like this was another area where we were wrong."

"What are you talking about?" said Nick, his anger growing.

"Well, for one, from my own observation, and that of others, your relationship is more physical than it should be."

"What?" said Nick sharply. "I've done little more than put my arm around her waist and kiss her!"

"Nicholas!" Saul interjected loudly. "Mind your tone! You are talking to your leader!"

"Hmph!" said Nicholas.

"That may seem innocent, Nick," said the reverend as if there'd been no interruption, "but we are more concerned with where it may lead. Just as we're concerned that intimate dinners held alone in her apartment may be innocent, but can lead to other things."

"So, Sarah *has* been getting word around," said Nick, half under his breath.

Rev. Sam continued with relentless serenity, "Pamela is a good sister in the Lord, and has been with us for many years, but even the best of us can be swayed."

Nick summoned what little remained of his patience and said, "What are you saying?"

"Just this: that I think the two of you should slow down. Take some time to reflect and pray...perhaps not see each other for a while."

"You're out of your mind!"

"Nick!" said Saul, but Nick paid him no attention: He was on his feet and confronting the seated reverend.

"If you think that Pam and I are going to stop seeing each other because you say so, you're out of your mind! I don't know what the hell is going on here, or what you're trying to do, but I can tell you one thing: Not only am I going to go on seeing Pam, I'm going to do everything I can to get her out of this nutty group! And I don't just mean out of your church, I mean out of the whole damn neighborhood!"

Rev. Sam stared up at him, unmoved. "Pamela is strong in the Lord and knows her commitment. I have not been trying to upset you or hurt you..."

Nick once again had a sudden twinge that the reverend somehow knew what he was thinking: Only now he realized it was a talent—a talent for making accurate stabs in the not so dark.

"...I am merely trying to follow the leading of the Lord."

Nick stood his ground, looking down at the reverend, then with quiet rage said, "The hell you are."

"Nicholas!" said Saul. "You're way out of line!"

The reverend shook his head sadly, though his smile remained, and said like a disappointed parent, "Surely I've gone very wrong. The lack of respect I've been shown lately is very disheartening."

"Oh, please..." said Nick disgustedly.

Rev. Sam looked up. "Michael was going down the wrong road and was very disobedient. Look what happened to him."

Nick stepped back and paused. "Is that supposed to be some sort of threat?"

For the first time, the reverend looked somewhat confused. "Of course not, what are you talking about?"

"And how in the hell could Michael have been disobedient? He was the meekest person I've ever known."

Regaining himself, the reverend shrugged and said, "He called Danny's mother and brought the police into this Community, despite the fact that I told him there was nothing to worry about."

"Well, you were wrong about that, weren't you!" said Nick, his anger long since having gotten the better of him. "Danny was dead, so there was something to worry about! And I'll tell you something else you were wrong about: I don't believe Michael was 'backsliding' with anyone—he was just confused and unhappy, and you helped make him that way! And at his worst, he wasn't disobedient to you! He didn't call Danny's mother, *I* did!"

With this he stormed out of the house.

Saul let out a little gasp.

The reverend was no longer smiling.

WHILE NICHOLAS flared at his respective leaders, a much calmer meeting was taking place in the apartment of Pamela Frazier and Sarah Bennett. Sarah had buzzed the detectives into the stairwell, and stood waiting in the doorway of the second-floor apartment, the door opened about eleven inches, her slender body wedged into the space.

She wore a yellow knee-length dress, crimped around the waist by a two-inch-wide tan belt with a large gold buckle. From her stance it was evident that she was prepared to repel all boarders: or at least resist all boarders. Her bony fingers curled around the edge of the door, looking as if she could either swing the door open or slam it shut.

Ransom noticed as they reached her that her eyes held a mixture of fear and what he suspected was low cunning. She looked as if she were eager to see Ransom, and disappointed when she noticed he wasn't alone.

"You're the police, you say?"

"Yes. I'm Detective Ransom, this is Detective White."

She hesitated a moment and said, "I know Saul said you'd be talking to all of us...but...do you have any identification?"

Both the detectives pulled out their badges and showed them to her. She seemed to take an inordinate amount of time over them, without appearing to take them in. She stood staring at the badges until Ransom was fed up enough to slip his back in his pocket without a word. Gerald followed suit.

"May we come in?" said Ransom.

Sarah paused demurely, in a way Ransom suspected she'd picked up from watching film versions of Tennessee Williams plays.

"I don't know," she said, the door wavering in her hand, "Pam's not home yet, so I'm alone here."

Ransom hoped he hadn't noticed a coquettish note in her voice.

"I assure you you'll be perfectly safe."

Sarah glanced back into the apartment and then pushed the door open.

"I suppose it'll be all right," she said, leading them down the long hall and into the living room.

The room was decorated nicely, which Ransom thought he could attribute to Pamela's influence. The furniture didn't exactly match, but it was close enough to pass casual inspection. The colors were soft, the plush carpet old but clean, and the walls were adorned with framed watercolors of southwestern scenes.

There were two good-sized windows overlooking the street, and one on the north wall through which the church was visible. The church immediately caught Ransom's attention. It was clearly not as old as the rest of the buildings on the street, but by no means new. It was as if it had been built as an afterthought once the neighborhood was established, then forgotten as an idea that was better left unmentioned. Until, of course, the Community had purchased it.

As the detectives took seats at opposite ends of the maple coffee table, Sarah went around the room and systematically turned on all the lights. After she had worked the switches on the two floor lamps, the desk lamp, and a small accent lamp that was perched on the wide windowsill, she moved a straight-backed chair a few feet away from Ransom and sat back, trapping her long, straight hair between her back and the chair's. She placed her knees firmly together. Gerald did his best not to smirk.

"You know why we're here, of course?"

"Yes."

"You know that we're investigating the death of Danny Lyman, and…did you know that Michael Franklin has been killed?"

"Yes, praise the Lord."

Her face was impassive, giving the detectives no clue as to the meaning of this statement.

"I beg your pardon?" said Ransom.

"'In all things give praise,'" she replied, folding her hands in her lap. "It's in the Bible. We're supposed to praise the Lord for all things, good or bad—because all things are working together in God's plan."

Ransom had the sneaking suspicion that he was meant to be dazzled by her knowledge. He chose to remain unbeguiled.

"Do you mean that you weren't affected at all by these murders?"

"Oh, yes, I was simply devastated by Danny's death." Her right hand fluttered to her breast, and her face became sad.

"Why by Danny's in particular?" asked Ransom, raising an eyebrow.

"He was very special to me."

"How so?"

"Well…" She glanced at Gerald and noticed for the first time that he was taking notes, then turned back to Ransom. "Well, this isn't really for publication…"

"Oh?"

She leaned toward him, releasing her hair from its imprisonment. "Yes, because nobody knows about it. Not even the leadership." She glanced Gerald's way again, quickly.

"Gerald," said Ransom, "there's no need for notes on this part."

"Sorry," said Gerald, closing the notebook with a smile in Ransom's direction that was missed by Sarah.

"There, now. You were saying?"

She cleared her throat with a little soprano gurgle and said, "Well, I haven't told anyone about this, not even Pamela...but Danny and I were going to be married."

It took an effort, but Ransom managed to hide his surprise. Gerald's features seemed to come a little closer together.

"You were?" said Ransom.

Sarah nodded.

"The two of you were keeping it a secret?"

"*I* was."

"*You* were? Wasn't Danny? Did he tell someone about it?"

"Oh, he didn't know."

"He didn't know..." said Ransom, with a glance at Gerald, "...forgive me, Miss Bennett, but I don't see how it's possible for you to be engaged without your fiancé knowing."

"I didn't say we were engaged."

"You weren't engaged," said Ransom in the tone he usually reserved for mental defectives, "but you were going to be married."

She sat back and smiled, her face taking on a childlike innocence that Ransom was sure she had practiced in front of a mirror for just such an occasion. "You see, the Lord showed it to me in a dream. He showed me that Danny was the one for me. And I didn't tell anybody about it. I was cherishing it in my heart."

Ransom paused while he mentally rolled his eyes, then said, "And you didn't tell Danny about this?"

"Oh, no! But I watched him. He didn't show any sign of knowing yet on his own. So I just watched and prayed that the Lord would reveal it to him."

Ransom wondered how many of the single "sisters" had prayed the same prayers.

"Miss Bennett, have you ever had similar dreams about any of the other single men in the Community?"

"No…" she said uncertainly, her cheeks turning pink, "…not really."

"How about Michael? You were here when Michael joined the Community, weren't you?"

"Yes…but I knew Michael wasn't for me," she said quickly.

"Ah! You knew about Michael's 'problem'?"

"Of course, we all did. We prayed for him together."

"What can you tell us about Danny's relationship with Michael?"

"Well…they were very close…" she replied in a tone that reflected more than a little jealousy, "but that would have ended soon enough. Soon as Michael and Barbara finally got married."

It wouldn't be soon enough for you, thought Ransom.

"Miss Bennett, we're looking into the movements of everyone in your small group on Wednesday night. Can you tell us where you were?"

Sarah's eyes widened. Ransom thought this was perhaps the first honest reaction he'd seen from her.

"You can't suspect me!"

"No. We're merely following routine. We believe that Michael was killed on Wednesday night, so it's only natural that we'd be interested in where all his friends were at the time."

"Friends?" she said with disdain.

"His small group," Ransom amended.

"I don't believe anyone in our Community had anything to do with this."

"Then you have nothing to fear."

"I have nothing to fear but fear itself," she said with an earnestness that convinced Ransom she thought she was quoting from the Bible.

"So, Wednesday evening?"

Sarah sighed. "I suppose you know we have a regular meeting on Wednesday nights."

"Yes...?"

"Well, the men scheduled a work party for Wednesday night, and so the sisters were going to get together and do something. We hadn't decided what yet. But early this week the work party was canceled, 'cause Rev. Sam said the Lord put it on his heart to have a leaders' meeting instead."

She said this last as if she might have resented the Lord's interference.

"And that threw everything into a tizzy—and it didn't need to, because *I* felt that we sisters should just go ahead and have our get-together and let the men fend for themselves." She sighed again. "But Nicholas and Pamela wanted to use the opportunity to be alone together, as if they needed any more. And so did the Claytons, and Barbara was hoping that Michael would want to do something, so everybody went their separate ways."

"And you?"

Sarah looked acutely embarrassed, and more than a little angry.

"So I was left alone. As usual. I just sat here and read my Bible, 'cause I think you should do all you can to learn about the Lord. But it was really frustrating, especially since they changed their minds anyway."

Ransom narrowed his eyes and said, "What do you mean?"

"Because after all our plans were changed back and forth, they ended up doing it anyway."

"I'm sorry," said Ransom, leaning forward, "they ended up doing *what* anyway?"

"Having their work party," she said, her voice taking on a slight whine. "I figured, as usual, I was left out. Nobody told me the plans changed again. And I was..." her lower lip trembled "...I was kinda hurt. And I didn't say anything about it, 'cause I didn't want them to know. But I told the Lord."

"Miss Bennett, are you telling me that someone *did* work in the church Wednesday night?"

"Yes."

"How do you know?"

"I can hear them when they work. I could hear them hammering. The church is just next door. They were doing it awfully late, too."

"What time?"

"About ten-thirty."

Ransom paused for a moment, his mind racing. "You said you could hear *them*. Did you hear several people hammering?"

"Well…" She thought for a moment, then said, "…not really, but that doesn't mean anything."

Ransom knit his eyebrows. "What do you mean?"

"With all the changes, and everybody making different plans, they probably couldn't get everyone to come."

No, thought Ransom, it was probably a party for two.

AFTER LEAVING SARAH Bennett, Ransom and Gerald went next door for their first survey of the outside of the church, which was bordered on one side by the apartment building, and on the other by the river. It was a small, round building with a square entryway, which made it look not unlike a concrete igloo. There were the obligatory stained-glass windows at regular intervals. However, these did not bear the usual religious pictures. Instead they were made up of random geometric forms.

The detectives peered through one of the windows, and received a multicolored view of the sanctuary. Then they wandered around to the back of the church, where they found a small cement staircase leading down to a plain door with a small window.

"The famous basement," said Gerald.

They went down the steps and looked in. They saw, framed through the window, a basement in the process of having its floor raised. Rows of joist were already in place, with the as yet unused two-by-six planks stacked in neat piles along the south wall. Thick sheets of wood leaned against the opposite wall. Those that were already used spread out from a staircase that apparently led up to the sanctuary, making it look as if the floor was in the process of creeping along the parallel lines of joist toward the door through which the detectives peered. Boxes of various kinds of smaller building supplies were scattered here and there over the finished part of the floor, and there appeared to be some materials shoved way back under it. The overall effect of the room as night fell was one of approaching gloom.

Ranson stepped back from the window and fell into silent contemplation. Gerald seemed to speak for both of them when he said:

"Empty churches give me the creeps."

"Obviously childhood trauma," said Ransom.

Gerald smiled and fell silent himself while the wheels and gears of Ransom's mind worked. After a few minutes he finally became impatient and said, "What next, Jer?"

Ransom folded his arms and tapped an index finger beneath his nose. After another moment's silence, he said, "I think it's time we had a little talk with the reverend...on our own ground."

SAUL WAS STILL with the reverend when the detectives returned. Ransom respectfully requested that the reverend accompany them to area headquarters. It was put in the form of a request, as he did not yet have any evidence on which to arrest him. It was Ransom's fervent hope that once out of his own lair, the clergyman could be pressed into a more forthright conversation.

Reverend Draper agreed to accompany them with the carefully measured reluctance of a saint enjoying his martyrdom. As the detectives led Draper to their car, Saul protested the action in terms that Ransom would have thought would be reserved for the arrest of Christ in the Garden of Gethsemane. Ransom smiled to himself at the thought. Emily would have been proud of him for calling this reference to mind.

FOURTEEN

NICK WAS STILL fuming two hours after his meeting with what, in his mind, he already referred to as his ex-leaders. He had dressed in navy blue slacks, light blue shirt, and topped it off with a rag-knit sweater in a shade of blue somewhere between the other two. Pam liked him in blue. She especially liked him in what she called his "elegant-casual" attire, in which she said he looked more natural than in a suit. He appraised himself in the mirror of his too-small bathroom, and ran a comb through his hair, though it didn't need it.

Pam had called him just a few minutes ago, her soft, warm voice going a fair way in calming him down. She had just called to say she was running a little late and would be there in about twenty minutes. He told her that was fine, and when he hung up there was a smile on his face.

Nick rested his palms on the sides of the sink and looked at himself in the mirror. He wondered if Pam would be hard to deal with: She was not difficult on any subject other than the Community, and she wasn't exactly responsible for that. The problem, he knew, was internal. She had been with the Community so long that the ties that bound her to it were as strong as a child's to a dysfunctional family. He knew that if he were to cut them, it would have to be as gently as possible.

He shook his head at his reflection. He couldn't be gentle. The ties had to be cut. If Pam couldn't understand the subtler reasons for their need to secede from the union—namely the increasingly overbearing leadership that to his mind was growing out of control, as evidenced by the meeting he'd had tonight—surely she would see that these murders were reason enough to get out while they could.

But Nick experienced some doubt. Pam had been in the Community for a long time and the emotional roots had grown very deep. But he had to get her out. The alternatives were unacceptable. If they stayed with the Community one of two things would happen: Either they would have to separate, at least for a time, as "suggested" by the reverend, or they would defiantly stay together and face the subtle ostracism of their fellow members. There would be nothing overt: no silent treatment or anything of that nature. Just the careful looks and reticence meant to tell them that they were not "walking in the Lord." The worst of it was that most of the pressure would be brought to bear on Pam, being longer with the group. Nick was no longer smiling. Whichever way it went, Pam would be hurt.

The doorbell rang. She was a little early. Nick went to the door of his apartment and pressed the white button that released the lock on the door in the lobby. He opened his door and called down, "Hi, honey."

He returned to the bathroom, removed the towel from the doorknob where he'd left it while he dressed, folded it, and hung it on the towel rack. He switched off the light and went out into the living room. He was surprised to find that Pam hadn't reached the apartment. He went back to the hallway and called "Pam?" but there was no answer and no sound of footsteps. Nick's forehead wrinkled for a moment, then he shrugged and went back into his apartment, closing the door behind him.

He had barely stepped into the room when it happened: Something extremely hard came down on the back of his head with a loud crack.

REVEREND SAMUEL DRAPER sat at the bare table in the interrogation room, his large hands folded with Sunday school precision and resting on the table. He had refused the offer of a cup of coffee or glass of water. Ransom sat directly across from him, drumming his fingers on the table, which Gerald took as a bad sign. Gerald sat in a chair pressed into one corner of the room, his legs crossed and his notebook propped on his knee. They hadn't been there all that long, but Ransom already suspected that they weren't going to get much further. He wished he had a cigar.

"Mr. Draper, we have discussed the murders of these two boys with you on several occasions now. I can't say that I think you understand the seriousness of this situation."

"Murder is a terrible thing," Draper droned, "but I don't know anything about it."

Ransom stared at him for a couple of minutes, long enough to unnerve the most unwilling suspect, but it had no visible effect on the reverend.

"Tell me, after your meeting on Wednesday night, did you happen to stop by your church to do a little work on the basement?"

The reverend looked affronted. "No, I did not. I went home, as I told you."

"There were about two hours before your wife returned home. Two hours unaccounted for. Two hours for which you have no alibi."

The reverend's thumbs pressed against one another. "I have accounted for them. I told you what I did."

"You have no one who can corroborate your story."

"I don't need anyone to. I don't lie. I'm a man of God. My word is enough."

"Not in a court of law," said Ransom with a smile. "Now, do you know if any of the men in your Community went to the church Wednesday night?"

"No," said Draper, knitting his brow, "not that I know of. Why do you ask? What does our renovation have to do with it?"

"Someone was heard hammering there late Wednesday night."

Draper shrugged. "I suppose anyone could have stopped by to work. Our men are very dedicated."

Ransom paused, then said, "I don't think that's the kind of work that was being done."

This seemed to stop the reverend. His eyebrows arched at their centers. "What do you mean?"

Ransom released a deep sigh and said, "I think that Michael Franklin was being murdered in your church basement on Wednesday night."

There was a very long pause during which Reverend Draper seemed to silently turn to granite. At last his lips moved. "In my church?"

"Yes."

They stared at each other across the table. The reverend's eyes were pointed at Ransom's, but he seemed to be gazing at some other place. Ransom wondered if the place existed somewhere in this world or in God's. When he thought the staring contest had gone on long enough, he said:

"We have the medical examiner's report on Danny. As near as he can tell there were sharp objects—nails, if I'm not mistaken—driven through his hands and feet—while he was alive. And after that, his brains were bashed in. Michael was exactly the same condition as Danny. Two boys—two boys who were essentially in your care—were tortured and then brutally murdered. In your church, if I'm not mistaken."

There was the slightest pause. "I don't know anything about it," said Draper in the monotone that he'd used since they'd brought him in. It was truly beginning to get on Ransom's nerves. The one saving grace was that although the reverend gave no outward sign, Ransom would have sworn he'd been affected by the details of the deaths.

Ransom placed his right elbow on the table and rested his head against his hand. "Mr. Draper, for someone who claims to be the spiritual leader of this group, concerned about all their comings and goings, it seems there have been some rather drastic things going on right under your nose without your knowledge."

"As I've said before, I can't keep an eye on everything."

"With selective blindness like yours," said Ransom with a curled lip, "you could be President."

"I see no need for sarcasm, Detective."

"Oh, I see every reason for it. The members of your church are being killed off one by one, and you refuse to do anything about it."

"I've told you everything I know."

Ransom gazed at him for a moment. If he was the killer, his stoic nature was not serving him well: The one thing that was perfectly legible on his face was that he was not telling all he knew. If he wasn't the killer, his immobility was even more infuriating. He was, thought Ransom, a detective's nightmare: a witness or suspect who wouldn't talk.

"Mr. Draper, there is a killer in your Community. Whatever you may think about justice in this life or the next life or whatever the hell it is, let me tell you this: You bear part of the responsibility."

"I bear all the responsibility for what happens in my Community."

"That's not what I mean. We don't know why these murders have happened. Without knowing why, we don't know whether or not there'll be more. Now exactly how do you think your Lord will take it if someone else is murdered, and you could have prevented it?" Ransom let him think about that for a minute, then added, "Let alone Michael."

"Michael?"

Ransom nodded. "Who knows whether or not he could have been saved if you'd listened to him."

"The Lord alone chooses the day of your death."

Ransom leaned in toward the reverend. "The Lord has an unfair advantage in your Community, Mr. Draper: He's getting help. I think it's time we even the playing field. Now, we know why Michael came to you, and we think we know why Danny came."

Draper's expression didn't change.

"It was Michael, wasn't it? Danny came to you to try to get you to stop trying to change Michael—to let him be himself."

Draper's eyes dropped shut. He was silent for a moment. Finally, he spoke:

"When Michael came to our Community, he felt completely lost. He had an ineffectual mother and a father who made it quite clear how Michael would be treated if it were found he was homosexual. He wasn't happy the way he was."

"Very few of us are," said Ransom. "Some things you can change, some you can't."

The reverend's eyes burned, and he repeated, "Michael was unhappy the way he was. When he came to us, he found for the first time in his life the acceptance he needed—the Lord's acceptance."

"And yours?"

"And mine."

"You accepted him?" said Ransom wryly.

"Yes."

"And then took away that acceptance the minute he joined your merry band by telling him he needed to change himself."

Though the reverend and Ransom were approximately the same height as they sat opposite each other, Ransom knew the reverend was attempting to look down on him.

"We are told to love the sinner, not the sin, Mr. Ransom."

"And how did Danny enter into the discussion?"

"He was Michael's friend. Michael told Danny how we were shepherding him. Danny, of course, objected…in the strongest possible terms. He came to us and told us we were making Michael miserable—that Michael was a good person, and that was all that mattered. But it wasn't."

"Hmm?"

"He said that Michael was created the way he was, and God loved him. Danny was mistaken."

"About God loving Michael?" said Ransom quickly.

"No," said Draper, his voice droning on, "about that being all there was to it. Danny was young in the Lord, and couldn't see the bigger picture."

"Perhaps you could explain it to us," said Ransom, almost managing to keep the disdain out of his voice.

"Just because Michael was born that way doesn't mean that he didn't need to change. We're all born in sin. He was like the man who was blind from birth."

He stopped. If Gerald hadn't been so disgusted by the man, he would have smiled. The reverend appeared to enjoy being prompted almost as much as Ransom.

"Yes?" said Ransom.

"Jesus met a man who was born blind, and the disciples asked him what had caused the man to be blind—his own sins or the sins of his parents. And Jesus said, 'Neither hath this man sinned nor his parents: but that the words of God should be made manifest in him.' You see, some people are born with afflictions just so the miracles of God can be shown. If Michael had believed and been cured, it would have been another sign of the Glory of God."

Ransom glanced at Gerald and was silent for a moment, then he said, "I take it Danny didn't agree with your interpretation of the matter."

"It isn't my interpretation, it's right there in the Bible in black and white, for all to see."

With measured patience, Ransom said, "Danny didn't agree."

Draper looked at him. For the first time the reverend looked as if his own patience were being tried.

"Danny didn't agree," he said evenly.

"And that was unacceptable to you?"

Draper sighed. "I have nothing to do with it. Danny could disagree with anything he liked and it would have been of no consequence to anyone else if he had just kept it between himself and the Lord."

"And you," said Ransom with a smile.

"And me. But he wasn't content with that. And he wasn't obedient. He compounded his sins by leading Michael astray."

"In what way?"

"By trying to convince Michael that he was all right the way he was and didn't need to change. He confused Michael more than you can imagine."

Ransom was tempted to challenge the reverend on exactly who it was who'd done the confusing, but he let it pass.

"So, Michael had to die because he was backsliding, and...why was it that Danny had to die?"

The reverend's eyes had not wavered from the detective's. "Because he was leading Michael astray. It says in the twenty-eighth chapter of Proverbs, 'Whoso causeth the righteous to go astray in an evil way, he shall fall himself into his own pit.'"

"Or be pushed," said Ransom.

The detective considered all of this for a minute. It was the link they were looking for, if you accepted the reverend's reasoning (and the interpretation of certain Bible passages, laid down in black and white, thought Ransom, interrupting his own ruminations with a touch of sarcasm). It made sense, in a way. Ransom had to remind himself that these people were by their own admission living in a world different from his own, and he'd found their reasoning to be skewed. His mind flashed back to Emily and *Through the Looking Glass*. Everything backward. But the lands that Alice visited were not without logic, they simply operated within a logic of their own.

Ransom said to Draper, "All right. What you're telling us is that Michael was killed because he was backsliding, and Danny was killed because he was leading Michael astray."

"Yes," said the reverend with a surprising degree of impatience. Then a curious look came over his face: His normally glacial features seemed to melt and slide, like snowcaps finally touched by the sun. There was a newly discovered hesitation in his voice when he added, "...at least, that's what I think."

Both Ransom and Gerald looked at him with intensely questioning expressions. Ransom believed that a great deal of this man was theatrics, that his usually unchanging, unreadable facade was cultivated by years of practice, and was designated to give the effect of holiness, knowledge, and depth—without letting on that it, in fact, revealed nothing. The steadiness with which he maintained this facade made it tempting to accept any break from it as genuine. But in this case Ransom was inclined to agree with the reverend: Temptation was dangerous.

"That's what you *think*," said Ransom sharply, "you mean, you don't *know* why they were killed?"

"It could have been..." he said haltingly, as if he were not sure whether or not the words should be spoken aloud, "...it could have been because they defied me."

FURTHER QUESTIONING was interrupted by a firm double knock at the door. Robinson poked his head in and signaled to Gerald. Gerald went to him and there was a short, whispered consultation, at the end of which Gerald nodded and Robinson withdrew, closing the door behind him. Gerald went over and whispered something to Ransom, who didn't look anywhere near pleased by the interruption.

"Excuse me," he said to Draper as he left the room with his partner.

As they strode to his office, Ransom said to his partner, "So she's on the phone. For God's sake, why not just take a message?"

"Robinson said she sounds really upset, and says she has to talk to you right away—it's an emergency."

They reached the office, Ransom picked up the receiver of his phone, pressed a button, and in a voice designed to let the caller know that this wasn't the time to chat said, "Yes?"

"Mr. Ransom?" said Pamela Frazier, the urgency in her tone palpable.

"Yes? What is it, Miss Frazier?"

"My God, it took forever to track you down! I've been trying for the past..."

Ransom cut her off. "Miss Frazier, what's wrong?"

There was a little gasp. "Nick is missing."

Gerald saw something on the face of his partner that he

didn't think he had ever seen before: Ransom was startled.
Then the expression changed to wariness.

"What do you mean, missing?" said Ransom, his heart
beginning to sink.

"I was supposed to meet him half an hour ago. He's
disappeared!"

Was that all? thought Ransom. "Maybe he's just late."

"No! No! You don't understand! I talked to him just
twenty minutes before I went over to his apartment—to tell
him I was running late. I told him I'd be there in about
twenty minutes. When I got there, there was no answer."

"Perhaps..."

"No! You don't see! He never would have left knowing
I was on my way. I stayed at his door about half an hour,
and I kept ringing the bell, but he never came back. And
then I came back home and tried to get you, but it took
them forever. Something's happened to Nick! I know it!"

Ransom knew it, too. But he thought they might just be
able to stop it this time, if they weren't too late. He thought
all of this as he grabbed a small package from his upper
right-hand desk drawer, and then scrambled for the car with
Gerald in tow.

NICK REGAINED consciousness little by little. His coming to
was hampered by the realization that the room he was in
was completely dark, and he'd been confusing that fact
with his semi-consciousness for some time. There was a
familiar stuffiness, or mustiness, about the room.

He seemed to be stretched out on some extremely uncomfortable apparatus. He tried to move his arms and
thought at first that they were weighed down by the stupor
in which he found himself. But as he regained more of his
senses, he realized that both of his arms had been spread
out at ninety-degree angles to his torso, and his wrists
bound to whatever it was he was lying on. Similarly, his
legs were straight, though his feet were turned slightly inward so that the ball of his right foot crossed the top of his

left. His legs were bound at the ankles in the same fashion as his wrists.

His mouth was excessively dry due to the cloth that had been stuffed so far into it and his throat that it was only with an effort that he didn't choke on it.

He began to wonder about the apparatus on which he lay. Whatever it was was lower at the foot and the head, with something extending across horizontally under his arms and shoulders that raised them and caused his head to loll backward. This uncomfortable position added to the feeling that his head was swimming. He tried to shift the bottom half of his body, the sound of wrinkling plastic beneath him, and suddenly realized that he was naked. It was this discovery that made him realize what the apparatus was.

He made a struggling sound in his throat, and was stopped immediately by a voice that was at once familiar and unfamiliar.

"You are very weak. Weaker than the rest. It took you much longer to come 'round than the others. Weakness."

Nick struggled against his bonds, which dug painfully into his wrists.

"It'll be better if you don't struggle as you go home. If you repent...as the one sinner who received the Lord's blessing on the cross...then today you will be with Him in the Kingdom of Heaven. Otherwise, God help your soul."

Nick was making a heroic effort to control the terror in his mind, which was difficult since he already knew how Danny and Michael had died. And the voice...the voice in the darkness was like one of those nightmare things that he couldn't believe was really there. But after a moment, even the hope that this might be a nightmare was robbed from him. The voice said, "Let us pray," and launched into a long and rambling prayer for Nick's soul. It was during the prayer that Nick identified who it was, and why he had sounded so unfamiliar: Saul Berne's voice was devoid of any of its usual bluff and bluster. Somehow, the quiet calm of that normally agitated voice chilled Nick to the bone, adding to his terror.

The voice came to a halt, the "amen" hanging in the air like a dead man in a noose. There was a sharp scratch and Saul's face flared up in the light of a match. The flame reflected off the leader's glasses as if his eyes were the gates to hell. He calmly lit a tall candle, and the church basement was very dimly visible.

"There is no hope for you," said Saul calmly, "we've tried, but you can't be saved. You fly in the face of the Lord."

Nick tried to speak, but found himself capable of little more than an ugly gurgle.

"Even now," said Saul, "you show your disrespect for your elders. I can't let you defy our holy man anymore. It has to be stopped, before your immortal soul is ruined."

Saul began to move quietly around the room, his movement furtive and fluid, apparently collecting things. Nick tried to see his own arms and legs, and realized that he was bound to two two-by-six boards—the type they'd used for floor joist—which were put together in the form of a cross.

The effort cost his whirling head. He let his head fall back to the board, and then rolled to the left. He saw his left hand, tied at the wrist with cord, palm up. As he watched, Saul hovered into the dim light. Something in his hands glimmered for a second in the light of the candle. Saul turned the object around in his hand, then placed the point in the center of Nick's palm. It was a sixteen-penny nail. With a movement so swift that Nick barely saw it, Saul wheeled a hammer around with his other hand and drove the nail in.

RANSOM'S STOMACH churned so hard you would have thought it would have driven the car on faster. He removed a plastic-tipped cigar from the box he'd retrieved from his desk, lit it, and puffed furiously on it, his teeth clenching on the tip. He was unable to savor it, but he believed it was the only thing that kept him from exploding. Gerald drove

full-tilt without the siren, since they didn't want to disturb
whatever was going on in any way: They thought the noise
might serve to agitate the killer, urging him further on, or
cause him to simply flee. Neither of which were options
that Ransom wanted to entertain.

They arrived in Albany Park in what both detectives felt
would have been slightly longer than it would have taken
them to fly to the West Coast. Gerald steered the car onto
the street on which Pamela lived—the street that ended in
the church—and sped to a space in front of it. The detectives raced out of the car and then quietly...as quietly as
they could, crept to the back door.

A large board—Ransom suspected it had been one of the
panels for the floor—had been propped up against the inside of the door, blocking the window. Ransom muttered
"damn," put his ear to the door, and heard nothing. He
would have liked to break the door down, sure as he was
of what was about to happen in there, but the last thing he
wanted to do was to prod the killer into action. He fingered
the key that the reverend had given them—at Ransom's
vociferous demand—and motioned to Gerald. They quietly
climbed the cement stairs away from the back door and
slinked around the outside of the building to the front door.
Ransom very carefully, noiselessly fitted the key into its
slot and turned it. It was as he was making the attempt to
open the door without sound that they heard the first strike
of the hammer. The detectives exchanged swift, startled
glances and flung the door open. They ran into the darkened
sanctuary and looked for a light switch, found it, and turned
it on if for no other reason than to avoid hurtling down the
staircase—whose location they were unsure of—all the
while hearing the steady strikes of the hammer. They saw
the stairs to their right, and ran down them.

There they found Nick, naked and tied to the makeshift
cross, his left hand hideously scarred and bleeding. Under-
neath the cross was stretched a large, cheap plastic drop
cloth. Saul was poised over Nick's right hand, hammer and
nail in place. Nick looked beseechingly at the detectives.

"Mr. Berne!" said Ransom loudly. "Stop!"

The leader paused for a moment, looking at the detectives like a startled animal. Then he swung the hammer upward and hit the nail. Nick's entire body contorted: all except his left hand, which twisted but remained held in place.

The action caught the detectives off guard, but only for a moment. Ransom threw himself at the little man, knocking him backward. The leader let out a startled howl as the two of them tumbled sideways across the parallels of the joists, thudding heavily over each plank. On Ransom's impact the nails flew out of Saul's hand and clattered against the back wall. Saul held onto the hammer with all his might, and with his arms wrapped around the detective, brought it down in the area of Ransom's left kidney. Ransom's back arched when the hammer found its mark, and he pushed himself up and away from Saul, who was on his back floundering against the joist. He grabbed two of them to lift himself up—but while his hands were occupied, Ransom seized the opportunity: He grabbed Saul's head with both hands and slammed it full force back against one of the joists with a loud crack. All movement stopped.

There was a sudden silence. It was broken when Gerald said quietly, "Thank God he's not dead."

Ransom pulled himself up with some difficulty, and it was not until he was standing and had turned around that he realized his partner had been referring to Nick.

"Call an ambulance."

RANSOM SAT across from the reverend, whom they'd left in the interrogation room. It was very late. The reverend's face had begun to sag as Ransom related the details of Saul's confession—well, it would be more accurate to say his ravings. The reverend's face lost its steadfast qualities in a morass of guilt that seemed to have continued the melting process until his face looked much heavier at the bottom than at the top. His jaw had slackened.

"You knew, didn't you?" said Ransom.

"I didn't know. I told you that. I didn't *know*—any more than you did."

"You knew," said Ransom, unwilling to give him an inch.

"I…suspected…his behavior…he's always been highly strung…"

Ransom did not miss that this was exactly how he'd described Michael, when trying to excuse his own actions.

"…But lately he's been worse…and he's been talking more about people not showing me the respect that I deserve…and…there have been other things, but nothing that one could pin down."

Ransom's eyes narrowed. It crossed his mind that he'd like to demonstrate on the reverend how Danny, and then Michael, and then Nicholas had been "pinned down."

"Why didn't you talk to us? Why didn't you tell us what you thought?"

The reverend didn't seem capable of meeting Ransom's gaze at first, but with an effort that Ransom came close to admiring was finally able to turn his eyes to the detectives. The reverend's eyes seemed to have enlarged, and his lower lids drooped.

"I know you won't believe me, but I didn't…I really didn't think anything of Danny disappearing. It wasn't until Michael…until Michael that I started to think something was really wrong." He stopped and released a sharp breath. "It's useless to try to explain."

"Try me."

"We have tried to morally and spiritually withdraw ourselves from this world, and live entirely in God's world, so we could try…at least try, to remain unstained. But we…I forgot that we can't really leave the world…we're not meant to. We are, no matter what we try to be, human…born of sin and living in a sinful world. I had hoped that my suspicions of Saul were wrong. I had only his actions and the fact that these boys disappeared after flare-ups in meeting with me. I didn't have any…what you would call…hard evidence. I did what anyone in my position would do. I prayed. I prayed alone that the Lord would either prove or disprove that Saul was involved, and I prayed that he would change.''

''The way you prayed for Michael?'' Ransom couldn't help but spit this back at him.

If the reverend had had the strength, he would have glowered at the detective. As it was, his voice merely hardened when he replied, ''Yes, like I did for Michael. And I tried to get Saul to tell me...to tell me if he was involved, but none of my...''

''Tricks?'' Ransom offered.

The reverend's face remained impassive. ''None of my influence was able to get the truth from him. So I prayed. I thought the Lord would take care of it. He didn't.''

That was an understatement, thought Ransom.

''You realize that you can be held for obstructing justice, and perhaps on other charges as well?''

The reverend's eyes traveled down to the floor, as if he could no longer support them.

He said quietly, ''It is not possible for me to obstruct justice...any more than it is possible for me to escape it.''

FIFTEEN

THE HOUSE WAS spotless. Ransom had been pleased when he glanced into the sitting room on his way to the kitchen. Everything was dusted, polished, and vacuumed to within an inch of its life.

He now sat in the kitchen with Emily, in their usual places. But for once they were not alone: Lynn Francis was in the process of finishing her extensive cleaning of the stove and countertops. She had agreed on short notice to pause in her duties as "charwoman to the rich and famous" to clean house for one of the not-so-rich and famous. She'd agreed partly out of gratitude for the kindness that Ransom had once shown to her lover. Ransom had assured her that it would only be a temporary arrangement while Emily recuperated, but Lynn didn't know about that: She liked Emily.

While Lynn put the finishing touches on her cleaning job, Ransom and Emily finished up a plate of cookies and a pot of tea. When Ransom arrived, Emily had taken one look at him and ordered a pot of very hot, very strong tea with lots of sugar. There was a long scrape on the right side of Ransom's face, and along one side of his left hand. The little finger of his left hand was broken and in a splint. He had a cracked rib.

Once they had settled in the kitchen, Emily asked him for an explanation of his condition.

Ransom explained how they had found Nick and Saul, then said, "Doesn't the Bible say something about vanity?"

Emily knit her thin gray eyebrows. Though she smiled, it was evident she was very concerned about him.

Ransom continued, "For some reason, when I yelled

'Stop,' I thought he would.'' He laughed and the movement cost him some pain around the hurt rib. He winced. ''When he didn't, I threw myself at him and something like a barroom brawl ensued.''

"Grown men," said Lynn with a toss of her tawny hair.

"How is the young man…Nicholas?" said Emily.

"He'll be all right, I think. He's suffering from shock more than anything. Of course, he had a nail through one hand and halfway through the other. But it could have been a lot worse.''

Emily clucked her tongue and took a sip of tea.

"Were you able to find out what this Saul person was hoping to accomplish?"

Ransom set down his cup and frowned. "You were, as usual, correct all the way around. From what I could fathom from all he said, he did it out of devotion: devotion to Reverend Draper. He thought these boys were more than just disrespectful, he thought they were challenging the reverend's authority and were therefore some sort of danger to him. You were right about something else, too: The motive was the important thing. We couldn't figure out what the first two boys had in common. I knew there had to be some connection between the deaths. As it turned out, it wasn't sexuality or anything like it. The connection between the first two victims—and Nicholas—was not to each other, it was to the reverend. The motive was their perceived disrespect of him.''

"How was it all accomplished?"

"Well…'' said Ransom, replacing his cup and warming to the story, ''we don't know how he lured Danny to the church, or for that matter, *if* he did. After all, he knocked Nick unconscious and dragged him to his car, which was in the alley. Anyway, he did tell us that he killed Danny late Friday night…for his sins, and the sins of others: the symbolism you were looking for, my dear Emily. Not only was Danny guilty of not respecting the reverend's authority, he was perceived as leading Michael astray. He wanted Danny to die the way Jesus did. So he made a makeshift cross out of the boards they were using for the floor, tied him to it, then drove the nails in.''

Emily shuddered.

"Are you sure you want to hear about this?" he said, concerned.

"Of course," she replied, her thin gray eyebrows rising.

"Anyway, it was much easier to get Michael there. All Saul had to do was tell him that he was expected to work on the church basement with him *after* the leaders' meeting—he was never let out of work parties, you know—part of his therapy, doing 'manly' things—then when Michael arrived, all Saul had to do was club him over the head, and there you go.''

Emily shook her head. "He sounds as if he was very clever, but one would hardly think you would adopt crucifixion as the method of choice.''

"I think once he found he could do it, he did it. They had tons of drop cloths handy, and he put one under the cross to catch any stray blood. When he was through, he pulled out the nails…''

Emily shuddered again, but motioned for him to go on.

"…shoved the boards under the finished part of the floor, and wrapped the body in the drop cloth and threw it in the trunk of his car. The forensics team is going over his car now.''

Emily took a sip of tea, her eyes reflecting that her mind was sorting through all of the information. At last, she said, "Why did he take them downtown?''

Ransom gave a rueful laugh. "No doubt the lawyers will have a field day with that one. He did it because he thought it would look as if they were killed there. And Saul called the bookstore the next morning, muffling his voice and claiming to be Michael calling in sick to make it look as if Michael was alive on Thursday. Remember, Betty said she hardly recognized him. It was a calculated risk. Any good prosecuting attorney would argue that that shows that he was in possession of his faculties when he committed the crimes. But…''

"But?" said Emily, her interest peaked.

"But in his…condition he failed to realize that the marks on the hands and feet would lead us right to the church. It's like a child putting its hands over its eyes and saying 'I'm hiding!'"

"Do you think he's insane?"

Ransom smiled coyly. "By the world's standards, yes. But in God's world, who knows?"

Emily clucked her tongue again and said, "There is nothing new under the sun. That's from Ecclesiastes."

"What do you mean?"

"Only this, my dear Jeremy: that there have been a lot of very bizarre things done in the name of the Lord and the church, and there probably always will be."

Ransom was silent for a minute, then said, "You know, the one thing I remember from my old Sunday school days is that saying, something like 'Everything works together for the good for those who love God.' At least it's worked out that way for two people in this mess."

"Hmm?" said Emily.

"Nick and Pam. This has been enough of a shock that it doesn't look like Pam will give Nick any problem about leaving the Community. If there's a Community left to leave."

Emily arched her left eyebrow. "You don't think the Community will continue?"

Ransom sighed. "I don't know. Reverend Draper didn't sound like he knew what to do next. This has shaken his foundation. But I wouldn't be surprised if he prays about it for a while and comes to the conclusion that the Lord wants him to continue. If this hasn't killed the Community, it may end up making it stronger."

Emily shook her head in none-too-firm disbelief. She had learned enough of the world in her seventy-odd years to know that what Ransom said was probably true.

"The reverend says he blames himself for what happened, and I'm fully inclined to agree with him, except…"

He shifted in his seat, which sent a little spasm of pain through his midsection.

Emily said, "Except what, dear?"

"Well, he said he didn't *know* who the killer was, he only *suspected,* and he couldn't do anything about that...and as much as I hate to admit it, he's probably right. If the police department can't do anything without proof, I don't know how we could expect him to."

"But that's not all that's bothering you, is it?" said Emily, the black flecks in her blue-gray eyes adding to their incisiveness.

"Well..." he said slowly, looking down at the newly polished floor, "...I can't help thinking that if I hadn't disliked the reverend so much I might have noticed that his sidekick wasn't all there."

Emily gazed at him for a moment, then said, "Jeremy, I think it was you who said that if killers acted guilty, your job would be much easier."

"I didn't say that," said Ransom with a smile.

"Well, whoever it was was right."

Lynn finished wiping out the sink, rinsed the washrag, and draped it over the tap.

"Is he always like this at the end of a case, Miss Emily?"

"Sometimes worse," said Emily with a twinkle, "but it's a sign of humanity."

Lynn laughed lightly and went to the doorway. "Well, I'm done for now."

"You did a marvelous job," said Emily. "I couldn't have done better myself."

"And that," said Ransom, "is the highest praise you'll ever receive."

"Thank you, Mr. Ransom," she said with a broad smile, then turned to Emily and said, "I'll be back next Saturday to move the dust around. I'm off to the hospital."

"Thank you, dear," said Emily.

Lynn looked at Ransom. Her eyes sparkled, and with a

toss of her hair she started out the door and called over her shoulder:

"See ya in church!"

Ransom smiled, and then grimaced as he shifted himself in his seat for a better view of Emily. She looked very tired, but she seemed to be coming back to herself: as if she'd woken from a drugged sleep, and would take just a little longer than usual to become fully awake.

Emily gently lifted the cup to her lips and took a sip of tea. She replaced the cup, folded her hands—which trembled just a little—on the table, and turned her knowing eyes to him. Her mouth pursed into a little frown.

"Now, Jeremy," she said, taking a deep breath, "I can tell you've been smoking…"

Death and Faxes

A MOLLY MASTERS MYSTERY

Cartoonist Molly Masters has returned to her hometown
with her two children…and steps smack into trouble she
thought she'd left behind. Her scandalous high school
past—a scathing poem about a teacher had made front
page of the school paper—comes back to haunt her. Now
there's a letter from the teacher with a cryptic message,
but poor Mrs. Kravett is dead before Molly can respond.

Then come the death threats—by fax.

Leslie O'Kane

"O'Kane's engaging mystery takes a slanted
entertaining glance at high school figures we all
loved to hate." —*Publishers Weekly*

Available in September 1997 at your favorite retail outlet.

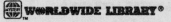

A MOST DEADLY

RETIREMENT

First Time in Paperback

A Laura Michaels Mystery

When one of Timberdale Retirement Center's residents makes a 6:00 a.m. run through the woods to the nearby convenience store to stock up on cigarettes, she never makes it back. Bludgeoned. But by whom?

Laura Michaels, the center's manager and social worker, is intent on doing something—at least stopping the media from sensationalizing the horror. But as more untimely deaths occur, it's clear that something terrible is happening and retirement has become most deadly.

JOHN MILES

"The author...has created some real characters..."   *—Sunday Oklahoman*

Available in October 1997 at your favorite retail outlet.

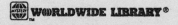 **WORLDWIDE LIBRARY** ®   WMOST